DUST

AND OTHER STORIES

P9-BIT-810

WEATHERHEAD BOOKS ON ASIA

WEATHERHEAD BOOKS ON ASIA

Weatherhead East Asian Institute, Columbia University

For a full list of titles in this series, see pages 265–66.

DUST

AND OTHER STORIES

YI T'AEJUN

TRANSLATED BY JANET POOLE

COLUMBIA UNIVERSITY PRESS   NEW YORK

Dust and Other Stories is published under the support of the Literature Translation Institute of Korea (LTI Korea).

This publication has been supported by the Richard W. Weatherhead Publication Fund of the Weatherhead East Asian Institute, Columbia University.

COLUMBIA UNIVERSITY PRESS
Publishers Since 1893
New York   Chichester, West Sussex
cup.columbia.edu

English translation © 2018 Janet Poole
All rights reserved

Library of Congress Cataloging-in-Publication Data
Names: Yi, T'ae-jun, 1904–1956. | Poole, Janet, translator.
Title: Dust and other stories / Yi T'aejun ; translated by Janet Poole.
Description: New York : Columbia University Press, 2018. | Series:
    Weatherhead books on Asia | Includes bibliographical references.
Identifiers: LCCN 2017037821 | ISBN 9780231185806 (cloth :
    acid-free paper) | ISBN 9780231185813 (pbk. : acid-free paper) |
    ISBN 9780231546348 (e-book)
Classification: LCC PL991.9.T3 A2 2018 | DDC 895.73/4—dc23
LC record available at https://lccn.loc.gov/2017037821

Columbia University Press books are printed on permanent and durable acid-free paper.
Printed in the United States of America

Cover design: Chang Jae Lee
Cover image: Construction Site Dreg 03, 2012 © Jung Jihyun

FOR MY MOTHER, WHO LOVES STORIES

CONTENTS

TRANSLATOR'S ACKNOWLEDGMENTS   IX

TRANSLATOR'S INTRODUCTION   XI

Omongnyŏ   1

Mr. Son, of Great Wealth   16

The Rainy Season   27

The Broker's Office   50

The Frozen River P'ae   67

A Tale of Rabbits   81

The Hunt   96

Evening Sun   108

Unconditioned   134

Before and After Liberation: A Writer's Notes   147

Tiger Grandma   189

Dust   207

GLOSSARY   263   VII

TRANSLATOR'S ACKNOWLEDGMENTS

This translation was initially undertaken with the help of a grant from the Literature Translation Institute of Korea. I was greatly encouraged when the project was selected for a Banff International Literary Translation Centre Residency Fellowship at the Banff Centre for the Arts. I would like to thank the then directors Katherine Silver and Hugh Hazelton for their encouragement and for introducing me to such an inspiring group of translators. In particular, Russell Valentino was kind enough to offer helpful suggestions during the Banff sessions.

I know that I am the most fortunate translator in the world to be able to call upon Hwang Jongyon and Jiyoung Suh whenever I am perplexed by Yi T'aejun's prose and colonial references. I cannot thank them enough. In the final months of preparing this manuscript Bae Gaehwa generously shared with me invaluable resources on Yi T'aejun's original publications. I am also grateful for the suggestions I received from Amanda Goodman and two reviewers for Columbia University Press. Finally my deepest thanks go to Jennifer Crewe and Christine Dunbar at Columbia University Press for their continued support of Korean literature in translation.

TRANSLATOR'S INTRODUCTION

In August of 1946 Yi T'aejun (1904–?) boarded a Soviet army plane in Pyongyang, circled over the city that had recently become his new home, and flew north, across the border with the Soviet Union and over the tall buildings of Vladivostok, before landing in a small town on the outskirts of that city, where his delegation from the Soviet-occupied zone of northern Korea was to be placed in quarantine for five to six days before journeying on to the capital of the Soviet empire, Moscow. Yi was taking part in a two-month-long tour of the Soviet Union, organized by the Pyongyang-based Korea-Soviet Union Cultural Association. Over a period of two months, the delegation of farmers, laborers, scholars, artists, and politicians was to be based in Moscow, with side trips to Leningrad to the west, and Armenia and Georgia to the south, returning to Moscow via Stalingrad, before finally making its way home to Pyongyang via the Trans-Siberian railroad. Later that year, Yi published the diary he kept during his journey. The book was titled *Record of a Journey to the Soviet Union*, and photographs inserted at its front record the journey of the delegation from a newly liberated land: pictures of the group inside the Kremlin, exiting from a government building in Armenia, and at a farewell reception; an article from the Moscow Cultural Newspaper with a photograph of Yi T'aejun, the writer Yi Kiyŏng, feminist activist and journalist Hŏ Chŏngsuk, and other members of the delegation meeting with Russian writers; Lenin's mausoleum and a scene of the night sky lit up during the first September 3 celebration of victory on the Pacific front by the side of the Moscow River. Ordinary snapshots of neatly suited dignitaries standing in line for the obligatory group shot are juxtaposed with the sturdy stone of the Red Square walls and the dazzling lights of the celebrating capital city. The novelty for this group of being received as representatives of a liberated nation should not be forgotten. During their stay, several members of the group purchased newly printed maps of the world, on which Korea and Japan were now depicted as separate nations. As Yi looks down upon the tiny country of Korea, dwarfed by the enormous breadth of the Soviet Union, he is enthralled by it being depicted there in its very own color.

In the preface to his diary, Yi suggests the significance of this trip, timed to coincide with the first anniversary of Japan's defeat in war and Korea's release from a colonial occupation lasting more than three decades:

> As someone who had barely been freed from a long life of slavery to old things in an old world, on this trip to the Soviet Union I was like a bird flying through the sky for the first time, having been freed from a cage. Those few months were truly enchanting. Everything old and bad connected to humans had disappeared; it was a new world with a new culture, new customs, and the new daily lives of new people. Moreover, although it was new by the day, the Soviet Union was moving forward without end, just like a great river flows toward the eternally stable ocean.[1]

The repetition of the word "new" is striking; it portrays Liberation with a sense of joyous rupture, which turns everything that came before and all that is expected afterward into the old and the new. The new world here lies foremost at the heart of the Soviet empire. For Yi, a former Japanese imperial subject who had previously only traveled back and forth between metropolitan Japan and its Korean colony, Liberation allowed travel into new worlds in the most literal of senses. In the few brief years before he was sent into internal exile in the emergent Democratic People's Republic, Yi took part in official trips to the Soviet Union and to China.

But these journeys were preceded by a shorter journey that would prove life changing: his decision to move from his longtime home in Seoul, by this time occupied by the United States, to Pyongyang in the summer of 1946. At the time, he would not have known this journey would prove irreversible: that four years later a civil war would erupt that still has seen no armistice more than sixty years on, and that his many works would, as a result, be banned south of the thirty-eighth parallel until 1988, erasing him from the pages of written history in South Korea. Neither would he have realized that he, along with so many of the artists and writers who chose to move from the South to the North at this time, would fall from favor so quickly as power consolidated around Kim Il Sung in the mid-1950s, leaving his work equally unpublished north of the thirty-eighth parallel and his final whereabouts and date of death unknown.

In 1946 the journey to the Soviet Union was a journey to a new world that seemed full of hope and promise. Yi describes life there as one of culture, leisure, and pleasurable labor. Perhaps what he saw, however, was not so much the reality of Soviet life, hard enough to grasp in any event within the confines of an official tour, but the life he dreamed of for himself, which contrasted sharply with his current life in the chaotic midst of a forcibly divided country and the aftermath of colonial occupation by an empire at war. This dream life sought stability at the same time that it thrived on the excitement of the new. In Yi's preface, too, this sense of newness is, in this supposedly foundational moment, not singular but accompanied by a notion of eternity. Yi's description of his time in the Soviet Union brings to mind Baudelaire's famous definition of the modern in "The Painter of Modern Life": where the modern is composed of two sides, so to speak, the contingent or ephemeral and the eternal, as if to be truly "modern" it is not enough to be merely new.[2] This suggests that Yi's move to what was to become North Korea is best understood as a search for the authentically new, a search that had characterized his entire literary career.

By the 1930s Yi had already earned a reputation as a dedicated writer, editor, and teacher. One of colonial Korea's foremost writers of fiction and anecdotal essays, Yi left behind a voluminous oeuvre. As an editor, Yi curated arts pages for national newspapers and cofounded a literary journal that championed Korean-language literature after the vernacular press had been shut down by the colonial authorities in 1940. As a teacher, he wrote several popular writing guides and taught at schools. He was a founding member in 1933 of the Group of Nine (Kuinhoe), a short-lived but famous grouping of modernist poets and fiction writers who had shocked colonial society with their commitment to experimentation with literary form and the Korean language at a time when writing was more properly understood to be an instrument for national and socialist revolution.[3] Yi was always conversant with the new, even when the new was what seemed most old. For he was also an antiquarian, a collector and lover of old things in an age that was just beginning to recognize what was being lost in the rampant drive to modernization.

Yi's stories record that sense of loss at the same time that they explore the new spaces and experiences of colonial Korea: its capital city, Seoul, where Yi lived; provincial cities, such as Pyongyang and Kyŏngju, that were undergoing the first wave of imperial tourism; and destitute rural villages, which provoked an intense sense of nostalgia in the urbanite Yi. The materiality of these spaces is less his focus, however, than the sentiments they inspire and the mental life of his urbane protagonists, especially his oft-used alter ego, Hyŏn. Yi's stories revolve less around plot than around mental contemplation and the processes of thinking, reflecting an intellectual response to the changing urban environment that characterized modernisms around the world. Those stories that focus on rural, lower-class, or female characters equally eschew the drama of narrative incident to reflect Yi's urban male gaze, which seeks in these characters' naïveté, morality, and especially their colorful language, the simplicity and authenticity of a different world and a different life. Indeed, the centrality of female characters and old men to Yi's stories suggests they provided integral forms through which he explored the rapid changes in contemporary life. The critic Yu Chongho once characterized Yi T'aejun's stories as a "dictionary to humankind."[4] Yi believed in character as the focus of the short story form, and we can see this lifelong interest clearly in the stories selected here: from Yi's very first published short story from 1925, which describes the canny but destitute temptress Omongnyŏ, to characters from his later works, such as the indomitable Tiger Grandma, who stars in his tale of the nationwide literacy campaign launched in North Korea soon after the end of colonial rule. Whether depicting the inner thoughts of a sensitive writer or the often humorous antics of figures struggling to cope with modern life, Yi's short stories were considered among the best of his time. He was acknowledged as an accomplished writer, whose attention to style and the texture of language—especially in the frequent dialogues featuring different dialects and representations of class—brought him the admiration of readers, colleagues, and students alike.

Yi produced his best writing in the short literary forms of the anecdotal essay and the short story, in which he seems to have found his own style during the mid-1930s.[5] He was also a prolific writer of long serial novels, which appeared in the national newspapers, but he often complained that economic necessity forced him to concentrate too much time on these popular novels; time which he would rather be spending on the work he called "art"—the short story or the dream of an "authentic" novel. In 1930s Korea a contract to serialize a newspaper novel was a major and most welcome source of income for any writer. Yet Yi also valued the short story form for reasons beyond its supposed freedom from the drudgery of commodified labor. He once wrote, "In environments such as Korea, where one encounters a variety of difficulties when trying to handle the general situation either spatially or temporally, it is no exaggeration to say that the most partial and fragmented form of the short story has to be the most appropriate literary form."[6] This is the closest that the rather dilettantish Yi came to acknowledging the constraints upon artistic production under colonial occupation. More often he would claim that art "blooms from the individual alone," as if that individual him or herself existed in isolation from any social or political situation.[7]

One of Yi's contemporaries, the critic Sŏ Insik (1906–?), provides a helpful context for the individual that was Yi, and especially for the nostalgic sentiment that so permeates his work. For Sŏ, writing in 1940, nostalgia was the sentiment of the age, so pervasive that he even came up with a typology of three nostalgic forms he believed to be significant in late colonial Korean literature.[8] The first of these he termed a "feudal" nostalgia, which turned obsessively to the past and old things as a way to avoid the problems of the present. He cited Yi T'aejun's interest in antiques and practiced archaic writing style in his anecdotal essays as a primary example of this. Sŏ described a second type of nostalgia as "modern" and diagnosed it as a generational phenomenon suffered by those who had come of age in the early twentieth-century rush to enlightenment only to find their options foreclosed by state mobilization as the Second Sino-Japanese War and then the Pacific War took hold. This generation was not nostalgic for a distant past but for its own youth and the possibilities for the future that it had once seemed to hold. Finally, Sŏ isolated a decadent nostalgia, a general dis-ease with the past and the present, as a site for future hope in the way it sought to confront present contradictions rather than seek refuge in a comfortable past.

There is a way in which Yi T'aejun's work encompasses all three of Sŏ's nostalgic forms. Born in 1904, in the midst of the Russo-Japanese War fought partially on Korean soil, Yi belonged to the generation of modern nostalgics whose youth seemed in retrospect to have been a time of possibility and opportunity. This might seem ironic, because Yi was of the first generation of Koreans to receive their education in colonial schools, after the formal declaration of colonial rule in 1910. Yet the extreme rupture brought about by a modernizing colonialism paradoxically produced opportunities for some, while inflicting great violence on others. Yi was not from a particularly elite family, his father having been exiled to the Russian Far East after taking part in an attempted coup in the 1880s. Yi had been orphaned young and moved around the Korean peninsula in a rather nomadic style, before eventually traveling to the heart of the empire, where he managed to complete his education at Tokyo's elite Waseda University in the 1920s. At that time the imperial capital was the stage for dynamic social activism both in the arts and on the streets as avant-garde artistic movements and a colorful mass culture were taking hold in Japan's growing cities. Returning to Korea in the 1930s, Yi was to rise to the forefront of the literary scene in a decade when Korea would also experience a large increase in its urban population as its predominantly agricultural economy began to diversify and writing was to emerge as a profession for a very few. Increasing literacy rates had meant that readership of newspapers soared, and commercial magazines, as opposed to the small coterie journals of the previous decade, emerged and demanded material to fill their pages. Whereas publishing had previously been seen as an act of self-sacrifice for a patriotic cause, by this time writers were beginning to be paid by the printed page, and a small number of them, including Yi T'aejun, could earn a living by writing, editing at newspapers, and teaching in schools.

The life brought about by such upward mobility bred the very modern fantasy of the past having been simpler and morally pure, at the same time that few seriously wished to turn back the pages of time. In the mid-1930s Yi moved to the neighborhood of Sŏngbuk-dong, then located on the outskirts of the colonial capital. His stories detail daily life in a leisurely neighborhood, where older residents coexisted with up-and-coming young families such as Yi's, whose wage earners could commute into the inner city on the newly expanded bus lines and tramlines. "Mr. Son, of Great Wealth" is one of several character portraits Yi wrote during this period that gently portray the eccentricities of people living askew to the demands of the modern city. Yi's favorite characters were uneducated, sweetly naïve, and often old, as in "The Broker's Office," which depicts a trio of old men who feel unwelcome in a changing world and alienated from the values of the younger generation. Other stories from this time present the claustrophobic mental life of an intellectual protagonist, who appears to be thinly based upon the author himself. Such stories invariably locate the protagonist's concerns within the domestic sphere, even when he is wandering, flâneur-like, through the capital's streets, as in "The Rainy Season," or attempting to forge a livelihood, as in "A Tale of Rabbits." While the public life of the city appears increasingly cut off to these colonial subjects, the stories depict a domestic life emerging during this period, which is recognizable to readers today with its economic uncertainties, gentle bickering, and slightly sentimental tone.

Yet the arc of Hyŏn's life in "A Tale of Rabbits" suggests a violence increasingly encroaching upon Yi's rather sentimental world. The nostalgia that accompanies the sense of an end to a time of growth and opportunity does not merely refer to middle age here but is decisively shaped by the larger geopolitical situation. As a decidedly nonsocialist aesthete, Yi had been unaffected by the first roundups of Korea's top socialist thinkers in 1931, roughly coinciding with the so-called Manchurian Incident and the founding of the Manchukuo puppet regime. When in January 1935 the leaders of Korea's proletarian arts movement (Korea Artista Proleta Federatio, or KAPF) declared its official end under intense suppression, the waning of its dominance over the literary scene might even have been welcomed by Yi, who valued the noninstrumental celebration of the arts. But a self-made man such as Yi could only have been devastated to watch an ever-tightening surveillance unfold. His fortunes had risen with that of the printed Korean word, but that print's public life came under threat with the onset of war in China in 1937 and the opening of a second front in the Pacific in 1941. The response of the Japanese state was to move toward a regime of total mobilization, including the attempt to violently assimilate its Korean colony into the "Japanese nation" through a host of new policies. In 1938 Korean was declared an optional language of study in Korea's schools, with Japanese established as the national language and Korean eventually equated with the status of mere dialect by colonial bureaucrats. In 1940 the major vernacular daily newspapers were closed down, along with many of their sister magazines, and subsequently the spaces for Korean print shrank dramatically. From 1938 Koreans were allowed to "volunteer" for the Imperial Army, but from 1942 they would be drafted, while writers were induced to take part in propaganda tours recruiting support and volunteers for the ongoing war. A guaranteed livelihood, writing in Korean, and soon freedom from the fear of colluding in or dying for the colonizer's war now all became legitimate objects for nostalgia.

The stories at the center of this collection date from this period of great uncertainty, which was paradoxically Yi's most productive time as a writer. The impulse for the journeys into the countryside that form the settings for "The Frozen River P'ae," "The Hunt," "Evening Sun," and "Unconditioned" lies in the unease with everyday life in the capital, which was more closely associated with the economic and political regime of the empire. The nostalgia for a past that is simpler and less commercial is one way of registering Yi's disquiet with his present, but also forms the creative impulse for imagining alternative fictional worlds. "The Frozen River P'ae" and "Evening Sun" take their protagonists to the provincial cities of Pyongyang and Kyŏngju, respectively: both cities were associated with a decidedly feminized and exoticized past, which was at the time becoming the focus of commercial tourism.[9] Visitors from throughout the empire traveled to see Kyŏngju's temples and ancient burial mounds, or to Pyongyang, where they hoped to consort with the famous *kisaeng* performers, supposedly the most beautiful women in all of Korea. Yi tends to be unsparingly critical of this commercialization of the past, but he was hardly free himself from the contemporary craze for tradition and all things old. From 1939 until 1941 he worked as editor for the journal *Munjang* (Writing), one of two Korean-language literary journals that managed to publish past the closure of the vernacular newspapers. *Munjang* championed Korea's new young writers, but had a decidedly antiquarian bent, from its cover and interior designs to its rediscovery and serialization of Korea's literary classics, and explorations of the nature of traditions. In "Evening Sun" we see a hint of a decadent nonreconciliation with the present, which Sŏ Insik had cited as the potential for a future-oriented politics, but we also see how the story ultimately diffuses that conflict and returns Hyŏn to the capital at its end. The story thus provides material for contradictory claims that were later made about its author: (1) that he disdained the world-changing power of colonialism and protected the nation's traditions, and (2) that he adopted a fundamentally "passive" stance to life that colluded with the imperial power. Such claims were to exert real-life effects when Japan's colonial rule came to an end.

"Before and After Liberation" is often read as a documentary witness to life during the final months of the Pacific War and the imperial state's efforts to mobilize writers to its cause. In the story, Hyŏn escapes to a rural village in 1943, where he lives a rather dilettantish life of fishing and reading until news comes of Japan's defeat in war and he returns to Seoul. The story reads equally, and not accidentally, as a kind of apology for a life of passivity and a public declaration of Yi's transformed attitude to life and politics in the post-Liberation world. By the time the story appeared, one year after Liberation, Yi T'aejun had moved to the northern zone and was touring the Soviet Union as a representative of what would later be called the Democratic People's Republic of Korea. There is no mistaking the difficult real-life maneuvering demanded by Yi's past actions and new location. As Liberation soon revealed itself to be the rapidly polemicizing landscape of national division, the question of how one had lived under colonial occupation was a charged one in both the northern and southern zones, with potentially deadly accusations of collaboration thrown about widely. Yi was undoubtedly trying to preempt the criticism of his behavior that would surely be thrown at him by colonial-era socialist writers. But "Before and After Liberation" also stands as a literary testimony to dividing forms and language. As the scene shifts in the second part of the story, so does the sentence length, style, and language. The uneasy gaze at the retreating figure of Headmaster Kim at the end of the story bids farewell to a much larger realm of old things, thinking, and knowledge that must be routed with the rupture brought on by the new world.

Two other stories included here suggest that the revolutionary power of the new world was far from total and that it was not so easy to discard the past. If "Tiger Grandma" offers an entertaining take on Yi's long-held fascination with colorful subaltern characters, the longer "Dust" recalls the figure of the antiquarian and an old man struggling to reconcile to his present. That present is now a divided land, and the old man takes center stage, but is afraid of becoming a mere speck of dust caught up in the turmoil of historical change, as a recurring metaphor describes his situation. Are we correct to read Hyŏn into the old man's thoughts, or has Hyŏn merely disappeared in the writing of a good story? Throughout the quarter century of Yi's career represented by this collection, his fiction verged on autobiography to an ultimately undeterminable degree. There is no reason to believe his works written in the North are any less fictional than the earlier ones.

In retrospect, many critics have been flummoxed by Yi's decision to move to the socialist zone, but in this he shared a decision made by many of the colonial era's most well-known modernist writers and artists. The majority believed the authentically new lay to the north, and we should perhaps consider this a legacy of the exploitative nature of Japan's colonial rule, which caused socialism to be seen as a more viable prospect by many, even by some who shared Yi's previously rather noncommittal political thinking. Despite his early acceptance by the northern regime, however, by the early to mid-1950s Yi began to be subjected to extreme criticism for "bourgeois thinking," a charge that would be hard to deny, given the amount of evidentiary proof left by his voluminous works. Finally, he was sent into exile: a fate shared by so many of those who had crossed from the South, although less severe than the executions that felled others. His whereabouts thereafter are unclear, and, despite many poetic rumors of him ending up working in a print shop or even a brick factory, the circumstances of his final years and death remain unknown.

Throughout his career, Yi T'aejun had despised above all the instrumentalization of art, despite having himself relied upon it for his own livelihood. He was probably most aesthetically in tune with the diffused literary world that emerged after the suppression of socialism and the proletarian art movement. As a member of the Group of Nine he had explicitly criticized the attitude to the arts of some of the proletarian writers, and as a newspaper editor he had championed the poetry of Yi Sang (1910–1937), whose abstract work had scandalized the public with its incomprehensibility and attracted demands that it not be published. It was in this sense that Yi T'aejun had demanded a literature that arose "from the individual alone"; not from the demands of the Communist Party, but neither from the propagandistic desires of the wartime state or the capitalist market. The vicissitudes of mid-twentieth-century Korea were to provide little space for an artist such as Yi.

This collection of Yi T'aejun's short stories aims to introduce some of the best of his fiction. It also strives to present work from across his entire known career. Extreme censorship has silenced his work in the two states on the Korean peninsula that he called home: he is unpublished in North Korea today and was only belatedly lifted out of oblivion in the South with the relaxation of laws in 1988, which had prevented the publication of works by those artists who chose to go north either before or during the Korean War. Although freely read in South Korea today, collections of his work invariably separate stories written after he went north into a separate volume, reinforcing a sense of their illegitimacy, both political and literary. The field of English translation has followed, and fallen behind, these publication practices, with the result that works written in the North are rarely translated at all and often refused the title of "literature" in a legacy of Cold War thinking. This collection thus attempts to conjoin two things rarely read together—the before and after of Liberation. Despite the polemical divides of before and after, and North and South, we can see many continuities in Yi's work that point to a writing life, a coherent aesthetic ideal, and an ongoing love of the written word.

In 1933 the poet Kim Kirim (1908–?) praised Yi's work by labeling him a "stylist" in a move that has occasionally worked to undermine Yi's achievements as a writer of fiction.[10] But if we understand "style" to mean the riches of creative experimentation and attention to language at a time when literature in the Korean language was still barely established, then the term captures some of Yi's unique qualities and innovation as a writer. To the translator, "stylist" signals a challenge of a different dimension, of course. I have attempted to match Yi's quiet and measured prose, for though a stylist, Yi was not ostentatious in his use of language. I have suggested his nuanced play with words where possible, but Yi often played with the multiple languages in use in colonial Korea, and it is not easy to reproduce the tiers of meaning between the imperial language of Japanese and its colonial Korean counterpart when translating into English. Even harder to convey is Yi's profound love and use of dialect, especially when depicting colorful characters from different classes and regions of Korea, but neither does it seem right to ignore this. When we consider that the Korean Language Society had announced the first attempt to standardize the written Korean language only in 1936, when Yi was entering mid-career, we can see that his explorations with dialect, newly visible in response to the standardization of language, constituted more than mere personal taste. On this point, however, the translator is doomed to fail. I have tried to gesture toward Yi's different languages, but exchanging them with supposedly equivalent ones from other worlds seemed untrue to Yi's claim for their particularity.

The move north for Yi proved to be not only a political move, but also a stylistic one. A striking change in tone divides a story such as "Before and After Liberation," where the two halves of the story and their different aesthetic worlds demand a differentiation in everything from style to worldly references and diction. If the language in my translation of the second half of that story, and of the later story "Dust," seems somehow less opaque and more instrumental, this is because it attempts to follow Yi's Korean, which became noticeably streamlined in adapting to a new reality. In the 1930s, Yi often wrote about the significance of the long sentence as a guiding post for the organization of his style and as a characteristically Korean creative form. I have thus tended to keep to Yi's sentence breaks, even where others might be more inclined to break up the long sentences into more palatable bites for the Anglophone reader. I am mindful also that the Anglophone reader of Yi's time would probably have had more patience with his sentences' meandering form. A translation will always necessarily remain an approximation, but I hope at least to have suggested some of the nuance and creativity of the stylist Yi T'aejun.

Finally, I should add a note on the multiple versions of colonial-era texts. Many of Yi's stories were first published in journals in the mid to late 1930s. Early in the 1940s they were often republished in single-volume collections of his short stories, and yet more single-volume collections appeared in the aftermath of Liberation. With each new publication the stories were altered to various degrees. Some of these alterations seem to suggest the author tidying up repetitions or awkward phrasings, whereas others suggest the changing landscape of censorship as the historical situation unfolded. In South Korea the practice is to refer to the last version of the text touched by the author. I have, for the most part, followed this practice, except in cases where it seemed clear that censorship of content rather than the polishing of style had brought about changes, for example, in "A Tale of Rabbits," where I translated the first version from 1941. I have used a later version of "Unconditioned," where Yi added a lengthy final section when he republished the story in 1943, one year after its initial publication. The title "Unconditioned" may seem obscure at first, but refers to a Buddhist notion of liberation from the conditioning of everyday life, something to which perhaps the main character aspires. In the case of "The Frozen River P'ae," sentences from the 1938 version were removed in 1941, rather than rewritten, and I have been able to include them in parentheses to allow readers to draw their own judgments on the kinds of changes Yi made.

All but one of the stories I have translated date from 1935 or later, despite the fact that Yi made his literary debut a decade earlier. During that first decade he wrote some two dozen stories that would perhaps be best described as minor sketches, a passage toward his later achievements. There are simply too many to include here, but I have included the first version of "Omongnyŏ," a story that Yi republished with significant alterations in a 1939 collection. In this case his alterations seem to record an interesting shift away from the presentation of the flamboyant personality of the lead character and toward the movements of her husband and lovers in response. I have preferred to translate the earlier version as a record of a dynamic female character, who seems to disappear from Yi's writing for a while only to make a spectacular return in the early years of the Democratic People's Republic in the form of Tiger Grandma.

A brief glossary at the end of this volume identifies the many contemporary figures of the Korean writing scene that are mentioned by pen name only in the stories "The Rainy Season" and "A Tale of Rabbits." Although references to other writers also appear in other stories, their significance is explained within each story itself, and I have not included their details in the glossary.

NOTES

1. Yi T'aejun, *Ssoryŏn kihaeng* [Record of a journey to the Soviet Union] (Seoul: Cho-Sso Munhwa Hyŏphoe, Chosŏn Munhakka Tongmaeng, 1947), 1–2.

2. Charles Baudelaire, *The Painter of Modern Life and Other Essays*, 2nd ed., trans. Jonathan Mayne (New York: Phaidon, 1995).

3. For a more detailed discussion of Yi's work and late colonial Korean literature more broadly, see Janet Poole, *When the Future Disappears: The Modernist Imagination in Late Colonial Korea* (New York: Columbia University Press, 2014). On Yi and other members of the Group of Nine and their thinking about language, see Christopher P. Hanscom, *The Real Modern: Literary Modernism and the Crisis of Representation in Colonial Korea* (Cambridge, Mass.: Harvard University Asia Center, 2013).

4. Yu Chongho, "In'gan sajŏn ŭl ponŭn chaemi" [The pleasure of reading the dictionary of humankind], in Yi Sŏnyŏng, ed., *1930 nyŏndae minjok munhak ŭi ŭisik* [The consciousness of 1930s national literature] (Seoul: Han'gilsa, 1990), 293–307.

5. Yi T'aejun's most famous collection of anecdotal essays has been translated as Yi T'aejun, *Eastern Sentiments*, trans. Janet Poole (New York: Columbia University Press, 2009).

6. "The Short Story and the Conte," in Yi T'aejun, *Eastern Sentiments*, 61.

7. "For Whom Do We Write?," in Yi T'aejun, *Eastern Sentiments*, 53.

8. Sŏ Insik, "Hyangsu ŭi sahoehak" [The sociology of nostalgia], *Chogwang* [Morning light] 6, no. 11 (November 1940): 182–89.

9. Nayoung Aimee Kwon has written about the related prevalence of imperial nostalgia and what she calls "colonial kitsch" at this time in her *Intimate Empire: Collaboration and Colonial Modernity in Korea and Japan* (Durham, N.C.: Duke University Press, 2015).

10. Kim Kirim, "Sŭt'aillisŭt'ŭ Yi T'aejun ssi rŭl nonham" [On the stylist Mr. Yi T'aejun], *Chosŏn ilbo* [Chosŏn news], June 25–27, 1933.

DUST

AND OTHER STORIES

OMONGNYŎ

This place called Sŏsura is a port located at the northernmost tip of Northern Hamgyŏng Province, far beyond the towns of Wŏnsan, Sŏngjin, Ch'ŏngjin, and Ŭnggi.

If you travel about ten ri further north of Sŏsura you reach the Tuman River, and there, right on the east coast, lies a small town called Samgŏri. There are no more than forty households, all farming families, as well as a police substation; four or five inns; a barber shop; a dry goods store run by some Japanese selling cigarettes, alcohol, sweets, postage stamps, and the like; and a house operating something along the lines of a brothel.

In one of those four or five inns, situated at the top of the town, lives Chi Ch'ambong.

Ch'ambong does not refer in this case to the title of a government appointment. Chi has been blind since childhood and has been known as Chi Ch'ambong, or "Blindman Chi," for as long as everyone in the town remembers. He tells fortunes and conducts exorcisms on the side, but in such a small town there are not so many exorcisms or fortunes to deal with, and so he also runs an inn, but this being a remote border town far from the railroad, no more than five or six people show up on foot, even in a good month. The blind Chi Ch'ambong has in fact lived a life of destitute poverty. His household numbers two: Chi, now over forty, and a girl called Omongnyŏ, who is barely twenty years of age.

Everyone thinks that Omongnyŏ is his daughter. But as an aging bachelor, Blindman Chi had paid thirty-five won for a nine-year-old Omongnyŏ and brought her up with the intention of making her his wife. For the past five or six years already, Blindman Chi and Omongnyŏ have been living as husband and wife, and their neighbors have no idea whether they have married or not.

With just the two of them living together, Blindman Chi has grown to love Omongnyŏ to a frightful extent, but though she may well have allowed him thirty-five won worth of her flesh, when it comes to her affections she is barely worth thirty-five chon. This is no great surprise, of course, for how could a young woman to whom the future seems as bright as a flower not but feel dissatisfied living with a blind man old enough to be her father, no matter how she came to be sold?

If she gets hold of some tasty snacks, it's not in Omongnyŏ's nature to share them with her husband. They sit facing each other at mealtimes, but she's not the kind of woman who feels at all sorry about gobbling up everything herself, regardless of whether her blind husband eats a proper meal or not. This may well be why Chi looks as gaunt as a dried pollack. Two sunken eyes are affixed to his greasy face. The end of his tiny, green-chili-sized topknot is covered in white dust, and yet he always sits around wearing a horsehair headband. By contrast, Omongnyŏ has put on some weight since growing up, and her fair complexion invariably sports two rosy cheeks on a roundish face. Not really a beauty as such, she might perhaps be best described as soft and plump, a blessed woman? In such a tiny, remote town, this is enough for her to wag her tail and act like a great beauty. Omongnyŏ is one fine-looking woman, but she grew up in desperate poverty, and now that she has become used to tricking her blind husband out of both money and food, she has developed a habit of deception. If she wants something, even something that belongs to someone else, then she simply steals it and hides it away. Whenever guests show up or she shows signs of morning sickness she always manages to procure a tasty meal without spending any money.

It is the middle of August, and tomorrow is Omongnyŏ's birthday. She has bought a gourd-full of rice and gathered some seaweed, and now she is on the lookout for some fish, making her way through the darkness. She has come down to the seashore under misty moonlight and is stepping lightly across the soft sand with bare feet, a basket by her side. She stops in front of a boat on the shore, coughs, looks around, and then once sure that no one is about, she jumps aboard.

Omongnyŏ has been stealing from this boat whenever she feels like eating fresh fish or clams. The boat's owner is a bachelor named Kŭmdol, who moved here from Ŭnggi two years ago. As the son of a fisherman he is used to the sea and has been making his living as a fisherman since moving to this town. Kŭmdol takes the fish and clams that he has caught during the day and divides them into two parts, half to sell that evening and the other half on the following morning; while he takes the evening's share into town, he leaves the remaining fish on his boat and does not return until deep into the night after he has sold everything. Omongnyŏ has been taking advantage of this time to steal his fish and clams.

This evening too she casually jumped into the boat and was loading up her basket with fish and clams when—ah!—the boat suddenly moved. She hurried to the side only to discover that the boat was already so far from the shore that it was impossible for her to jump down.

It happened that Kŭmdol's catch that day had not been large enough to divide into two, and, having suffered from several recent thefts, he had decided to sell his entire catch the following day and wait in the evening to find out who was stealing his fish. When he discovered it was Omongnyŏ, known as the flower of the town, he could not believe his luck at the treasure he had caught. The best strategy, he decided, was first of all to set sail, and so he pushed his boat out into the water and began to row. A wide-eyed Omongnyŏ had no idea what to do. There was little point in shouting out, and she couldn't jump from the boat; a fish caught in a net would have better options.

The boat's anchor was only lowered once far enough from the shore to be out of sight on this misty moonlit night.

Kŭm: "M'lady?"

O: ". . ."

Kŭm: "Now don't be frightenin' yourself. What is it you think I'll do?"

Omongnyŏ's expression quickly changed and she smiled at him. Then she said,

O: "Boy, what're you up to? Take this here boat back to shore."

Kŭmdol smiled as he moved to her side, where he placed his trembling hands on her shoulders and pointed with one hand toward the moon, which was shrouded in soft clouds. Omongnyŏ did not try to evade him, but instead turned her head at his command to gaze up at the misty ocean moon, just as if she were meeting a promised lover. And then, in a low voice, she murmured:

O: "Take this boat in, d'you think there's anything I won't do if you just take the boat in . . ."

But the boat did not move.

A couple of hours later, it quietly slipped back to shore.

Omongnyŏ returned home deep into the night, her basket chock full of fresh fish and clams.

The following morning, she both roasted and boiled fish, and spread it out alongside fresh slices of clam, and that day even Blindman Chi ate well. This was the first time ever that Omongnyŏ had prepared such a birthday feast.

After meeting Kŭmdol, Omongnyŏ's dissatisfaction with Blindman Chi grew ever stronger. She had no idea why, but she always found herself comparing the two men. Chi was blind, old, and listless; if he had anything going for him it was this one thatched hut. Kŭmdol, on the other hand, could see perfectly well, was young and full of energy, and, though it was no home, the two of them fit quite snugly into his boat . . .

She wanted to see Kŭmdol again. She wanted to eat fresh fish and clams again. She thought of what Kŭmdol had said, as they left the boat on the night before her birthday and he dropped his hands from her shoulders, "Come back, will you? No one'll know. I'll expect you tomorrow night, so make sure you come."

She pined to see him, with the thought that he might produce something even better than fresh fish as a welcome.

More than ten days after she had celebrated her birthday, Omongnyŏ finally went back again with her basket. This time the boat stayed ashore even after she had climbed aboard. Although she had set off in the early evening, it was late at night by the time she returned home, her basket full of fresh fish and clams, naturally.

After this second meeting, she began to visit Kŭmdol whenever she was bored, just as if she were popping next door to see a neighbor. If Blindman Chi happened to make a little money telling a fortune, she would take the money and head off to the wine shop carrying a bottle. But Blindman Chi would not catch even a whiff of alcohol that evening; instead a tipsy Kŭmdol would be banging on the side of his boat, as if playing a drum, and pestering Omongnyŏ, who had fallen in love for the first time in her life.

This being a border town, the police keep a strict control on inns, on account of the armed bandits and smugglers who operate in the area and deal in opium, kaoliang liquor, and tobacco. Inn owners have to report the arrival of any guest to the police substation within the evening. And if they forget just once? Then the inn owner is thrown into jail or fined, and naturally the inn is put out of business.

Whenever a guest arrived at Blindman Chi's house, they too would have to fill out the guest information book that same evening, and Omongnyŏ would then take it to the substation. Altogether there were three officers stationed here: the chief, who was Japanese, and then constables Yi and Nam. This Constable Nam harbored indiscreet thoughts about Omongnyŏ whenever he saw her. When he thought of his slowly shriveling wife, who had now given birth twice and was losing her spirit as well as amassing wrinkles on her face, and then he saw Omongnyŏ, plump and at her peak, he would grow overexcited. He even believed that, given the opportunity, and Omongnyŏ's aging husband, he would be able to fulfill his desire for her with little resistance.

August soon passed. One evening in early September, a traveler arrived at Blindman Chi's house and ordered dinner, looking to stay overnight, but when he heard the foghorns of the boats entering Sŏsura Port, he set out immediately after dinner without sleeping over, having grown worried that he might miss the next morning's boat. There had been neither time, nor any need, to fill out the guest information book. This just happened to coincide with the substation chief taking advantage of a holiday coinciding with a Sunday in order to go on a three-day hunting trip and Constable Yi escorting a couple of gamblers to Ch'ŏngjin to hand them into custody. Left by himself, Constable Nam had been trying to devise some plan that would take advantage of this golden opportunity, when he heard that a guest had eaten dinner at Blindman Chi's house but no guest information had been provided. He took Omongnyŏ into custody that very evening and locked her up at the station. Then he went to see Blindman Chi, and this is what he said: "Ch'ambong, why didn't you bring us the information? The chief's angry, but I'll soon talk him round. We'll take care of this no problem, so don't you worry yourself too much."

Blindman Chi had no idea what was going on and apologized a hundred times. He begged the constable to talk to the chief and bring Omongnyŏ home quickly. The rotten Constable Nam told Chi not to worry with a swagger that suggested he had all the power.

Nine o'clock passed, and it was near ten by the time the lights in the houses in town began to go dark one by one and Constable Nam quietly slipped out to unlock the station cell. His voice quivered, "Omongnyŏ? I'm goin' to put you in the night duty room, the chief won't know."

He told her to use his quilt and sleep by herself in the night duty room, while he would go back home. Then he locked the storm door so she couldn't escape, and she heard him walk away.

Omongnyŏ had been crouching in the chilly cell for a while and was grateful for Constable Nam's kindness. The small room had been newly wallpapered and the furnace was neither too hot nor too cold, so that it was as warm inside as a spring day. A thick Japanese quilt covered with Shandong silk was spread out over almost the entire floor. A kind of vain curiosity arose in Omongnyŏ, who had never owned even a cotton quilt. When she placed her hand between the quilt and the futon, the soft warmth made her heart thump and her chest pound even more than when Kŭmdol's burning breath would evaporate over her face. But when she began to wonder why Constable Nam had shown her such sympathy, she suddenly recalled an incident from the previous winter. She grimaced as she realized she had been in this room before.

A constable named Pang had preceded Constable Nam. He would beat people terribly whenever he drank, whether they were guilty of any crime or not. This Constable Nam also beat people, abusing men old enough to be his father and strutting around the streets as if he owned the place, but in general he had a reputation for being an improvement on Pang. Last winter when Pang was still in town he too had been left alone for several days and had visited Omongnyŏ's house for no particular reason. Upon discovering that Blindman Chi was away at an exorcism in some other village, he had arrested Omongnyŏ and humiliated her here in this very room. Afterward he had harassed her relentlessly until sometime in March when he had died crossing the Tuman River. This Nam had arrived from Ch'ŏngjin as Pang's replacement.

Omongnyŏ closed her eyes as she recalled the incident and guessed that Constable Nam had brought her in with similar intentions, and not for the crime of failing to report a guest. She wasn't in the least bit frightened however, but considered this an honor bestowed upon her alone. She fell asleep, fully dressed, on top of that plump Shandong silk quilt while waiting for Constable Nam to show up. He still had not arrived by the time the clock in the office struck twelve. His wife must be nagging him not to go out again when he only slept at home alternate nights, at least that's what Omongnyŏ thought, and forgetting all about him, she extinguished the furnace, removed her jacket and skirt, and slipped beneath the quilt.

As the soft warmth swept over her bare skin, Omongnyŏ's lustful body shivered with excitement. "Kŭmdol'll be waiting for me later tonight," she whispered to herself, and then she even tossed her coarse underwear to one side before falling asleep.

This was the first time that she had ever slept in the nude and stretched out beneath a Shandong silk quilt at that.

She had been asleep no more than thirty minutes when something unfamiliar touched her lips. She was experienced enough to recognize the lips of a bearded man even while sleeping. She opened her eyes wide. But in the dark she could only hear the sound of somebody next to her, removing his clothes. Although surprised, she spoke quietly in a low voice that would not be heard outside the room, "Oh, now who's this stray?"

"It's me . . . shhh, shhh . . ."

It was without a doubt the voice of Constable Nam.

Omongnyŏ finally emerged from the room at dawn the following day. No sooner had she hurried out of the gate than she unfolded some paper clutched in her right hand. There were two one-won notes. After glancing back just once with a sense of satisfaction, she made her way home, all the while thinking to herself, "Oh, a person's looks gives everything away, that old bastard Pang, now d'you think that bastard would give me money? Calls me to the cell, does his business, and then locks me back up! Good job he's dead, good job . . . now this Constable Nam, he calls me Omongnyŏ and m'lady, with that other bastard it was 'bitch this,' 'bitch that' . . . and then that quilt! That was quite something, if only I could sleep under a quilt like that every night . . ."

Sometime later, a slightly inebriated Constable Nam entered Omongnyŏ's kitchen in the evening, only to hear several voices in her husband's room. The combined kitchen and parlor was empty. The constable listened at the door and overheard some youths from the town, who had lost their hawk on a pheasant hunt and come to discover whether the cards would say he'd gone east or west. Perfect, thought Constable Nam, and he quietly tried the door to the backroom, when Omongnyŏ's hand reached out to grasp his and pulled him inside, the door closing behind the both of them.

The cards quickly concluded the hawk had gone north. The disheartened youths soon scattered, "Signs are we'll never catch that hawk . . ." North from here meant the mountains across the Tuman River, and to go there meant almost certainly to be shot dead. After he'd sent the young men away, Blindman Chi went to lie down in the warm parlor, but as he fumbled around for his wooden pillow, his hands landed on an unfamiliar pair of shoes. A blind man with many thoughts and well aware of Omongnyŏ's behavior, he held on firmly to those shoes as he pressed his ear to the backroom door. Two people were breathing evenly, but no voices were to be heard. His ears were as sharp as his eyes were dull, and there was little that escaped his suspicion. They had stilled their breath so that no one would hear, but nothing escaped Blindman Chi. He knew that such shoes could only belong to a constable in a town like this. He suppressed the urge to rush straight in with a knife and cut the couple up, knowing well that any rash move might lead him, who could not see, to let the man slip away without discovering his identity. And so he waited, with just one shoe in his hand.

Not long afterward, Omongnyŏ's laughing voice rang out, and the door opened. The couple saw Blindman Chi sitting in the parlor. Omongnyŏ retreated into the backroom, while Constable Nam crept around Blindman Chi, keeping his distance, and would have made a run for it, but for the fact he was missing one shoe. Chi called out, "Who's there?" And then shouted, "Don't you need your shoes, hey, who's there? Who . . . is there no one human in this town?" No matter how he thought about it, Constable Nam had to act quickly. Soon everyone in town would come running, and his job would be at a greater risk than his shame even. He thrust several banknotes into the blind man's hands, and then brought the affair to a safe conclusion by tempting, pacifying, and threatening him all at once, with the promise that if Chi didn't keep quiet, a fine of one hundred won for not reporting a guest would soon follow, whereas his silence would be rewarded: Nam promised to confer with his boss and somehow force the other inns to shut down, leaving Chi the only inn owner in town.

From this moment on, even when Omongnyŏ visited Kŭmdol's boat, Blindman Chi presumed she was with Constable Nam. And several days later, just as Nam had promised, one of those other inns was ordered to close on account of its rooms having been found unclean. Blindman Chi gave the issue some more thought and decided his inn might be the only one left within a matter of months. From then on he said nothing when Omongnyŏ went out only to return during the night or early the next morning.

M eanwhile, Kŭmdol was growing impatient. Omongnyŏ had been visiting him eight days out of every ten, but now she was skipping two or even three days at a time. One morning he had gone to the police chief's house to sell his fish, when he caught sight of her coming out of the night duty room. That's how he discovered the reason for her less frequent visits. That day Kŭmdol bought five or six measures of rice, as well as soy sauce, firewood, drinking water, and a small iron pot, all of which he brought onto the boat without Omongnyŏ knowing. Then he waited for her to show up.

Omongnyŏ finally appeared the following evening, carrying her basket. When she jumped in her usual fashion into the boat, where Kŭmdol had been sleeping on a straw mat, he got up and pushed the boat away from shore. He began to row. That evening, the boat landed at a small, deserted island some ten ri away.

N o matter how long Blindman Chi waited, Omongnyŏ did not return home. One day, two days, three days passed, and there was still no sign of her. The old man thought Constable Nam must be playing some kind of trick.

When Omongnyŏ did not return on the fourth evening, Chi called Constable Nam to his house to have it out with him. He was ranting, "You bastard, if you haven't hidden her away, then who's done it? You bastard, you're killin' me, how can I live alone when I can't even see? I don't care if I have to go to prison for not reportin' a guest, I'll file a complaint against you." Blindman Chi was so angry that he charged at Constable Nam, and even his sealed eyes seemed to blink. Nam was left with no choice but to set some kind of trap. If Omongnyŏ had run away, she was unlikely to return. . . . And so, in the end, he came up with a plan. He seemed to confess that everything was his fault.

"I've got nothin' to do with what's happened to that wife, but I can't just stand by and do nothin', can I? I'll find her in three days. It must be hard for you. I got paid today so I'll go home and come back with some money. There's nothin' to worry about. I'll have her back in three days . . ."

Nam's behavior seemed reasonable. When he assured Chi he would find her within three days and mentioned his salary, it seemed as if Omongnyŏ had already been found and some money would appear that evening too. Judging from his face, the old man seemed appeased, "Then be on you way . . ."

But instead of going home, Constable Nam went to the substation. Once his boss had left and he was alone, he sneaked into the office and took some opium and a bottle of kaoliang liquor, which had been confiscated from a smuggler. When all the lights in the town were dark and everyone had gone to sleep, he went to Blindman Chi's house.

Nam: "It's late, uncle. I went to get a bottle of kaoliang liquor."

Chi: "No, where on earth did you get hold of that? You're a smart one, Constable Nam. I tried some of that once when I crossed the river to the west . . ."

Nam: "If word gets out, there'll be trouble. Shall we go to the backroom?"

Chi: "Anywhere . . ."

And so Blindman Chi was lured into the backroom by the taste of kaoliang liquor.

Nam: "Now this is strong stuff. I had myself two cups at breakfast yesterday and had to sleep it off."

Chi: "Well, it's best to sleep after a drink. Those travelers I see who drink and don't sleep, they just don't seem human. Sleepin' a few drinks off is the gentleman's way . . ."

Right in front of Chi's unseeing eyes, Constable Nam mixed the opium into his drink. The blind man collapsed before drinking even three cups of this special kaoliang liquor.

The constable knew all about the way corpses are examined in order to distinguish between a murder and a suicide, and so he took a kitchen knife and stabbed Blindman Chi clumsily in several places around the throat. In this way, he made it look to someone else as if this were a suicide. The rogue Constable Nam then had another thought. He took Chi's seal out of his pocket and created a bond of debt. For the amount he wrote forty won, with Blindman Chi as the debtor and himself as creditor. He dated the bond a couple of months previous.

Blindman Chi's body was discovered the following afternoon by someone who had come to have their fortune read and then reported it to the substation. The chief's two subordinates, Constables Yi and Nam, both attended the scene and, after examining the body, concluded without a doubt that the man had committed suicide: he was a blind man, there was no food in the house, and he had clearly grown despondent when his wife had apparently left him. That evening they ordered the district head to have him buried in the public graveyard.

Constable Nam showed the forged bond of debt for forty won to his boss, and easily took possession of Blindman Chi's house.

Omongnyŏ and Kŭmdol enjoyed more than twenty days on the deserted island. With no one to watch her other than the passing birds, this island was paradise, an incomparably ideal environment for the debauched and lustful Omongnyŏ.

But then the days grew colder and their rice ran low, so that they had to leave their island paradise.

Omongnyŏ was satisfied with Kŭmdol as her husband, and of course he was happy too, so they promised each other they would return to the town to buy some more provisions and take some household goods without Blindman Chi knowing, and then they would go live in Vladivostok. Thus Omongnyŏ and Kŭmdol returned to Samgŏri for the first time in more than twenty days.

This was when Omongnyŏ discovered that Blindman Chi was dead. She was overjoyed, as if she had made it to heaven.

When Constable Nam heard that Omongnyŏ had returned to town he immediately went to see her, worried that the house would cause a problem.

Nam: "Ah, so what've you been up to? Not even knowin' that the husband's dead and gone. Well!"

O: "Good job that! I was in Pangjin, but had to come back again because I'm not so well."

Nam: "Pangjin, why? Did you go there to get yourself a husband? Ha, ha!"

O: "What, one of those good for nothing travelers? Why would I be on the lookout for a husband when there's Constable Nam now? Mmm! So now I'm a constable's wife as well."

Nam smiled, as if that really were the case.

Nam: "I've bought this house!"

O: "No! Who sold it?"

Nam: "Well, who was there to pay for the old man's burial? We had to do something. So the chief sold me this house to pay for the funeral, and the rest went to public funds."

O: "You mean that rest can't be found anymore?"

Nam: "Are you crazy or what? The old man died when you went away, I managed to stop them lookin' for you, they were goin' to put you on trial, so don't talk to me like that. If the boss doesn't get his way, there could still be a trial now . . ."

O: ". . . for that . . ."

In this way Constable Nam managed to resolve the problem of the house to his satisfaction.

Omongnyŏ and Nam looked at each other lovingly for a while without saying a word, while Omongnyŏ thought about that Shandong silk quilt. As a new plan took shape in her mind, she pressed her smiling lips to Constable Nam's ear, whispered something, and laughed raucously.

Constable Nam laughed too. It was nothing other than the happy thought of setting up another home in his new house with a concubine. And so that Shandong silk quilt was spread in Blindman Chi's backroom that night.

However, Constable Nam did not show up, even as the night grew dark. Omongnyŏ heard later that his wife had given birth. Instead, Omongnyŏ and Kŭmdol took advantage of this opportunity to move everything worth possessing to the boat, including the Shandong silk quilt, the pots, and even clothing.

And then the newlyweds Omongnyŏ and Kŭmdol set sail for Vladivostok for good.

Translated from *Sidae ilbo*, July 13, 1925

M r. Son is quite the popular guy in Sŏngbuk-dong. There's
nowhere he fails to show up whenever something's going
on: whether it's a wedding or a funeral, clearing out a plot of
land or digging a well, or even in the midst of the hubbub that
arises when somebody's child falls over and gets hurt. He has
no fixed occupation but is a stroller by nature who enjoys chatting with others, and even though you may sometimes hear
some inappropriate gossip when he calls out nonsense to you,
on the whole there's no one better suited to a lively occasion
than Mr. Son. It's his habit to go running toward any conspicuously loud sound of a creaking gate, and if something's going
on that demands a lively atmosphere, whether wedding or funeral,
the people here invariably go and fetch him to their homes
themselves.

Yet I have never seen him stumble around drunk or fail to
turn around at once to politely greet the slightest acquaintance
who happens to pass by, no matter how enthusiastically he might
be chatting away with someone else. "On your way to the
office?" "Finished work now?" He always greeted me morning
and night, even before we got to know each other.

I've forgotten now whether it was one day in the spring or early summer of last year when Mr. Son came to our house for the first time.

"Is anybody at home? U-um . . ."

He walked into our yard, chattering as if to himself and carrying a large piece of board, which if it were a book would be about four to six times the usual size.

"Welcome."

"Oh, so sir is here, that's good timing."

"What is that?"

"Well, uh . . ."

He blinked and grinned for a while before saying,

"I came to ask whether you might write on a nameplate for me."

"My goodness, what kind of nameplate has to be so huge?"

"Well, I can't just write my name, can I? There are other kinds of things that need to be written now."

"Other kinds of things?"

"Would you mind writing down what I say?"

Without further ado I fetched a brush and ink stone out onto the veranda and took hold of his piece of board.

"Okay, so tell me what you want me to write."

"Hold on a minute . . ."

He glanced back toward the gate and waved his hands, as if to chase some kind of animal away,

"Oh, darn it . . . damn kids . . ."

I turned around to see his two sons, who were always traipsing around in a line on his tail. One of them poked his head around the gate briefly, all the while sniffling and swallowing his own mucus, and then a second one poked his head around before disappearing again.

"I see your children have followed you."

"Oh, I can't even take a shit without those damn kids coming after me."

"Let them be, what does it matter? Please, tell them to come in."

He called out to them,

"Come on in then."

And he tutted.

At close glance one of them looked to be around ten years old and the other five or six, but both their faces were the spitting image of their father's: eyebrows thin and eyes as long and narrow as blades of oat grass, but with broad catfish grins.

"So, what shall I write?"

"First, we must write Sŏngbuk-dong, mustn't we?"

"Well, yes. But shouldn't we add the number too? And just write the name of the household head in large characters. . . . I think that's how we did it here?"

"No, that won't do. It's a bother to write all the names one by one. Let's put everyone in one place. Then could you write the total number of men and of women, followed by Eldest Son and his name, and Second Son and his name? Then if the census inspector shows up, we won't need to talk with him for long."

"Oh, I see now . . . that's why you brought such a large piece of board."

"Of course."

And he patted his sniffling, narrow-eyed youngest on the bottom.

I had never been asked to write such a nameplate before and was amused by his idea of it acting as a shield against the census inspector, but I was also somehow curious about his naïveté. First, I wrote "Koyang County, Sungin Township, Sŏngbuk Village" at the top, and then I asked, "And what number are you?"

"We don't need to write the number, do we?"

"But why not write it? Ah, how can we not write the number when we're going to write out the names of the eldest son, second son, and all that?"

"We don't have a number yet."

"Don't have a number?"

"Our house is built on the bank of the stream. What I mean is it's state-owned. Get my meaning? So we don't have a number until someone comes from the township and gives us one."

"Well, if that's the case . . . are you the head of the household?"

"Yes. Write Household Head and, underneath, Son Kŏbu. That's *son* as in the country, *kŏ* as in huge, and *bu* as in wealthy. That's right."

"Well, that's a name for a full stomach."

"And yet, I worry that we go hungry so often."

We both laughed. I wrote Household Head and Son Kŏbu, just as he asked.

"So, shouldn't we write your wife's name before that of your eldest son?"

"What do we need to write something like that for?"

"Something like that? Your wife's part of the family, isn't she?"

"Heh heh, there's nothing to write. I mean . . . do broads like that count as people? Where on earth . . ."

"I see, but it's because of your wife that you have these sons, isn't it? What is your wife's last name? And her first name?"

"What, well there's nothing to write, as I said. We've lived together twenty years and I still don't know her name."

Both he and his sons grinned.

"So leaving out your wife, what's your eldest son's name?"

"It's this rascal here, and he's called Taesŏng."

"*Tae* as in big and *sŏng* as in achievement?"

"Yes."

"And your second son? That one?"

"Yes, he's called Poksŏng."

"*Pok* as in happiness and *sŏng* as in achievement?"

"Yes."

"Those are two very fine names."

"The Village Head down there came up with them."

"And he did a fine job."

"Huh!"

Mr. Son spat and said, "But what's to say we turn out like our names? If that were the case, I'd want for nothing."

"Well, you never know if the day of great wealth is yet to come."

"That's where you're wrong. There was never any hope from the beginning."

"Why not? You just have to make some money from now on. . . . So, next you want me to write the number of men and women?"

"Yes, together with my sons there are three men, and one woman."

"No daughter?"

"We had one but we lost her."

"You lost a precious daughter among many sons."

"It's a good thing she died. Unless you have money or some standing in society, a daughter ends up living a shameful life, doesn't she? What kind of a scoundrel sells his own daughter as a street girl or harlot because he wants to? That's what happens when you don't have money or standing."

"When you think of it like that, then daughters really do live shameful lives, but . . ."

"Oh, I know. You're going to ask whether people don't sell sons too, when they need the money? But isn't that exactly why everyone has wanted a son since the old days?"

He patted each of his two kids on their heads, which were more burnt red than yellow, as if they were truly precious.

"You really love your children, don't you?"

"Of course. Do I have the riches that others have? Do I have a great big family? I just have the joy of raising these two."

"There, it's all done. Shall I read it through once?"

"Yes, please."

"Koyang County, Sungin Township, Sŏngbuk Village, Household Head Son Kŏbu, Eldest Son Taesŏng, Second Son Poksŏng, Three Men, One Woman, that's it. Is that okay?"

"Yes, that's wonderful. But aren't you going to put the total at the end there?"

"The total?"

"That the total population is four people."

I wetted my brush with more ink.

"Population? Wouldn't it better to say members of the household?"

"Please write Total Population Four People."

And just as he asked, I even added "Total Population Four People."

From that day on, Mr. Son became a frequent visitor to our house, whether for any particular reason or not.

"Did you know that the house cleaning inspections are on the XX day of this month?"

Or,

"Did you know that this month they're vaccinating at the school down there on the XXth?"

He would tell us all the news far more quickly than the village officials ever did.

"They say that the land over there with the apricot trees just sold for eight won a p'yŏng."

And,

"Did you hear the rumor about the burglar . . . he got away last night, over the back there at the paddy cave?"

He would come to see us on purpose to tell us such things.

Once he showed up and said, "I'm not here today to tell you anything, I've come to consult with you about something."

"Consult? Then, please come and sit down."

"Thank you."

He pointed at the eldest of his two children, who had as usual followed upon his tail, "This rascal here is exceeding my expectations. I think he's going to do better than his own dad."

"That's good, isn't it?"

"Ah, but he keeps saying he wants to go to school. D'you think I should send him?"

"Can there be any doubt? It's already late, isn't it?"

"Well, in this world they say you have to study if you want to get on in life without people looking down on you . . . so I went and explained everything at XX School down there, and they said to bring the child who's to be a student in tomorrow."

"Well, that's good then."

"There's no doubt at all that it's good to send him to school?"

"Ah, well you really should. Even those who are really struggling to get by should try to send their children to school."

"That's decided then . . . I just wanted to stop by and hear your opinion as I wasn't quite sure."

The following morning, Mr. Son stopped by our house, wearing only his everyday *chŏgori* jacket, albeit washed and neatly ironed, and explained that he was on his way to the school.

"If you have an old hat sir, I would greatly appreciate your lending it to me for a while."

"You mean to wear now?"

"Yes."

"Do you not have a coat either?"

"Does it matter? It just doesn't seem proper to go and introduce myself bareheaded. . . . I mean, if his father were to go into the school bareheaded it might discourage him. D'you see what I mean?"

"I understand. Please borrow my hat."

I don't know whether his head was too big or whether he hadn't put the hat on properly, but my felt hat perched on top of his head most precariously as he walked away in high spirits. His two sons followed close behind, looking up at him and giggling away.

After that the little rascal Taesŏng would pass by each day clutching a bundle of books, apparently on his way to school, and Mr. Son showed his face much less often than before.

"What's been going on? We haven't seen much of you recently."

I asked him one day.

"Ah, everything's changed now that one of them's at school. First he asks for books, then the monthly tuition, he's always asking for money. And then, well, it's not so bad if we go hungry, but how can we send him to school on an empty stomach? That's why I'm running here and there after all kinds of jobs."

With that he rushed off again. Once I met him walking back up the hill with blood dripping from his hands.

"My goodness, what happened?"

"I was doing some work at the quarry and scratched myself on some stones."

"That looks bad."

"It's the thumb, phew . . . I don't know if I'll be able to use it again."

It wasn't long after that I climbed up the hill behind us to go for my morning walk when I heard someone crying in the ravine over by the Buddhist shrine. It was a child's voice and judging from the way he was screaming his head off, he was being caned. I quietly crept over toward the noise and saw that Mr. Son had brought his eldest son up there to beat him.

"You little bastard. . . . Your dad goes without food to send you to . . . to send you to school and you, you little bastard, you skip classes to go roaming around the town in Chin'gogae . . ."

Having tied his son's wrists to prevent any escape, Mr. Son was holding a piece of wood so huge it looked more like a club than a cane, and he walloped his son on the back with a ferocity that made all the veins protrude on his own neck. Just then his pregnant wife, who looked as if she might be about to pop at any moment, staggered up to him dragging her feet.

"What, why . . . are you trying to kill him? What's he done wrong, eh? What's he supposed to do if the school tells him to stay away, eh . . ."

The son was immediately swept up into the mother's arms, and Mr. Son could only spit and put down the cane, unable to continue.

"And why did the school tell him to stay away? Oh, because we didn't pay the monthly tuition, and we didn't pay the support fees . . . that's just the little bastard's excuse . . ."

"What do you mean, excuse . . . the kid from the bleaching place came by and said the teacher had told him to stay away because he couldn't understand what teacher was saying, so that's it . . . I've never heard of a damn school like that . . . if he can't understand, why don't they teach him . . ."

Later that day I met someone from the school and asked about Taesŏng.

"The kid's mentally deficient. You can't teach him much of anything. He's just got a really thick head . . ."

Several days later, Mr. Son dropped in, once again holding in his hands the nameplate on which was written all kinds of other things, to use his words. Naturally, Taesŏng and Poksŏng formed some kind of a line behind him.

"Welcome."

"Thank you . . . I . . . Well, I had another son the day before yesterday."

"Really! And is your wife all right?"

"Yes, she's eating her rice and seaweed soup."

"Oh, I'm glad to hear that."

"Please sir, I was wondering if you'd mind making up a name? I need you to write it on the nameplate here anyway, so I took it down and brought it with me."

"A name?"

"Yes. . . . Seeing that Taesŏng and Poksŏng both end with *sŏng*, could you write another one that ends with *sŏng*, please?"

"You're not asking the Village Head?"

"He's not around at the moment. If you could please choose a good first part, anything will do."

"Anything good? What do you hope your third son will become, Mr. Son?"

"Who says that you turn out like your name?"

"Still . . ."

He stared at the hills in the distance for a while and then said, "I'd like him to be good at writing and earn a government stipend."

"Government stipend? Then, let's use *nok*, the character for stipend. As *nok* can also mean happiness, Son Noksŏng will be a fine name."

"Noksengi . . . that's a good one. Son Nokseng . . . just saying it sounds right. . . . So you'll have to add Third Son Noksŏng on here."

"That's right, and add one more to the total population."

I took out my ink stone and brush and wrote "Third Son Noksŏng" on his nameplate, and then I corrected "Total Population Four People" to "Five People." Taesŏng wanted to play with the ink stone, so I asked him, "You little rascal, aren't you going to school?"

Mr. Son sounded surprised, and said, "Goodness! I meant to tell you but completely forgot. . . . I've decided not to send that rascal to school."

He continued with his explanation before I could ask "Why not?"

"Well, you have to send them as far as university, don't you? Otherwise, they'll just end up temping at some company or store, and what's the point? It's more comfortable taking any job that comes your way. Isn't that so? The school keeps telling me to bring him in and I was going to, but then last night I decided for good not to."

"I see . . ."

I knew that Mr. Son was telling a lie, because I had seen him beat Taesŏng up on the hill and because of what I'd heard from the teacher at the school, but I could do no more than pretend to be listening properly.

"Noksengi, Noksengi, I'll have to practice saying that and it'll come more easily. Ah . . . thank you very much."

Mr. Son took his nameplate, with the new son's name added, and walked away at the head of his other two sons, looking very satisfied with himself. Before he went out the gate, he turned around and added, "Oh, don't forget the day after tomorrow we have to fly our flags. They're going to check up on everyone that day. Be sure to put yours out. Really . . ."

First published in 1935; translated from *Kamagui: Yi T'aejun tanp'yŏnjip* (Hansŏng tosŏ, 1937)

"Since you're just lying around, why don't you try opening up the closet?"

"What are you moaning about now?"

"Well, what will you do if all your books rot?"

My wife is dusting the mold from the cord of her electric iron, which she keeps hidden away somewhere.

"Why don't *you* get the books out while you're at it and dust them off too?"

"Do you think I have nothing else to do?! Why don't you take care of your own things, instead of keeping on at me . . ."

"All right . . . that's enough. If we go on like this, it'll be last night all over again."

I get up from the veranda floor and sit down in an easy chair. The chair is so damp it feels as if it has been boiled. When I wipe the armrest with the tie of my thin *chŏksam* jacket, it turns black with mold and dust as if a bug has been squashed into it. It's only then that I remember I had put on a clean jacket this morning; I hurriedly hide the tie and glance in my wife's direction. She's still busy wiping the cord of her iron with a dry cloth. If she'd seen me, she would invariably have grumbled, "Do you have to act like a child? Someone else has worked hard to wash that for you . . ." If I'd uttered so much as one word in reply, ten or twenty would have streamed out from her mouth.

Bickering like an old couple is generally a sign of having grown tired of life. But for a young couple like us, arguing back and forth as if trying to catch each other out in order to make some point, it seems almost a necessary tonic to clear the air from time to time.

Perhaps it's because of the rain that has kept me at home for the past couple of weeks, but our silly arguments have undoubtedly become more frequent. As a general rule, marital arguments come to seem trivial over the course of time (at least in our not-so-long experience), and so it was with our argument the previous evening, which had begun on such flimsy grounds. The flashpoint was our daughter, Somyŏng, having gone through four changes of clothing in one day. The child had been smacked for going out in the rain so often when there was no hope of the sun reappearing and all our wet clothes were sprouting mold; now she was wailing at full decibel. She was making so much noise I just had to stick my nose in. I told my wife that surely children have to play outside in the rain in order to develop resistance to things like colds, so what kind of nonsensical, irresponsible parent would confine them indoors just because it was hard to dry their clothes? But she was not to be defeated and countered that since I had brought up the question of responsibility, why was it that only mothers were held responsible and not fathers? Moreover, why was it that we could not buy any new clothes when the child was getting through so many outfits each day? And, why couldn't we build a house that was perfectly equipped to dry wet clothes before they turned moldy? And, given this situation, what kind of nonsensical, irresponsible father and husband would do nothing but sit and lecture so loudly? She went on to point out all the imperfections in our home finances as if she had them memorized, placing special emphasis on the phrase "why couldn't we" and rebuking me for all my inabilities.

In these circumstances, the only way to shut her up would be to maintain full composure while asking, "And what kind of broken promise is this? Who was it who promised before we were married that she wouldn't complain no matter what material difficulties we encountered?"

And if she continued complaining even after that, I would launch my final shot, "Then just do as you please."

There were so many hidden meanings contained in this phrase that she would be unable to suffer it in silence.

"Just do what as I please?"

If she asked for an explanation, I could make so many explosive declarations in return that this proved by far the most effective way to make her really angry.

Yesterday we'd reached the point where I explained the phrase with the result that she became so furious that her anger had still not abated by morning and rendered obsolete the saying that no one remains an enemy after a night's sleep.

Now it looks as if the rain might be drawing to an end. I take my shoes out from under the veranda. They are covered in white mold, both inside and out.

"Hey, honey?"

This is the first time since the previous night that I've tried conferring with her about something.

She merely glances in my direction.

"Honey?"

"Can't you say anything without calling me?"

"Is mold animal or vegetable?"

"Oh, you . . ."

To tell the truth, I can sometimes be quite irksome.

It's a long time since I've looked in a mirror in order to straighten my tie, and I find there a beard as unruly as the weeds in our yard.

Should I shave before I go out?

I take out a razor blade, but it's covered in rust. If anyone else had been using it, I would probably blame them, but this razor can only have rusted because I didn't wipe it dry before putting it away. It would take a lot of scraping to clean it up. Asking for water to be fetched, and then for some soap, seems like all too much trouble. I think of Yi Sang and his beard, which stretches from ear to jaw just like Lincoln's. A prickly beard with a hint of the wild is not such a bad look after all. But my beard is on the thin side. In photographs my father's beard is quite long, but clearly he did not pass that on to me.

It's still only eleven o'clock, but if I were to go now to Nang-nang or the Myŏngch'i Bakery I would probably find Yi Sang or Kubo, sporting far thicker beards than mine and sitting looking bored in front of coffee cups, being free from employment as they are. If I were to walk in, they would greet me enthusiastically, as if they'd been expecting me. And maybe they would even tell me a story or recommend something they had recently read to stimulate my creative impulses, which are now also covered in spores of mold.

I leave the house. When I reach the front of the grape field, I look down at the stream without forgetting my usual thought: "If only the bus came as far as this stone bridge." After several days of rain, the water is clear enough to brush your teeth in it. A woman walks by and exclaims, "Oh, it's perfect for washing."

I lament the sad customs of Korea's women, who can only look at such crystal-clear water and think, "It's perfect for washing."

There's not a single spot of blue sky in sight. As I climb up the hill, the sky seems to fall even lower. The windows are closed at Pockmark's store, and an ice cream container forgotten by time has rolled out into the road, obstructing any traffic.

"Who d'you think you're kidding. . . . I've got all the orchids, just look . . ."

Pockmark's wife's voice is as shrill as that of any twelve-year-old. I call it Pockmark's store, but other people usually call it the hunchback's store, on account of the wife. If only she weren't a hunchback, she would have been a beauty far beyond the reach of Pockmark: her skin is as white as a roundworm, and her tiny eyes, nose, and mouth as pretty as can be. Once deformed she probably had no choice but to come to Pockmark and his ice shop here on the hill, but she still retained a sense of pride, which deep inside made her scornful of her husband. Judging from what occasionally catches my ears as I pass by, she's often complaining in her childish voice about "the likes of you" doing this or that. Her husband, so dark and rough in contrast, then glares and chases after her, shouting, "You little . . . ," and grabbing onto her until a noise somewhere between a scream and a whine can be heard long after I've passed by. He's all too large and sturdy compared to her slender body and legs, which are bent like those of a grasshopper. Once I saw him riding his bicycle back from the market carrying a full load of bananas and pop, among other things; he didn't stop once between the Posŏng school at the bottom of the hill and the front of his store at the top. Maybe she finds some secret pleasure in being held roughly by such a strong young man while she screams in her whining voice. Perhaps they're the ones living a blessed life in this world full of worries, for they sit together and play cards, betting on suits and the like, no matter whether they are running out of food or no customers show up on account of the rain.

That rain starts to fall again. Namsan is shrouded in a light mist. Walking down the hill is always more pleasant and conducive to thinking than walking back up.

Someone must have acted as a go-between for this disfigured husband and his bent-up wife, because they surely could not have shaken each other's hands by themselves, all the while thinking, "Since I'm pockmarked, a hunchback is fine," and "Since I'm a hunchback, a pockmarked husband will do." The go-between would have visited one side first to report that the groom was pockmarked and then visited the other to report that the bride was a hunchback.

What thoughts passed through the young bachelor's mind when he heard that the girl he would marry was a hunchback?

Just thinking about it makes me feel sad.

But I still have further to go before I reach the bottom of the hill.

What about when we got married?

I try to recall our own past. I was from Kangwŏn Province, and my wife from Hwanghae Province, and until I was twenty-six I had neither seen nor even heard of her. We had been brought together by an acquaintance of mine, a Miss Cho (now also a teacher), who was also a close friend of my wife's. Yet, it was not the case of us seeing each other by chance because of Miss Cho and then a romance developing. Even if there had been such an opportunity, my wife does not have the slightest natural ability to be the heroine of a romance story, though I might. Miss Cho had brought us together from the very beginning with the question of marriage in mind. I don't know how she had introduced me to my wife-to-be, but to me she'd said, "First of all, she is from a decent family, and though she has not suffered any hardships, she does have an ability to compromise that will help her cope with any situation. She is a new woman, but not at all a modern girl, and although she majored in music that was only as a hobby, she has no ambitions for the stage. She's not exactly a beauty, but when you meet her I don't believe either of you will be disappointed."

I asked for a chance to meet her, and Miss Cho had set up a date immediately. I shaved, shook the dust off my Western suit, polished my shoes, and set out. Because of my embarrassment at being looked at at least as much as I was doing the looking, I'd spent most of the time staring down at the table, but I could tell that in general she was not hot-tempered, seemed modest, maybe even a little shy, and that her face was shaped like Kujō Takeko's. All in all, I was not disappointed.

They say that you have to fall in love to be married. If that's the case, then when are we going to fall in love and really be married? Since we met from the outset on the premise of marriage, there's no way for pure love to raise its head. However much we come to like each other and play out the kind of love scenes that appear in movies, ours will always be a development from an arranged meeting with marriage as the goal, not a romance . . .

I came to regret having met her. As I trusted Miss Cho's character, cultivation, and friendship, I could have left everything to her and gotten engaged to someone completely unknown, and if I'd done so, how sweet would that most traditional, foolish pleasure have been, that of seeing my wife's face for the first time at our wedding. To this day I still regret having missed out on that experience, but since we had already met once I felt that we should get to know each other a little better, and so I requested the chance to take a walk together. The reply came back that she would like that too and could leave her school for three hours between two and five o'clock on a Saturday afternoon, and that she disliked crowded places like parks and theaters.

I had met her at the tram stop on Sŏdaemun Hill, but did not know which way to walk.

"Which way should we go?"

"I don't know."

She looked all around, blushing madly. I got the sense that she was worried she might bump into a friend or a teacher and would like to move on quickly.

"Shall we walk up to those walls?"

She began to walk ahead in silence. After a while, I pointed to the top of Hyangch'on-dong and asked, "Why don't we walk up this hill?"

"My friends often go for walks up there," she replied.

Out of necessity I remembered the path up to Chin'gwan Temple, where I'd gone on picnics in middle school. Back then, once we had walked past the Sŏdaemun Prison and crossed over Muhakjae Hill, the stream coming down from the Segŏm Pavilion had been crystal clear, and the riverbed had been clean too. The two of us had met in autumn, and I thought we would enjoy the scents of the ripening grain, the asters, the clear blue sky, and the white sandy path. And so we suffered the dust that covered our feet as we walked past the prison and over Muhakjae. But my belief that the path on the other side of the hill would be clean and follow alongside a crystal-clear stream turned out to be nothing but an illusion. No matter how far we walked, we just kicked up dust. Then the night soil cart passed by, churning up even more dust alongside its piercing smell. Whenever a car or the like passed us, we could barely open our eyes or even take a breath for a while. We'd already wasted almost an hour. We hadn't been able to exchange even one quiet word. And it looked as if we'd have to walk a lot further before we would find that stream flowing down from the Segŏm Pavilion. The sun's rays were striking at the hottest possible angle. I looked around the hill. All I could see were rocks burning in the heat. But we had no choice other than to climb the hill and try to find somewhere to sit. We looked for some shade, only to find some pine trees eaten up by crimson caterpillars. When we finally found somewhere to sit down, a crowd of women was doing their washing in a thread-like trickle of water and creating a clamor as if trying to catch fish. We had to raise our voices just to hear each other speak above the noise of the pounding washing sticks.

When my wife first came to Sŏngbuk-dong she had laughingly asked me why I had not known of a good place for a walk back then, and added that as a novelist I was certainly not qualified to write love stories. My defense had been that we had not fallen in love.

She was upset with my answer and replied, "Then why don't you try falling in love and get it off your chest?"

To tell the truth, from time to time I do wish I could fall in love. This is probably an eternal hunger common to us all. And most likely it's a desire we can never fully satisfy, no matter how often we try.

The bus toys with me again today. It pulls out just as I'm folding my umbrella in order to run. I turn away, determined not to watch the disappearing bus or feel any duty to remember the name of even one of the products advertised on its despicable backside.

For three years now I have left my house almost every day to take the bus, but I haven't once managed to time my arrival in order to hop right on without having to either run or wait. It would actually seem more natural if out of those several hundred journeys at least once or twice events had gone my way, but I've yet to experience that sense of being natural.

Where should I go first?

I ponder for a while and decide to take the first bus that arrives, regardless of its destination. It's going to the Government General Building. The vehicle is quite old. I push my way on and sit behind the driver, but the bus seems to need oiling because an awful screeching sound pierces my ears each time the driver tries to stop or start the bus by pushing and pulling on this thing that's as big as a spade. Yet the most unpleasant aspect of the route to the Government General Building is that we have to pass through the Tonhwa Gate. The bus has to wait there for the inspector's permission to continue on its route, and he has yet to keep the bus moving speedily, not even one out of every ten times I've been on the bus. All eyes fix on him as if to say, "You bastard, let us go quickly," but sometimes I start to count "One, two . . ." as if I'm sitting in the hot bath, and I generally reach seventy or eighty before the bus moves on. Not only that, but often he'll suddenly tell us to switch to the bus in front or the one behind, so that you start to hear the words *baka yarō*, "you idiot!" falling from the mouths of short-tempered passengers, and then for tall passengers such as myself, who had barely managed to find a seat and sit down, the worst scenario is when we change to a different bus with no empty seats and have to stand up, pretending to look out the window as we can't even straighten out our necks.

"Damn him, what kind of inspection takes this long?"

"Whatever time of the day or night all the bastard does is to tell us to get on the bus in front . . ."

Curses flow of their own accord, but of course if we thought about it, our friend the inspector is not being willful; he's merely enforcing the organization and control necessary for all the passengers' sakes.

But let's leave such sociological thoughts for later, for now we are all busy just trying to reach our destinations and it's hard not to curse and glare at him. Perhaps it is the case that Korean society is full of too many elements who lack public morality and cultivation, including myself, but it has to be said that being a bus inspector must be on a par with being a detective or a customs officer when it comes to making friends.

Luckily, today we are not told to change buses, but if I had counted I probably would have reached seventy before the bus moved on.

I change to the tram at Anguk-dong. It's called Anguk-chŏng now, but it still doesn't feel right to say that. I have more than a few complaints about the all-encompassing change of neighborhood administrative units such as *dong* and *ri* to *chŏng*. Regulating culture for the purpose of business efficiency is nothing more than an absurd import from the Nazis. What's more, to say Sŏngbuk-*chŏng* instead of Sŏngbuk-*dong* seems as frivolous as calling an elderly gentleman Yi *san*, instead of Yi *chusa*. If it carries on like this, in a few years they'll say that Yi, Kim, Pak, Chŏng, and all the other family names create chaos, and they'll find some way to regulate citizens' names as well.[1]

A culture that kills off any sign of individuality can never be said to be of the highest order.

"This is the *Chosŏn Central Daily* Building."

As the stop was announced, I decide to get off here instead of going all the way to Chongno. I know more people here because I used to work at the newspaper for a year or so, thus I've made a habit of always stopping by when I'm not too busy, even if I've no other business than to exchange the usual greeting "Everything all right?," which has become as meaningless as a sigh these days.

But once I go inside, it always turns a little sour. I used to be like that too; after they've shaken my hand once and offered me a chair if there's one handy, they soon lower their heads to continue whatever they're working on. They'll be talking with me and have to answer the phone. Even as they shake my hand, they'll be calling out to the office boy, "Hey, find out how we're doing the ads today!"

Whichever way you look at it, it's a tragedy to see the ethereal poet Yŏsu sat at his desk as head of the Society section, frowning at the title of some article about a robbery or a rape. It's been a long time since the novelist Pinghŏ began rotting away in the

---

1. Four years after Yi wrote this story, the Government General did indeed issue an ordinance exhorting Koreans to adopt Japanese-style names.

same position at the *Tonga Daily*. And the poet Suju spends his days at some women's magazine.

Is this how ignorant they are about people?

To put it kindly, they've no idea how to exploit their employees' skills to the best effect. I start to feel indignant on behalf of all those rotting in their jobs and on behalf of the newspapers and journals themselves, and I'm sure that if I ever became the head of a newspaper or magazine, I would do a much better job at placing people in the right position.

"Oh, are you leaving already?"

"Yes."

As usual I flick through several editions of the *Tokyo Newspaper* and then, seeing that they've no time to talk to me, get up rather awkwardly.

"Why don't you send us several installments of your novel in advance?"

"Sure."

I reply with ease. But I haven't written anything in advance and don't really feel like doing so. This is a really bad habit of mine, which needs treatment. I grow truly despondent as I wonder whether I'll ever write a real novel if I continue like this, rather than some newspaper serial.

I go down to the printing section. My friends here are just as busy. Sinbok (he still uses his childhood name) looks the very model of a busy person, crouched barefoot on top of a rotating chair, which has been raised up as high as it will go, flicking the ash from his cigarette with one hand and scratching away with his pen with the other.

"Thank you for the manuscript."

"What manuscript was that?"

I've received several requests but can't recall having written anything.

"He means thank you for the one you're about to write now."

The interpretation was proffered by the children's fiction writer Yun, who's also shut up in here.

"Okay, then I suppose I'll write something right now."

As soon as I utter these words, Sinbok swings his chair around, gets down and brings me a pen and some manuscript paper.

"How about writing a short essay?"

"On what theme?"

"How about the sea?"

I end up having to write for at least an hour.

"The sea!"

In the distance I can see Pukhan Mountain shrouded in rain. The only sounds are water running off the eaves and the rotary press turning in the printshop.

"The sea!"

However much I try saying the word out loud, I would have to travel 550 ri to the east to find the sea that I was trying to conjure up. I write one line and cross it out noisily, and then another line and cross that out. . . . I mustn't be so harsh with the students in my writing classes. A fly lands on the back of my hand. This rainy-season fly wriggles along with a slimy sensation, like a maggot. I shoo it away, but it comes straight back. If I had smeared lime on the back of my hand that fly would now be stuck to it and regretting that he'd not flown far away at my first warning. In the midst of this, I completely forget that I'm supposed to be writing about the sea.

"Mr. Yi?"

"Yes?"

"Do you know when next month's issue of *Morning Light* will appear?"

"I've no idea."

Even if I did know, this is the correct answer. Rivalry between magazines is even more blatant than in the newspaper world. I'm always asked such questions as I visit both *Central* and *Morning Light* quite often, and they may even be watching out for me. Not just maybe, I should actually presume that is happening. It's a little unpleasant. And then I realize that I have forgotten about the sea once again.

I feel like chatting with someone. I consider stopping by the *Morning Light* office. But decide not to bother. This is how it usually goes. Nosan is never there unless you arrange by phone in advance to meet up with him; the novelist Ilbo is overwhelmed by editing work in a quantitative kind of way; and the illustrator Sŏgyŏng might appear to be free from work while he is staring at a blank sheet of paper, but he's also busy, in a qualitative kind of way.

I go straight to Nangnang, where for some reason there's no sound of a record playing. But I think that if I just push open the door there's sure to be someone there who will look happy to see me. I walk in expectantly and take a look around. There are very few customers to begin with, and all the faces merely glance in my direction before feigning ignorance and turning away again. I go inside and take a corner seat. This is most unpleasant. Everyone who glances at me is a regular customer. Even though we don't greet each other, we recognize each other's faces. Such familiar faces often seem less interesting than new ones. When I walk in, those faces seem to say, "Oh, it's him again!"

"What does he do that he can be entering a teahouse at this hour?"

I would do the same in their position, but they seem to harbor some kind of unnecessary scorn and pass judgment on me when they're no better themselves. It's more than a little unpleasant.

I order a cup of coffee that isn't mixed well and doesn't taste so good. I'd like to drink a cup of coffee that has been prepared with a scholarly conscience at every stage, from the choice of ingredients to the method of brewing. And then I'd like to talk to my heart's content about nothing in particular.

I call the errand boy.

"Go upstairs and tell the boss to come down."

"I don't think he's up yet."

"Whatever is the time? Go and wake him up."

"Who shall I say wants to see him?"

"Just go and wake him up . . . it'll be okay."

Only after I insist does he go upstairs.

The boss was a friend from my Tokyo days—Yi, known to us as the "Knight of Tears." He was so good at crying that he would sigh "Oh my!" at the slightest thing, and tears would start to gather in his eyes. He was in and out of teahouses night and day to the point where, even though he'd been offered a fairly high position at the Hwasin department store upon his return, he had complained that they didn't understand artists and quit to open this teahouse called Nangnang.

Whenever we met he would tell me that he needed to discuss something in private. One night he had dragged me upstairs to his room and told me that he was in the midst of a love affair. He tearfully explained that the object of his affections was a beauty of great repute revered by all the young men in Seoul, that he was the one man fortunate enough to possess the key to this high window, which attracted everyone's gaze, and that over the past year or so he had spent all the income from Nangnang on trying to reach this point and repel the evil hands of all sorts of other men. And then, he had asked me to answer honestly, "As you know, I have a wife and children. What should I do?"

If it were me, there was only one possibility, so I answered without much thought, "You have to give up."

"Which one?"

His eyes focused on me with greater intensity.

"Your lover."

"But I would die . . ."

"Then continue the affair . . ."

"You mean without telling my wife?"

"Well, how can your wife interfere in an affair she knows nothing about? Maybe if you wanted to marry her it would be different . . . do you want to marry her?"

"Of course . . . of course . . ."

He bowed his head. I tried to leave, saying, "As you say you would die without her, you're clearly going to continue, so what does it matter what I say?"

Suddenly he grasped my hand and asked, "Our relationship is still pure. Can't we continue to love each other in a spiritual way?"

"That's not really giving up, but it is a beautiful idea."

"Idea? You mean it's impossible?"

Then he showed me her portrait and burst into tears, "Isn't she beautiful?"

The next time I met him some time later, he was not looking too good and had a bandage wrapped around one of his ring fingers. I asked him what had happened and he replied, "I had an abscess."

There was something unnatural about his reply. I suspected that, emotional and softhearted that he was, he had cut his finger on account of his love affair, but I couldn't probe any further in front of others. He seemed to be down about everything and asked whether I might recommend someone to take over the teahouse: business was so bad that he wanted to sell up and try a change of scenery in Tokyo. I haven't seen him since then, but when the errand boy finally returns he says, "The boss must have gotten up and gone somewhere. He probably went home to eat."

"Home? You mean he eats at home usually?"

"When he wants to eat Korean food that's what he does."

There's no sign of either Kubo or Yi Sang. The rain is still pouring down. The record player starts up. I just want to meet someone, anyone. Maybe if I go to the Osakaya or Japanese-Korean Bookstore, I'll run into Wŏlp'a or Ilsŏk.

Friends?

I exit Nangnang deep in thought and walk along the sidewalk in the rain. I consider Nangnang's Yi to be a friend. But when I was told that he'd most likely gone home, I couldn't even begin to imagine what his home is like. As for his mother or father, I've no idea what sort of people they are, neither do I know where Yi was born or which elementary school he attended, or even what kind of child he might have been. I'm completely in the dark. Even if I were to hear that he had lost his father, I would have little sense of the old man who had passed on. And I'm equally in the dark about his ancestors or what his young children look like.

Is this what you call friendship? Can we really be called friends?

I think some more. But the more I think about it, couldn't the same be said of all those people I saw at the *Chosŏn Central Daily* today, and also of Kubo and Yi Sang, and Wŏlp'a and Ilsŏk, whom I was hoping to meet right now? I had either met them because we worked at the same newspaper, or were at the same school, or as a member of the Group of Nine; that was all there was to it. Because I met them often at work or on business we had exchanged greetings, and as we did that frequently we began to shake hands and that was all really. Where was the plaintive longing to see each other, where was the affection? All those phrases about "between friends" being like this and that, aren't they simply embarrassing? Then I thought about several of my childhood friends.

Yonggi, Hŭngbongi, Haksuni, Pongsŏngi. . . . Could they really be called friends? We grew up swimming naked in the same streams. Because of this I know that Yonggi has a scar on his leg and I know how many moles Pongsŏngi has on his back. I had grown closer to Haksuni after we'd paired up in the three-legged race at sports day and won first prize. I know exactly what their grandparents are like and I know all about their parents. Even the smallest details of their homes are familiar to me. I even know who has a pear tree in their yard and who has a sweet apricot tree on the hill behind their house . . .

That reminds me! That letter from Haksuni last spring . . .

I realize that I still have not replied. That I've even ignored his requests. I had failed to reply immediately not so much because I was busy but because I had simply wanted to ignore the letter. I still remember its contents.

I read in some magazine that you've published a book of stories called *Moonlight*. Why haven't you sent me a copy when you know how much I like storybooks? And what kind of title is that? Wouldn't it be more elegant to have something like *Shades of the Autumn Crescent* or *A Moonlit River's Night*? It must be a love story? Anyway I'd like to read it. I hope you send me a copy, and let me ask you another favor as well. I can't send any money, but if you could buy one of those little clay pipes and send it along with *Moonlight*, then I'll be able to smoke some cigarette butts. I heard they only cost about ten chon at the night market . . .

He hasn't left our farming village since elementary school, so it wasn't really surprising that he would compare a short story collection to a storybook like *Shades of the Autumn Crescent*, but I still found it a little unpleasant, and even if I were to send him *Moonlight*, it was clear that it would not meet his expectations, and so I had quietly forgotten even the request for a pipe.

I regret this now. I regret the fact that my foolish pride had triumphed over the simple kindness of sending him a copy, no matter whether he would understand the book or not.

I walk to Chin'gogae and take a look at the clay *matroos* sailor pipes. There's nothing in the realm of ten chon. They're all at least five or six won. They seem even less appropriate for him than *Moonlight*.

I move on to the Osakaya bookstore. Before I even turn to the books, I take a look at the people in there, but there's no one I know. Nothing stands out among the new books either, and then a store employee comes along and starts beating the books with a duster, though what kind of dust could have settled in the rainy season is beyond me. Driven away, I go into the Japanese-Korean bookstore, but I can't see anyone I know there either until, from the midst of the unfamiliar faces, someone approaches me, shaking the rain from a glistening raincoat.

"Isn't that Yi?"

As I listen to the voice, I gradually recall a face from the past, without the glasses he's wearing now.

"Kang . . ."

I have the right name. He'd been in my class at middle school. He grasps my hand, and as he shakes it seems to be recalling times gone by, so that he keeps on shaking my hand for quite some time before leading me off to the Ponjŏng Grill. When we remove our hats in the cloakroom, I see that he has a crew cut, and when we remove our coats I notice the Japanese national flag pinned onto the collar of his Western suit. He runs his fingers along that collar, while we ask for a table and sit down.

"I've been keeping up with your *katsuyakuburi* in the press over the years."[2]

And then he asks, "So, have you made some money?"

2. Typical of elite Koreans in the later years of Japanese colonial rule and indicative of his own collaborative stance with the occupying Government General, Kang injects many Japanese words and phrases into his sentences. Here *katsuyakuburi* refers to Yi's "activities."

"Money?"

I force a smile, which harbors several different layers of meaning, and then I ask, "So you've done well?"

"Let's see, I've caught a few nice fish . . ."

He keeps urging me to drink and empties a glass himself, before affecting a laugh and adding, "No doubt you're already aware of this, but the ways of the world are just like fishing, d'you get my meaning? You need some bait . . . ha, ha."

He seems to be quite a man of the world.

"I've been out on the coast of Hwanghae Province, working on the mud flats."

I've no idea what he's talking about.

"Ah, I see that you're a gentleman of the inner room."

According to his explanation, his work involves blocking off the outer limits of wide marshes to stop the tide coming in and out in order to reclaim land.

"I've made something like four to five hundred acres so far."

And looking disappointed that I seemed to have no notion of the value of such work, he added, "If I do well, I could make as much as five hundred thousand won. I'm getting well known at the High Command."

"High Command?"

I know this cannot be the term that means the opposite of a mistress, but I don't know what it does mean.

"Ha, you're wasted in Seoul you are, you don't know the High Command? The Government General!"

He revels in my embarrassment. And then he brags that when he visits the Secretary-General for Political Affairs he can say anything he likes, after all isn't he increasing the national territory by creating fine fields and rice paddies out of places that are merely marked as ocean on a map?

"I haven't tried yet, but if I make an effort, I could get a county magistracy for sure."

He calls for the waiter and suggests we order lunch. But after we've ordered, he changes his tone.

"Hey?"

"What?"

"Aren't you connected with some girls' school?"

"Yes, that's right."

"Why don't you help me find a wife?"

His affected laughter resounds once again. This is getting really unpleasant. If only we hadn't already ordered, I could get up and leave.

"Listen, don't you want to help make a friend comfortable? I'm not joking, this is for real. I'm single at the moment."

I don't ask whether he's merely not yet married, divorced, or even widowed, but I come to my senses in a flash at the word "friend." He uses that term way too freely.

"We're friends meeting up after a long while, so have a drink."

He pushes another beer on me, belches, and adds, "If we weren't friends, would I ask you such a thing, having just bumped into you like this?"

Our lunch begins to appear. I can't forget his earlier words, "The ways of the world are just like fishing." Maybe I'm the one being caught right now. Maybe it's me who's swallowing his bait.

"When it comes to women, first of all looks are important . . . what do you think?"

I think, "Okay, he's beginning to fish now," and hesitate, "Well . . ."

Then I think that with fishing the benefits are not all the fisherman's to reap. It's not impossible for the fish to simply pull the bait off the hook and eat it. I decide to fill up on all the expensive dishes that he orders and urges me to eat.

Later on he says, "As you're a literary sort, I bet you're better than me at love, marriage, and those kinds of things. If it's someone you choose, I'll go along with it unconditionally . . . this isn't a joke. This might seem like I'm boasting, but one of my friends at the High Command . . . that's right, do you know Minister X?"

"Does it seem like I would?"

"In just a few days he's going to become a provincial governor. People like him have introduced me to daughters from wealthy families, but it's your introduction that I want. Can't you recommend me a superb new woman, the kind that you read about in novels? I won't make her life difficult."

He continues, "I'm only telling you this because we're friends, but since I've been single naturally I've associated with women of the demi-monde, and not only is it bothering my body but it doesn't look very good, and . . ."

He then gives me his business card and explains that he has no choice but to stay at the Pijŏnok Inn when he comes to Seoul for the sake of business, and he asks me to keep in touch. After we've parted in the street, he doesn't walk far before turning around and shouting out, "I'm relying on you!"

From now on, when he tells someone that he's caught a few fish, maybe that will include having fed me lunch today.

The rain keeps falling. My back is throbbing now that I've had at least two glasses of the beer that my body can't tolerate. I suppose this is all a way for me to study the ways of the world.

My wife must be in a better mood by now. But if I go home that coldness might return of its own accord.

"I won't make life difficult for her."

I can't forget Kang's words.

I'm a husband who makes life difficult for his wife!

I go around the back of Nangnang and enter Chinatown. Back when my wife was having trouble breastfeeding, someone told her to try eating pig's foot, like the Chinese do. We bought some to try, and her milk started flowing again. She grew to like it so much that even now she's no longer breastfeeding, she would be over the moon if I bought some for her. I go into the Garden of Heavenly Abundance and buy one of the biggest feet they have. Then, on the way home, I stop by the Han Bookstore. I decide to leave the pipe for another day, but first I send a copy of *Moonlight* to Haksuni.

The hills of our Sŏngbuk-dong are still shrouded in misty rain.

—The Ninth Day of the Eighth Month of the Year
of the Fire Rat, in Songjŏn
First published in 1936; translated from
Kamagui: Yi T'aejun tanp'yŏnjip (Hansŏng tosŏ, 1937)

Whoosh! Water came pouring out from under the fence of the house in front. The crash had caught Mr. An by surprise while he was busy counting on his fingers, and now he peered down into the drain over his broken glasses, eyes protruding like those of a chicken about to peck at its feed. There were all kinds of things mixed up in the pearly rinsing water: squash stems, eggshells, empty bean pods.

"So they're making mung bean pancakes, huh . . ."

For five or six years now, Mr. An had ended his sentences with a sneer and a "damn it" or "huh."

"It must be the Autumn Festival tomorrow or the next day, damn it."

He licked his lips unconsciously. Saliva had gathered in his mouth at the oily smell piercing his nose. Suddenly the old days seemed like a lie, those days when he had been doing all right and worried about things like toothache and tooth decay. Now his underused teeth felt as sharp as drill bits.

He ground down on those sharp teeth and looked up.

The sky seemed to stretch for a thousand miles or more with puffs of cloud drifting here and there. The white clouds dazzled his eyes, like clean, washed-out calico. He thought of his own dirty *chŏksam* jacket. He looked down at his sleeves and did not raise his head again for a while. A tragic sense of loneliness lingered on his face, of a kind that no piece of mung bean pancake or glass of rice wine could assuage.

He blew into his sleeves, dusted them down with his hands, and lay down with his head rested on a wooden pillow.

"Two fours are eight, four fives are twenty, that's a thousand . . . wait . . . a thousand? He said four, so that's four thousand, four thousand p'yŏng . . . if the land goes for as low as five won a p'yŏng that still means four won seventy-five chon left over . . . four fours are sixteen, sixteen thousand won . . ."

A recount brought the total to nineteen thousand won, that was how much he calculated he would make if he paid in just one thousand won, in which case how much would he make if he could pay in ten thousand won? He sat up with a start. His forehead pounded. He quickly unfolded his crossed legs and crouched like someone about to relieve himself. He squeezed his pack of Macaw cigarettes again, though he knew well that it was empty. Then he reached into his purse and took out ten chon; this was all that remained of the forty or fifty his daughter had given him three or four times already in order to mend his glasses but which he had squandered on cigarettes. His thin hand trembled slightly as it held the nickel coin. When he thought of Major Sŏ's rough hands, his own seemed all too weak and feeble. Yet he had never once envied Sŏ, who made his living brokering houses, even though he might accept drinks from him occasionally and slept in his office, treating it like his own room. Sooner or later, An still believed, something would turn up and he would once again live in his own home, eat his own food, and face the world with his own strength and sense of dignity.

He recalled the words of a physiognomist who had once told him, "Keep your fists clenched around your thumb and your property will never leave you." He tried hard to follow this advice, but whenever he happened to look down, his damn thumb was invariably wrapped around the outside of his fist. His fabric store had failed and then he had gone into business selling furniture, using his house as security, only to have that store destroyed by a fire.

"Bloody thumb! Go back in, damn it!"

He tried pushing his thumbs against his palms and clenching both fists until they hurt. Then he headed toward the tobacco shop, holding the ten chon coin firmly in his clenched fist if only for an instant.

T he three old men would meet up in the broker's office. The old man with the red face and big eyes, who always wore a horsehair hat and sat facing the street because someone might appear at any moment asking to view a house, was the owner, Major Sŏ. A former military man, after Annexation he had whiled away five years looking out for a moment that never seemed to arrive before acquiring this house brokering business to pass the time. At first the income had barely allowed him to avoid starvation, but from year eight or nine of Taishō (1920–1921) rich people from the countryside had flocked into Seoul, whether driven by taxes or for their children's education. At the same time money had become more plentiful, and houses in central areas, such as Kwanch'ŏl-dong and Taok-chŏng, were selling for over ten thousand won as long as they were not too old. These deals brought in an income of three to four hundred won during some months from spring through autumn, so that after several years Sŏ had been able to build a house with some dozen rooms in Kahoe-dong, and then after a few more years he had begun to acquire land in the Ch'ang-dong area. Brokers' fees had decreased considerably with the increase in the number of brokers and the emergence of large building companies, such as Kŏnyangsa, who made buying and selling directly the general rule. Nevertheless, since he had student lodgers in a house with more than twenty rooms, Major Sŏ wouldn't fall behind with rice payments or be pressed to pay for fuel even if there were no other income in any particular month.

"In life you get by somehow . . ."

This was what Major Sŏ used to say. It had once seemed as if even the mountains and rivers would step aside at his command when he had worn a sword at the military training camp. He could not help but shed tears of sadness when he compared his spirit back then to his situation now—a mere buyer and seller of houses, owner of a broker's office, everybody's errand boy, who had to obey with a "yes, yes" whenever *kisaeng*, prostitutes, or the like asked him to find them a room to rent. He liked his drink anyway, but more than once he had been overcome by memories and headed off to a bar alone.

Recently such memories surfaced less and less, perhaps because the vitality that constitutes the source of the military man's spirit was also draining from his body. One day he had been at home and about to eat lunch when he heard the calls of some peddler, but the voice sounded strangely familiar. He listened carefully as that voice gradually drew closer; it wasn't trying to sell anything, but calling out "Glass bottles, soy sauce tins bought here!" Surely that voice belonged to someone he knew. He stood up in order to look out of the window and watched a middle-aged man pass by, holding a couple of straw bags and a pair of scales in one hand while calling out, "Any bags, newspapers, magazines?" It was definitely someone he knew, but at first he could not remember from where, the man's name, or even what he used to do.

"Ah! That's it . . . it must be . . . really!"

After a while he nodded. Just as the call for "glass bottles and soy sauce tins" was disappearing into an alley, Sŏ had remembered who it was.

"My old comrade Major Kim . . . huh!"

Kim had been a young officer, much younger than Sŏ, full of knowledge and talent and owner of a commanding voice that earned plentiful praise from their superiors. Even a couple of decades later there could be no mistaking that voice and figure. Sŏ was deeply moved when he thought of the young Kim and how he looked today; he put down his spoon and took several gulps of cold water.

And yet the feeling did not last as long as it might have done in the past, when he had been younger and stronger. He watched his second son, now in the final year of middle school, return home and his wife lightly count out the dark blue notes for the rice store employee who had come to collect payment, and he said to himself: "You just have to live, there's no other way. Some people even have to hide their shame and wander around like that . . . ahem."

He was not lacking a certain pride in the fact that his position was fairly respectable compared to such desperate friends.

"What's the point of thinking about the past? As long as I'm alive . . . ha, ha."

He planned on living the rest of his life with a smile. To be fair he was somewhat shallow by nature, but he was also cracking more jokes recently. This aspect of his character did not match Mr. An's permanently sunken eyes and the sullen "damn it" with which he brought every sentence to an end.

"Hey, you old fool, shall I buy you a drink?"

Insulted at being called a fool, An would fly into a rage.

"Bastards like you don't know how to measure your drink."

"And d'you think playing cards day and night will bring your mother back to life?"

When Sŏ kicked his cards away, An gasped and flushed bright red before quickly picking up his belongings, which amounted to no more than a fan and a pack of cigarettes, and walking out with a scowl as if he would not return.

"If he were a woman, he'd have to be a concubine!"

Major Sŏ burst out laughing, but Mr. An did not reappear for a couple of days.

One evening An's daughter gave a dance performance. Her name was An Kyŏnghwa, and she had been in both Osaka and Tokyo as a member of the Saturday Society, before showing up in Seoul five or six years later having made a name for herself as a dancer. This was to be her first public performance back home. Sŏ had pestered An to go, and even An had straightened his shoulders with pride when his daughter's picture and story appeared in every newspaper. He got hold of as many free tickets as possible and handed them out to several other friends in addition to Sŏ.

"Huh, is that your daughter, the one in the middle lifting her leg up?"

The others all sat stupefied, but Sŏ spoke in a disapproving tone, as if he were watching something outrageous.

"They say that when it comes to dancing, the more civilized the country, the less clothes they wear."

This was An's attempt to block any further comment.

"Well, I don't know . . . men these days must be fools . . ."

"Why?"

This time the criticism came from a different friend.

"When we were young, we'd never have put up with anything like that . . ."

"Damn you . . . can't you act your age . . ."

An exploded with rage.

One dance had finished, and the bright lights had been turned back on.

"You should tell her to go back to being an actress. At least actresses don't run around exposing their thighs like that!"

"Why do you have to poke your nose into other people's business? So you know something about the size of inner rooms and side rooms, but what do you know about anything else? If you don't like it, just get out!"

An was furious. And at the condescending mention of inner rooms and side rooms Sŏ flew into a rage as well. In the end he stood up, but not before shouting, "And what do you know? You fool!"

After this incident, An did not appear at Sŏ's office for almost a month. And then it was only because Pak Hŭiwan went and fetched him.

Pak Hŭiwan did not sleep at the office like Mr. An but whiled away his time there regularly. In fact, he did not just come to pass time but to study as well. He had a nephew who worked at the courts, and ever since Pak had heard about the push to hire scribes who could write Japanese, he had carried around a copy of the *Fast Course in Reading the National Language*, from which he would recite in the same style in which one might read from the ancient Chinese classic *The Romance of the Three Kingdoms*.

"*Kin-sang dokko-e yukkiimassukka?* Where are you going, Mr. Kim?"

The cover of the *Fast Course in Reading the National Language* was covered with greasy fingerprints and even jet-black dirt from his hair, because he sometimes placed it on top of his wooden pillow and rested his head on it to take a nap. As a result the small characters that read "Compiled by the Government General of Korea" could no longer be seen, and certification as a scribe seemed as distant as ever.

"What's the good of you or me acquiring a trade when we're half-dead? What kind of time do we have . . . huh!"

If An had been shuffling his cards half the day and they still had not fallen correctly, he would vent his wrath by snatching the *Fast Course in Reading the National Language* out of the murmuring Pak Hŭiwan's hands and hurl it into the street.

"And what kind of luck are you hoping for when all you do is wait for the right cards to turn up day and night?"

"I'm just killing time."

Yet deep inside, An burned with greater worldly ambition than Pak. An's daughter went back and forth to Pyongyang and Taegu, even touring the provinces, and she seemed to make some money, but what with fixing the house and buying a gramophone in order to open a studio, and having to run around socializing, there seemed to be no room for her father in her budget, especially as she considered him a nuisance.

After observing his daughter's mood carefully, An had once ventured to speak, "Look at this, perhaps it's because the cotton padding's old, or the way it was sewn, but the lining's gone in my trousers. And sometime soon I'll have to get myself a new shirt."

"Of course, I've been meaning to buy you one."

She answered easily enough, but An did not see that shirt until winter had already passed. And when he had asked for just one won to mend the bridge of his glasses, she had gone out of her way to change a one-won note in order to give him a fifty-chon coin. He had paid five or six won for those glasses back when he'd had a little money, so there was no way the bridge could be fixed with just fifty chon. Of course, there were bridges to be bought for fifty chon, but it was in An's nature to buy something neat, and he hated buying something that did not match his face. Instead he resorted to tying his glasses with string and spent the fifty chon on cigarettes.

"Why didn't you get your glasses fixed?"

His daughter had asked him that evening.

"Umm . . ."

An did not reply. A few days later his daughter gave him another fifty chon. As she did so, for some reason, she added, "Father, your insurance payments alone come to three won eighty chon a month."

It sounded like she was asking him to die so that she could get the insurance money.

"What business is that of mine?"

"I did it for you, of course. Who else do you think I would have taken out insurance for?"

An had to force himself not to say, "If you're doing it for my sake, then why not give me at least a penny while I'm alive? What will I know about it when I'm dead?"

"Why isn't fifty chon enough to fix your glasses?"

He did not bother explaining.

"Father, are you really in any position to be so picky now?"

But again the fifty chon all went on Macaw cigarettes. He had probably done this three or four times by now.

"What use are children? Especially daughters. . . . It's my own money that I need."

Each day An felt the need for money more acutely.

"Is this world only good to you if you have money?"

He had nothing better to do, and so he went outside for a walk; on every street high-rise buildings were under construction, and every neighborhood was expanding with picture-like modern culture houses. He had let his concentration lapse for a mere moment when a horn sounded at the back of his neck from a car shiny like a catfish that had just jumped out of water. He turned around to see the driver glaring at him—a fat, middle-aged man sat smiling in the back seat, his gold watch chain glittering.

"I'm almost sixty . . . damn it!"

An resented growing old. One way or another, before he got much older, he wanted to get hold of at least ten thousand won and bargain with the world again on his own terms. In this pitiful state what did it matter to him if modern houses sprang up, or if cars and planes increased like swarms of ants and flies? When he thought about it, his connection to the world had been broken the very instant that money had fallen from his hands.

"I might as well be dead, hadn't I?"

He had been asking himself such questions for a long time.

"Is there no hope?"

And, "You just need some kind of base, then you can get in the mix!"

And again, "Just because you've lost money, doesn't mean you can't make it."

In other words, he had the confidence that he could make money, if he could just find some kind of base.

And then, he heard the news from Pak Hŭiwan. It was secret information passed along from a certain influential person in government circles, who claimed that a second port city on the lines of Najin was to be built on the coast of Hwanghae Province. At this point only those in government office knew about the plans, but the land for the harbor construction was being bought up and there would be a public announcement from the authorities soon.

"Is it wasteland or farmland?"

An asked, his eyes wide open.

"They say it's dry fields."

"Dry fields? And how much is it a p'yŏng?"

"Apparently it's gone up a bit. When government officials buy, even country bumpkins notice something's up, don't they? But they don't know why the officials are buying, you see."

"Really?"

"Really, and apparently it hasn't gone up that much. . . . Maybe twenty-five or twenty-six chon a p'yŏng will do it. Even so, it's pie in the sky for us, right?"

"Hum!"

An's temples throbbed. If it were true, then the sooner one jumped in the more money was to be made. In Najin too, as soon as a rumor arose that a port was to be opened, land that had been worth five or six chon rose to over one hundred times that within a year, and, depending on the land, three or four years later the most strategic places had increased in value by over one thousand-fold.

"What's the use of delaying when I'm half dead? Even if I sold out in the first year, I could make at least five won a p'yŏng for sure . . ."

So An thought to himself, and then he sat down and asked more questions.

"Just where on earth is this place?"

"How would I know?"

"Well?"

"Only this one man knows. What he told me was that he had copied the plans and knows where the important sites are going to be, so if we could get ten thousand won in capital together, we could just buy those plots. And he doesn't want too much either, he's just asking for 20 percent of the net profit, not including expenses."

"I bet . . . Who would give such a tip and then step aside? . . . Twenty percent, you said? Twenty percent . . ."

The more An thought about it the more this seemed like the base he needed. Not only was there the precedent of Najin, but, according to Pak Hŭiwan, relations with China were becoming more intimate with the establishment of Manchukuo, and as a result even common sense dictated that a large port on the coast of Hwanghae would be needed, which would serve a similar purpose to Najin. This was common sense even An could believe in.

That day, for the first time in a long time, Mr. An bought expensive Pigeon cigarettes and smoked one all the way down on the spot before coming to the office. For some reason Pak Hŭiwan did not show up all day. An thought he must be running around trying to raise some money elsewhere. Major Sŏ had not yet returned, having left before lunch to try to strike some deal. An took his well-used cards down from the mantle of the sliding door.

"Eh, look at that!"

The cards did not usually comply with his wishes, but now they came up in the turtle shape first time. He wished someone were there to see it.

"Whichever way you look at it, this is extraordinary. . . . Luck seems to be turning my way!"

He threw a half-smoked cigarette into the street. He had now smoked several cigarettes on an empty stomach and his throat was dry. The discarded bean pods stuck in the drain of the house in front had now turned yellow.

"Just you wait, by next Autumn Festival . . ."

That evening he told his daughter what he had heard from Pak Hŭiwan. He might have encountered a few failures, but he was still the Mr. An who had spent more than ten years in business, and his way of exhorting investment surprised even his daughter. He sounded like a different person. She did not respond immediately, but must have been unable to forget what he had said, because the next morning it was she who brought the subject up first and asked even more questions, above and beyond what An had asked Pak Hŭiwan. An, in turn, had given detailed explanations beyond those given by Pak Hŭiwan, asserting that the net profit would at the very least amount to more than fifty times their initial investment, even if they settled accounts within one year.

His daughter was enthusiastic. Within four days she had turned her studio and house over to a trust company and borrowed three thousand won. An was so happy he wanted to jump up and down, as if he had become a millionaire or something.

"You bastard Sŏ, all this time you've secretly looked down on me. I'm going to have you find me a house even better than yours. People like you are house brokers by nature, what's so special about that?"

But on the day the money was released from the trust company, some young man he'd never seen before showed up and blocked An's way. This turned out to be the daughter's boyfriend. She did not let even one chon fall into her father's hands, but had the young man handle all the money. At first An could not contain his anger, but within a few days they agreed on a compromise; if they were going to accrue a net profit of fifty or sixty thousand from their three thousand won, what did it matter if ten thousand or so went elsewhere? And so, An followed unwillingly behind the young man, who was as good as his son-in-law.

One year passed.

It had all been a dream. And as dreams go this one was nightmarish. They had bought land worth three thousand won, but however much they pored over the newspapers everyday and kept their ears to the grapevine, news of a port being built surfaced neither in the newspapers nor any rumors. There was talk of land values in Yongdangp'o and Tasa Island rising thirty- or even fifty-fold, with millionaires being made overnight, but elsewhere there was no news for a while, and then later they found out through Pak Hŭiwan once more that they had all, even Pak, been tricked by this certain person in government circles. The entire scenario had been dreamt up by this person, who had bought up land too hastily when he heard about a survey of a proposed site for a port, and had then needed to sell it on when the plan had been abandoned due to some defect.

Although Mr. An had not been allowed to touch even one won of the money, the thunderbolt fell on him. He couldn't bring himself to eat, even when he had missed three or four meals, and he couldn't go home to eat anyway. All he could do was sigh.

"When money's at stake, can a child's filial duty really be discarded like the root of a cabbage?"

It was alcohol and cigarettes that he craved more than food. Needless to say, he could not get his glasses fixed. He could no longer get hold of ten chon, let alone fifty.

As the Autumn Festival approached, the weather was fine, as it was every year. The sky seemed to stretch for a thousand miles or more, with puffs of cloud drifting here and there. Some of the white clouds dazzled his eyes, like clean, washed-out calico. Once again, An thought of his own dirty *chŏksam* jacket. But this time he did not blow into his sleeves or give them a shake. Instead he quietly used those dirty sleeves to wipe away his tears.

The summer had been exasperatingly hot, but then the first frost had fallen unusually early, perhaps as an omen that the coming cold would be extreme too. The cosmos blooming over the fence of the Chōsen Industrial Bank residence, which Major Sŏ passed every day, was now shriveled and black, as if thoroughly parboiled.

The Major's head ached. It was most likely because the previous night he had tried to cheer up a tearful Mr. An by taking him first to a Chinese restaurant and then to eat some loach soup, with the result that they had been out until two in the morning. He had eaten a few spoonfuls for breakfast, but his mouth was still parched. An was surely feeling just as bad, and so the Major dutifully went down to his office, thinking he would drag An out for a drink to chase away their hangovers even though it was midday. Once there he discovered that the cloth banner bearing the words "Broker's Office" had not yet been hung up.

"Hey you . . . what time do you think it is to be snoring away?"

But there was not a snore to be heard. When he opened the sliding door, he received a shock. There was blood on An's lips, and his face was ashen grey. The air in the room was damp as a dirt cellar.

"No . . . ?"

First, Sŏ closed the sliding door behind him, and then he rubbed his eyes to take another look. An was long gone, leaving behind just his corpse and some kind of medicine bottle lying on the floor.

It took a while before Sŏ registered the tragic event.

"Oh . . ."

He thought he should go to the police, but then decided he should tell the daughter first, and went to fetch her from the An Kyŏnghwa Dance Studio, which he had heard about so often. He let her cry for a while before asking, "Shouldn't we tell the authorities?"

"No, please don't do that."

She flinched.

"Don't?"

"My . . ."

"Your what?"

"There's my reputation . . . ," she pleaded.

"Reputation? That's absurd, how can someone so concerned with their reputation let their father die like this?"

An Kyŏnghwa collapsed in tears again. She held onto Sŏ's legs when he tried to leave and would not let go.

"Help me!"

She repeated the words several times.

"All right, I'll keep this a secret, but will you do as I say?"

"Yes."

Sŏ sat down again.

"You took out some insurance for your father, didn't you?"

"Yes, I did, only simple life insurance."

"Whatever it is . . . how much will you get?"

"Four hundred and eighty won."

"Since you took it out for your father, you'll have to spend it on your father, all right?"

"Of course."

"Uh um, well. . . . He always wanted an undershirt. You need to buy him a good woolen one and a set of real silk burial clothes to wear on top. Do you have an ancestral gravesite? Somewhere to bury him?"

"No, of course not."

"Then buy a large, top quality plot in the public cemetery. . . . You'd better have a nice funeral, because if you do a shabby job, I won't put up with it. Do you understand?"

"Yes."

Only then did she open her handbag and wipe her tear-strewn face.

An's so-called funeral service took place in his daughter's studio.

Major Sŏ and Pak Hŭiwan drank rather a lot before they arrived. Pak had deposited something at the pawnbroker's in order to bring two won as a funeral gift, but when Sŏ saw this, he said, "There's plenty of money for the funeral, so don't you give that woman anything."

And they had gone to a bar for a couple of drinks.

A fair number of well-dressed mourners had gathered at the studio. There were even a couple of people in full ceremonial dress. They had not known the deceased, but appeared to have shown up to see An Kyŏnghwa the dancer. Some were even trying to staunch their tears with sobs, perhaps because they understood the dead man's sorrow or were simply affected by the atmosphere. With suitably tearful eyes, An Kyŏnghwa walked up to the coffin, dressed in some new Western-style mourning clothes made of plain black silk. She lit an incense stick and bowed. More than twenty people followed after her and bowed before the coffin one by one. Some were even chatting as they did so.

When the incense had almost ceased burning, Major Sŏ cleared his throat as if to speak and stepped forward, his face flushed bright red. He took a whole handful of incense and set light to it so that jet-black smoke rose up into the air. He blew on the flames to extinguish them, and then he stroked his beard and bowed. And then he cleared his throat once more and spoke his final words to the dead man.

"This is me, Major Sŏ, remember? Umm. . . . You're really going in style, in real style . . . you're better off dead, if you were still alive, would you be able to live in such style? There's no need to worry about fixing your glasses anymore. . . . Anyway . . ."

Pak stood up and pushed Sŏ aside, saying, "He's drunk, you know."

Pak felt frustrated too. He lit an incense stick and stood for a while, knowing that he would feel better if he could only say something, but instead he burst into tears and walked away.

Sŏ and Pak had planned to go on to the cemetery, but they did not like any of the people there, and so they went back to a bar instead.

—*Early Spring of the Year of the Fire Ox*
First published in 1937; translated from *Kamagui:*
Yi T'aejun tanp'yŏnjip (Hansŏng tosŏ, 1937)

THE FROZEN RIVER P'AE

There's not so much as a single bird perched upstairs, where two solitary and faded signs read "Most Beautiful Scenery, Floating Blue Pavilion." Hyŏn gazes up at the pavilion from where he strolls down below without climbing the bank, as if afraid that stepping into such tranquility would be to tear a painting.

Here and there the simple honesty of Yi culture flows out warmly from the thickly dented but still sturdy columns, from the ornamental carving at the top of those columns, and from the decorations on the eaves, which seem almost to have been thrown into place.

By contrast, the Taedong River seems all too cold. Even from the distance of the Floating Blue Pavilion it looks transparent, as if made from glass rather than water. He watches the gentle swaying of the green trapa leaves on the water and thinks he might even detect the breathing of a loach were it to lie flat between the pebbles. The water flows, but makes no sound. It passes through the Waterworks Bridge and around the Clear Stream Wall, and then it spreads out far and wide, like an enormous roll of silk, and the sky and the water are dyed equally red by the sunset as they disappear together into a distant rose bed. From the Ripe Light Pavilion onward, the black dots of paddleboats and flat boats are scattered here and there, none of them appearing to move. A sense of eternity surrounds the hills that dot the endless Taedong Plain.

Hyŏn tosses his cigarette away and adjusts the buttons of his *chŏgori* jacket. The autumn leaves have yet to turn, but his hands have grown cold without him knowing.

Why does nature in Korea look so desolate?

He recalls the lonely scenes in Puyŏ at the White Horse River and the Falling Flowers Rock.

M ore than ten years had passed since Hyŏn was last in Pyongyang. Whenever he set one of his stories in the city, he would resolve to visit again for some sketching before beginning to write, but in the end he had not made the journey even once. It was not so much his stories that demanded a visit, but a couple of friends who would write to him from time to time, urging him to come and see them. They were old school friends: Kim the businessman, who was also a city assemblyman, and Pak, a high school teacher of Korean and classical Chinese. But Hyŏn had not once taken the initiative from their letters. Pak's most recent letter had moved Hyŏn more than others, however, even though it did not request that he visit.

You can probably guess that my classes have been cut in half. At least I can take things easy. But now there are signs that they want to switch me from full time to an hourly basis. Given my subject I can't imagine that they will maintain my remaining hours for much longer either. When everything is gone,

I'll wash my hands of them for good, but until then I'm just hanging in there.[1]

After reading about the situation, Hyŏn felt a sudden urge to meet with Pak. He didn't have anything in particular to say, but he wanted to hold his hand just the once, and so he'd sent a telegram and set off immediately.

Pak showed up at the station looking a mess: he hadn't shaved for a long time and his frequent, almost habitual, scornful laughter was new to Hyŏn. It seemed that Pak was not only hanging in there at the school where he worked, but also in an age that no longer deemed him necessary. Hyŏn could see himself and his work in Pak's attitude, and wanted to cry with frustration.

They walked into the waiting room after finally releasing each other's hands. There was so much to say, but neither could find the words to begin. Hyŏn stood up again at once and said, "I'd like to walk by myself for a while."

He agreed to meet up with Pak again in the evening, together with Kim, at a restaurant by the Taedong River called The Best House in the East. Then he set off for Peony Peak alone.

On the way he glanced out the car window at the city streets. Row after row of new buildings passed by, none of which he could remember from before. One huge redbrick building was particularly impressive, crouching like some enormous grave on the corner of a main street but apparently neither a factory nor a prison. The driver told him it was the police station.

1. In March 1938 the Government General announced a third revision to the Chōsen Education Code in which Korean language was recategorized as a mere elective language at schools on the peninsula. This would have a major impact on teachers of the Korean language, such as the character Pak.

Hyŏn was perplexed to see no sign of the headscarves that women had once worn here. When he asked the driver about this, the reply revealed rather more self-satisfaction than explanation.

"Yes, good riddance, isn't it? Now Pyongyang is a match for Seoul."

Hyŏn had rather liked the headscarves the Pyongyang women used to wear. Simple but seemingly alive, almost like white butterflies but with ribbons resting naturally upon them like rose blossoms, they displayed a special kind of beauty that was something only those Pyongyang ladies could own along with their brightly accented speech. That he could not even witness such beauty in what was supposed to be its hometown reinforced the melancholic sense of ruin that Pyongyang impressed upon him.

H yŏn thought he might walk up to the Ŭlmil Lookout, but when he discovered soldiers there, apparently guarding the airstrip with lances poking out of their guns, he came back down to the river. He hailed an empty pleasure boat that happened to be passing. He wanted to go upstream to Chuam Mountain and back, but was told that was forbidden due to the proximity of the airstrip. Finally he settled on floating down the river to The Best House in the East—no rowing—and climbed on board.

By the time he had drifted like a leaf on the water, all trace of the sunset had disappeared, and the river was dark when he reached the restaurant.

The Best House in the East had been built upon a rock protruding out over the river. As the boat pulled up to the back entrance and he stepped up into the nighttime pavilion, awash in music, the scene was enough to rouse expectation even in Hyŏn with his gloomy state of mind.

He made a promise to himself, "I won't refuse a drink tonight, even though I can't handle alcohol! I'll do my best to cheer up Pak!"

Pak had already arrived with Kim and settled into place with two *kisaeng*. Hyŏn's spirits were lifted even more by the sight of Kim's plump, clean-shaven cheeks and the soft skirts the *kisaeng* wore.

"Hey you, why didn't you shave like Kim here?"

"What and make all the girls go wild for me!"

Pak smiled.

"So, how are things lately for our Mr. Kim, honorable member of the City Assembly?"

"Now then, we haven't seen each other all this time and you start with this mocking *hiyakashi*?"[2]

"You haven't changed one bit! When was the last time, wasn't it in Seoul the year before last?"

"That's right, I think . . . I know, I was on the way back from a tour of cities in the metropole . . ."

"So, I heard that you made a bit of money on some land in the west of the city, or was it the east?"

"Now then! What kind of a gentleman talks about money like that?"

"Why not? We have to feed ourselves."

"Feed ourselves, well, let's see who can eat the most tonight shall we, you or I?"

"Does that mean I'm a bystander at the Kyŏngsŏng-Pyongyang derby?"

"And we'll be the cheerleaders."

The *kisaeng* interjected alongside Pak.

2. Kim's frequent injection of Japanese words into conversation is not simply a sign of the times but indicative of his opportunistic collusion with the modernizing policies of the Government General. Here *hiyakashi* means "to mock" or "to tease."

"These provincial *kisaeng* are funny, aren't they?"

"Funny? But isn't this the capital of *kisaeng*? There must be something special in the vital forces of the land!"

One of the *kisaeng* smiled brightly, while the other was more coy. As Hyŏn looked at the smiling one he suddenly recalled another *kisaeng*.

"Hey you two?"

"What?"

"Was that twelve years ago already? Do you remember, when I was here and we went to Nŭngna Island and had that fish rice porridge?"

"My word, has it really been that long?"

"What was the name of that *kisaeng* back then? Either of you two remember?"

"Oh, I remember her!"

Kim had been leant back askew against the wall, but now he sat up in surprise and clapped his hands.

"That's who I should have asked for from the start!"

"No, but is she still around?"

"Yes, she's alive and kicking."

"And she's still working as a *kisaeng*?"

"Of course."

"Oh right!"

Pak slapped his thigh, as if he too had just remembered.

When Hyŏn had come down to visit that time the three of them had gone to Nŭngna Island to eat fish rice porridge. One of the *kisaeng* had been especially fond of Hyŏn, who was a literary type already back then and had written a poem for this Yŏngwŏl on her handkerchief. They had even had their photograph taken, just the two of them with the Floating Blue Pavilion in the background.

"But she must be getting on a bit if she's still working as a *kisaeng*, no? I do remember her, but I can't remember her name."

"How about one of you two go fetch her?"

"Who is it?" the *kisaeng* asked.

"Oh, now what's her name?"

"I don't remember either . . ."

Just as Pak was saying this, the boy appeared.

"The *kisaeng* . . . who's been here the longest, and who's the oldest?"

The boy had to give this some thought before replying.

"Would that be Kwanok? Or maybe Yŏngwŏl?"

"Oh! It's Yŏngwŏl . . . Yŏngwŏl. Give her a call."

Hyŏn's spirits rose still higher. The table was brought in. Wine cups were passed around.

"So have you learnt to drink yet?"

Pak asked Hyŏn, passing him a cup.

"Goodness . . . I didn't realize you could study drinking, where on earth . . ."

"You poor bastard! But I guess you guys have to be writing day and night, so there's no excuse for drinking parties! Today is on me . . ."

"By the way . . ."

Kim continued, as he held out a cup for Hyŏn.

"You should think about changing direction now too."

"What do you mean, changing direction?"

"Who's that? You know, that man who went to Tokyo to write?"

"I know."

"Now he had foresight!" Kim spoke with admiration.

"You bastard, take this cup. I don't want to hear about it."

Hyŏn quickly downed the cup Kim had offered him and returned the favor.

By the time Yŏngwŏl arrived they were all so drunk that Pak's eyelids were drooping. She was wearing a white *chŏgori* jacket and jade-green skirt and her hair was parted slightly to one side, neither dyed nor curled like the other more fashionable *kisaeng.* She sat down softly by the sliding door and looked around the table. Kim and Pak said nothing, but kept their eyes on Yŏngwŏl and Hyŏn to see what would happen. Yŏngwŏl's eyes passed quietly over Hyŏn, before skipping Pak and coming to rest on Kim with a gentle smile,

"Sir, it's been a long time."

"Hah! Your eyes must be failing you! It's not me you should be pleased to see."

"But a *kisaeng* does not greet the guest she's truly pleased to see."

And her eyes quickly passed over Pak once more to settle on Hyŏn.

"You are truly a great *kisaeng!* Quick with the repartee, eh . . ."

With that Kim held out his cup and Yŏngwŏl swiftly moved to the head of the table, where she picked up the wine bottle.

In her eyes there lingered a suggestion that laughter belonged firmly in her past; dark shadows clung to her eyelids, while her sunken cheeks and rough, parched lips revealed the deep traces left behind by the passing years.

"You . . . don't know me?" Hyŏn asked, as he stubbed out his cigarette.

"Please have a drink, sir."

When her eyes met those of Hyŏn, who held out his cup, Yŏngwŏl blushed and failed to notice the cup had overflowed.

"It looks as if you too have been exhausted by life?"

"Then we're just like everyone else. When did you arrive?"

Yŏngwŏl did not refuse the cup that Hyŏn had first emptied and then refilled to offer her.

"You wore a headscarf that looked like a white butterfly back then . . ."

"Oh, I wish I could be wearing that now."

"And you spoke with such a crisp and clear Pyongyang accent . . ."

"These days guests prefer it when we talk as if we're from Seoul."

"Worthless sons of . . . what do you think, Pak? How come there's not a headscarf to be seen in Pyongyang?"

"That's a question to ask of our Mr. Kim, the city assemblyman. It's these administrators who banned the scarves."

"Really, good grief!"

"Who knows what those jerks are . . ."

"Jerks, it's you who's the jerk . . . so what if those damn headscarves look pretty, do you two have any idea how much money was spent on those headscarves and ribbons each year in the city of Pyongyang alone?"

Kim sat up straight, adopting a more dignified manner.

"So, what if it was a million won? What do you bastards know about the value of culture . . ."

"That's what I mean, you writing types know nothing about the real world."

"What interfering bastards . . . why pick on Korean women? Just because they're trying to look nice? Why shouldn't women be allowed to look a little pretty?"

"But think of the money . . ."

"Hah! So they work themselves to death at home, bring up the kids, take care of men like us . . . and it's too much if they want to buy a ribbon once a year? Come on, do you know how much men spend on drinks and cigarettes? Reforming lifestyles, indeed . . . so that means cutting down on money spent on headscarves and ribbons? Administrators like you, you're just penny-pinchers! Picking on those who . . ."

"Damn you, you need to change your tune! You bastard, don't you know how important alcohol is out there in the real world?"

"I know. But is alcohol all we need? Don't we need our own unique culture too? You're just pigs . . . you wouldn't recognize a pearl if you saw one . . . huh . . ."

"*Hito o baka ni suru na*, don't take me for an idiot, you jerk."

"I can take you for an idiot if you are one . . ."

"*Nani?*"

"*Nani* . . . what the fucking hell is that? Just because you're buying the drinks doesn't mean I can't say what I want. You make me so angry . . ."

Hyŏn belched.

"That's all you've had, and you two are already drunk."

Pak put down his toothpick and offered Hyŏn another cup. Kim quietly pretended to be picking at the snacks.

Yŏngwŏl had made her living this way for long enough to be sensitive to her guests' moods, and now she called the boy and asked him to bring in a *changgu* drum. Picking up the drumsticks calmly with one hand, she banged twice on the rim of the drum with the other hand and began to sing.

"Oh yes, here we go. . . . Playing my zither on a moonlit night . . ."

Hyŏn stared at the raised veins on Yŏngwŏl's neck and undid the buttons of his jacket. With trembling hands, he tried beating on the table. But no melody came to him.

"Heh, heng, heh, heya ha, ora, dent it, the mortar . . ." Kim sang in reply, and Hyŏn seethed with anger once more. At times like this it would be such a relief to be able to sing a bit. The other two *kisaeng* sit quietly and watch Yŏngwŏl's lips. When she's finished, Pak says, "Well done."

He offers Yŏngwŏl a drink, while asking her to sing a *kasa*. Yŏngwŏl does not refuse, but picks up the drum that she has just pushed to one side and begins to play again.[3]

3. Yŏngwŏl begins singing a line from a long narrative poetic form that developed during the Chosŏn dynasty, known as a *kasa*. Pak replies with lines from a poem written in classical Chinese by the one-time anarchist and early twentieth-century nationalist historian Sin Ch'aeho.

"Parting from my love one morning . . ."

Pak clears his throat and replies with a line from a poem that suits the occasion, even though the melody is a bit off.

"Where the mountains and rivers all end, oh woe . . . though we want to sing and shout, it's just too hard . . ."

Pak finished with a sigh and tears welled up in his eyes.

The room was silent, as if a cold rain had passed through. Kim summoned the boy and ordered him to bring in a gramophone player. At the sound of jazz, the other two *kisaeng* took turns in dancing with Kim, as if this was now their world.

"Yŏngwŏl?"

Yŏngwŏl quietly moved next to Hyŏn.

"I never thought I'd see you again, I'm really happy."

"But who would take someone like me away from all this?"

"Are you sure you haven't set your sights too high?"

"What?"

She couldn't hear well over the noise of the gramophone player.

"Are you sure you haven't set your sights too high?"

"Not at all . . . you don't look so well."

"Mmm?"

"You don't look so well."

"Me?"

"Yes."

"Well, I've missed you . . ."

"It's only words, but still . . ."

"Hah!"

The dance had come to an end. Kim returned to his seat and turned to Hyŏn, "You should dance too, *odore!*"[4]

"But I don't know how. I've always despised people who dance with *kisaeng*."

4. Kim urges Hyŏn to dance in Japanese.

"I don't know anyone else as stubborn as you. If you can't dance, then why not just say so . . ."

"Huh! It's not that I don't like to give in . . . [but *kisaeng* are a Korean national treasure].[5] Hugging each other and shaking your bottom, screeching along to those damn popular songs, is that what it means to be a *kisaeng*, is that really entertainment? I bet our Yŏngwŏl here can't dance. Perhaps I should say won't dance, rather than can't?"

"Oh! Our Yŏngwŏl is a great dancer."

The other two *kisaeng* interjected, with a glance toward her.

"So you dance too?"

"I'm not very good."

"But, regardless of whether you're good or not?"

"What else can I do? I have to adapt to the tastes of all our different guests."

"Why is that?"

"I need to make money, of course."

"And what will you do with all the money you make?"

"A *kisaeng* needs to have her own money."

"How come?"

"Well, just think about it."

"I don't know. Can't you just find yourself a rich man?"

"And you think that a rich man will stay with me and not lose interest?"

"Well, why not?"

"A first wife knows that no matter how many affairs her husband has he'll come back home when he's old, so she finds her happiness in her children, doesn't she? But a *kisaeng* has to rely on just one person, so what happens when he doesn't come home? What hope does she have? How many *kisaeng* last long after

5. Brackets mark phrases dropped from Yi T'aejun's first version of 1938 when the story was republished in a collection in 1941.

they've set up home with someone? The best thing for a *kisaeng* is to make her own money and find herself a poor man."

"Yeah! Am I glad to hear that!"

Pak came and sat down by them. He took hold of Yŏngwŏl's hand and pulled her toward him, saying, "I don't have a penny to my name, and now my job is on the line too. My wife is so old she won't even grumble, so if you have some money, why don't we set up home together?"

"But pal, Yŏngwŏl belongs to Hyŏn."

"Well, I guess my only hope now is to find a *kisaeng* with money . . ."

And Hyŏn laughed too.

"You'd better skim the cream off the top from now on." Kim glanced over to observe Hyŏn's reaction.

["And how am I supposed to do that?"

"I mean write something that will sell. People have to know to read your stuff, don't they? Sometimes I give it a go because your name's on it, but it's so difficult . . . I don't know . . ."

"Bastard! . . . I don't need people like you to read my work. Change my direction . . . what . . . who says that writers have to be on the frontlines? That's shit from you . . ."

"What?"

Kim exploded. And because of that Hyŏn stopped joking, his eyes glaring.]

"You dirty scoundrel!"

"Hah, no matter how upright you pretend to be . . ."

"What, you bastard . . ."

And Hyŏn threw the glass of soda, which he'd been drinking in an attempt to sober up, straight at Kim. It wasn't only the glass that broke and rolled around. All the *kisaeng*'s eyes followed it. Even the boy came in.

"You bastard? Whether it's right or not, we, we . . . look we . . . [are artists! Art comes before everything. You bastard . . .]"

Tears welled up in Hyŏn's wide eyes.

"What are you doing in a place like this . . . you're drunk, get some fresh air."

Pak led Hyŏn out of the chaotic room and into the corridor, where Hyŏn took out a cigarette.

"What are you doing? Do you have to take offense at Kim's every word?"

"Phew . . ."

"What's the point in that . . ."

"I think I've drunk too much . . . I'm . . . Perhaps I'm sick of Kim? . . . You should go back in . . ."

Hyŏn leant on the railing for a while, and then he walked down to the riverside, still wearing his slippers. Not a single boat was on the water. He felt a chill down his spine, although there was no breeze. Frost was forming on the leaves scattered on the riverbank, and they sparkled like silver paper. He tried stepping on each leaf that sparkled.

"Step on frost and a hard ice soon follows . . ."

He suddenly recalled these words from the *Book of Changes*. The point was that ice follows upon frost. Hyŏn suddenly sobered up. He pulled the flaps of his jacket around him, but a cold air had pierced right into his chest. He wanted to smoke, but couldn't find a match.

"Step on frost and a hard ice soon follows. . . . Step on frost and a hard ice soon follows . . ."

The nighttime river was as cold and silent as a corpse.

—*The Eighth Day of the Eleventh Month of
the Year of the Wood Ox*
First published in 1938;
translated from *Yi T'aejun tanp'yŏnjip* (Chosŏn mun'go, 1941),
with additions from 1938 version

A TALE OF RABBITS

Before he could even rub the sleep from his eyes, Hyŏn fumbled around his pillow in search of the porcelain bowl full of rice water, which had stood there overnight. It tasted colder and sweeter than any beer steeped in ice. He recalled the way Sŏhae used to tease him, "Hyŏn, when you really start to drink, you'll discover the true taste of water." If Sŏhae were still here they would enjoy a drink together. But more than ten years must have passed now since his death.

Hyŏn stretched out his arms and stared at the flies circling the ceiling.

Back then he was working at the *Chungwoe Daily Newspaper*. It would already be dark by the time they managed to squeeze a hundred won out of the business department on payday and divvy out three to five won each, but even that would disappear before the shutters had been closed and rickshaws hailed when they passed down the line of bread, rice, and clothes merchants who waited outside the doors. Hyŏn was still a bachelor back then and had eked out a living for a couple of years, but Sŏhae, who lived with his mother, wife, and children in rented lodgings, could not feed his family on friendship and loyalty alone.

"I'm moving to the *Maeil*. Why don't you send us something from time to time? I know you don't have a family, but you still have to pay your landlady."

Hyŏn stayed at the *Chungwoe*, but from then on his landlady's complaints would be silenced by manuscript fees from the Government General-funded *Maeil News*. When the *Chungwoe Daily* finally closed down, Hyŏn dismissed it as a time waster and resolved to throw himself into his own studies: he began to reread the classics from the West, which he had not fully appreciated as a student, all the while paying for his board by writing a few short stories and trivial pieces for Sŏhae. Yet whenever someone gains a break, they are apt to set their sights on something even greater. Although Hyŏn had asked himself more than once whether he could inflict his lifestyle on anyone else, he ended up getting married with neither a job nor a home to his name. Supporting a wife turned out to be a burden, which sapped all of his strength and energy. His studies and art came a distant second and third. There was little choice but to return to what he knew, and that meant a newspaper company. Fortunately, he had procured a salaried position at the *Tonga Daily* before his first child was born. By writing serialized novels on the side, he managed to ease his housing worries with the purchase of a shack set on a two-hundred-p'yŏng plot. It was a twenty-minute walk from the tram to be sure, but back then one p'yŏng only cost two or three won. Later, when his land was absorbed into the prefecture and prices rose, he sold off half the plot and built a proper tiled house more than ten kan in area.

"Now that we have our own home, we just need to feed and clothe ourselves . . ."

Hyŏn's wife had taken a fancy to housekeeping. Just as they had paid off the monthly installments on a sewing machine and enrolled in life insurance, they heard that the neighbors had bought a phonograph player and promptly purchased one on installments the very next day. But if Hyŏn were to bring home a record or two, his wife would chide him.

"Why on earth did you spend three won on each of those . . . can we feed ourselves on music? You should give me that kind of money."

To ease his guilt at roaming here and there by himself all summer—thanks to his pass—Hyŏn would save up twenty won and tell his wife to take the children out for the day to somewhere nearby, such as Inch'ŏn. She would set off en route to Inch'ŏn but invariably stop off at Chin'gogae, have lunch at a department store, and return with the children carrying the pots, kettles, and other kitchen equipment she had bought.

This wife of Hyŏn's had graduated from the literature department of M Girls' School, which was located just over the hill from where they now lived. Even back in the days of the shack she had installed glass in each window, which she draped with flower-patterned curtains, hung Millet's *Angelus* on the wall, and arranged flowerpots morning and night. Sometimes she would sing the lullaby from *Jocelyn* to their sleeping children, or take a silk-covered book from the bookcase and recite Browning. But after their second child had been born, and especially after rows of those Kŏnyangsa houses had cropped up all over the place, she grew to dislike the frequent visits of her classmates from the nearby school, and buried herself in floor plans with the hope of pulling down that shack and building a solid new tiled house. Despite the dust on the *Angelus* and shriveling flowers, her daily schedule seemed full of things that were far more pressing.

Hyŏn would have one novel serialized in the newspaper each year. His ambitions did not really lie in serialized novels. He wanted to cultivate himself as a writer and exhaust himself with the kind of creative work that would satisfy his artistic desires, even if that meant a mere short story. He harbored a secret dream to go one step further and produce a major work that would forge a bridge onto the main literary thoroughfare from the minor path on which the new literature of this place still seemed to be lost. If he thought of a good name for a character, he would carefully write it down, and if he saw an interesting actor in a movie, he would take a cutting with a photograph to keep.

Yet all these things remained mere fancy as another year passed with him absorbed in the writing of a serialized novel.

Hyŏn's wife was even more delighted than his readers whenever he began a new novel. The pressure of unpaid bills would ease, and their household would feel quite flush with the unexpected cash, especially if the novel appeared as a single volume and, as sometimes happened, was even reprinted.

"I'm going on forty, the so-called age of decisiveness! Why am I wasting day after day like this? Wake up, go to the office, translate a dispatch or two . . . at best serialize a novel . . ."

Just as Hyŏn was reaching this resolute conclusion, the vernacular papers were shut down.

"Be bright!" "Be healthy!" Loudspeakers shouted out the new era. Hyŏn had returned home drunk the past several nights, bewildered and unable to hold himself together.

The rice water had freshened him up on the inside, but his head still felt heavy.

"Really start to drink and discover the true taste of water . . . umm, have I achieved anything during ten years at the newspaper other than discover the true taste of water?"

He picked up the bowl again but only the dregs were left. He knocked on the kitchen wall to summon his wife.

"Did you sleep well?"

"Some water, please."

She good-naturedly fetched some water and sat down. Then she stretched out her neck and burped, as if she had been the one drinking. Her breathing was already heavy. This was her fourth pregnancy, following upon the daughter and two sons, which they had believed to be perfectly sufficient already.

"I need to talk to you."

Hyŏn's wife was not one to scold normally, but from time to time she would become serious.

"It's not that I don't know how you're feeling lately. But this is the fourth day in a row that you've come home drunk . . ."

Hyŏn frowned as he silently ran his fingers through his thick hair.

"This resentment or anger of yours . . . if just a few drinks can make you forget, then why pretend to be angry or resentful in the first place? We women find nothing more disgusting and worrying than watching Korean men behave like this. We can't live on alcohol, can we? And you're not the only ones at home, are you? Just think about it, you've got a wife and all these children, now you have no job and there isn't even anywhere you could serialize a novel . . . can't you pull yourself together?"

"Oh shut up," Hyŏn grumbled and crawled back under the quilt. He returned home slam drunk that day and the next, perhaps as a kind of reaction. But to tell the truth, his wife's words had hit home; he knew that just because he was drunk did not mean the whole world would join him, and he could not keep on drinking alone forever.

Hyŏn agreed to his wife's request to set themselves up as rabbit breeders using the severance pay that had brought a chill to his heart, as if it had been stolen from the pocket of a corpse.

First, his wife had returned from someone's house, having seen for herself how just two rabbits had, within one year, reproduced so much that a fifty-p'yŏng yard could no longer hold them all. Then, she returned from someone else's house, where a couple had started with just two hundred won but were earning an average of seventy to eighty won each month just within a couple of years. And then, one evening Hyŏn had read a book on rabbit breeding, which his wife had acquired for him, and discovered that, although breeding rabbits would require his daily attention, it seemed far less of a burden than writing a serialized novel each day; and that, whereas writing a serialized novel left him no time to work on a serious novel, breeding rabbits would leave him with enough energy to read and work on the kind of novels he wanted to write, even if this meant only one every ten years. When he realized that this would also amount to the kind of bright and healthy life that the loudspeakers were screaming at him to live, Hyŏn's resolve to breed rabbits hardened still further. He accompanied his wife on a visit to her former classmate, who was now making seventy to eighty won a month on an investment of two hundred won.

The husband had once been a well-known pianist, whose photograph had taken up two columns in the *Tonga Daily* some years previous and whose performances several newspaper companies had been keen to sponsor. He greeted Hyŏn and his wife with rough, grass-stained hands unbecoming to a pianist. Once inside the courtyard they were surrounded by an uncomfortably warm smell, which reminded Hyŏn more of fetid flesh than manure. The rabbit cages looked like the boxes you leave your clothes in at the bathhouse: they were stacked in rows and together made a small yet tallish building that circled the yard. White rabbits crouched at intervals, their ears barely visible, rolling soft pink eyes and twitching their mouths. Hyŏn immediately thought of his children at home. This was the world of fairy tales. It seemed like a sideline more suitable to a children's fiction writer. Hyŏn and his wife listened for more than two hours to the pianist and his wife's various tales of raising rabbits before returning home with increased confidence. Soon they sent an order to the Kanebo rabbit-breeding division for twenty meriken rabbits, which were supposed to be the easiest to look after. They called the carpenter and had him build rabbit cages. Before he'd even finished, a telegram arrived to notify them that the rabbits had been dispatched. Hyŏn took the children up the hill to pick grass and acacia leaves. Then they got hold of left-over residue from the bean curd maker. They also ordered some dried food, because apparently the rabbits would get sick if fed only on wet food. Three days later the twenty tiny new members of Hyŏn's household arrived safe and sound in boxes with wire lids. They were breathing rapidly in the heat, other-wise their only movement was a calm twitching of their muz-zles while they avoided watching what was going on around them. They seemed to feel safer in their boxes. They looked more like some kind of chemical concoction created in a test tube than natural animals. While his wife and children rushed to unpack them with glee, Hyŏn stood back and felt guilty, ashamed even, to think that responsibility for the livelihood of five to six strong human beings was being placed upon these tiny, cute animals, which were as soft and white as the flowers on a gourd plant.

After the arrival of the rabbits Hyŏn did not have a moment's rest. Once he had fed them and finished all the preparations for the next meal as well, he tended not to quickly wash his hands and go inside. The next mealtime would arrive while he wan-dered about in front of the cages, and then it would be time to prepare the following meal again, and once that was done he would have to clean their cages. It was evening before he had any time to himself.

Slowly the long autumn nights began to draw in. Their house was out of the way, and few friends visited in the evening. Hyŏn enjoyed quietly turning on the lamp and breathing in his own world in solitude, even if that was only possible in the evenings. He reread the Western classics, which he had begun reading as a single man in a boarding house ten years earlier. Shining a lamp upon his bookshelves, he would feel his way through the vari-ous trends of thought in culture, literature, and the human race more broadly, he would observe the layered waves of modernity, and flush with pleasure as he continued to map out his novel, which he had barely been able to broach as each new trend had first hit and then passed through.

His library was not large, but Hyŏn could not help but feel awe whenever he leisurely perused his bookshelves. He could appreciate the saying, "To see a thousand years at one glance." Every day new books appear. Every day new books turn into old books. What had once seemed the pinnacle of human thought, making even the Buddhist canon and the Bible appear colorless, had now faded faster than a book cover. There was the new thing that had followed, and then the new new things that had followed thereafter; two or three ages in thought were neatly arranged on just one bookshelf.

Relics of old ways of thinking that have passed by! But are those books the only victims? And those authors? If only those books and authors had been sacrificed, then the human race might have lived as harmonious neighbors, but man had always felt the need to roam with the desire for some new and better order.

Whether for the sake of old things or for what was new, each new current of thought had always produced victims— sometimes many, sometimes few. The greater the significance of the trend, the larger the footprint left behind as it trampled upon part of the population. When he thought about it, material civilization was also the civilization of thought. The rapid dissemination of one thought had brought the rapid termination of another. In the past people might have suffered the chaos caused by a new trend of thought perhaps once in their lifetime, but how many times do we moderns have to live through this? More than once Hyŏn had smiled bitterly as he perused his bookshelves and remembered the words of the Qing poet Erjiao: "In his one life he suffers many lives and deaths." This was truly appropriate for modern times.

"In his one life he suffers many lives and deaths . . . thought is short and life is long . . ."

The rabbits increased rapidly, just as everyone had warned. By the time the acacia leaves had turned color, the initial twenty numbered more than forty bustling animals. Hyŏn envisaged this rising to fifty and had bought the timber to build more cages. And then a snag arose. Food. They had not been able to store enough grass and acacia leaves and had ended up relying largely on bean curd residue and dried food, but lately the bean curd maker sometimes skipped their delivery. Today he had again brought only about half the promised amount. And though they were sure to pay in advance for everything, including the delivery fee, the dried food hadn't arrived either. It was getting harder to procure soybeans, so bean curd production was down; consequently the number of people eating the residue instead of the actual curd had risen, making the residue even more precious than the curd. As for the dried food, that was made up of the husks of mixed grains, but certain grains were now being pounded until they lost 5 or even 7 percent of their weight, so there was no way any husks would be left over. They learned that they had actually been buying last year's product until recently. Hyŏn's wife ran about here and there, but even people raising chickens, let alone rabbits, were selling up and taking down their chicken runs.

His wife walked around with an angry red face, as she did whenever she'd been wronged, but finally she had to relinquish the idea of making a living from rabbit breeding. She set about trying to get rid of the rabbits, even at discount prices. There was no limit to the amount of rabbit skins that could be dispatched in one go, but when it came to live rabbits, the problem of food blocked every path. If they were to kill all forty at once, their home would be turned into a slaughterhouse. Not only did they not have enough boards to dry more than forty skins, but neither of them had it in their nature to pick up a knife and skin even one animal. Hyŏn might well be the man of the house, but he had never even cut a chicken's throat, and the only time his wife had bought a whole chicken that had just been scalded in hot water, back when they were still living in the shack, she had been so afraid of its glaring, dead eyes that she had to cover them with newspaper before she could wield her knife. As long as the rabbits didn't increase still further, they would have to dispose of them alive, even if it took more time. This decision meant they had to somehow prevent the rabbits from starving until they could be sold. By this time any kind of soft grass had almost completely disappeared. There were only radish leaves left over in the kitchen and clover to be found outside. A few days before the heavy frosts were due to fall, Hyŏn's wife suddenly remembered that the sports field at her old school, M Girls' High School, had always been covered with clover. She walked over the hill to the school, where they told her to come and pick the rampant clover by all means: the lawn was in danger of being swallowed up, even though someone was paid to take care of it. "If you don't want to go, I'll do it. How can we let such tiny creatures starve to death when we're all safe and sound?" Hyŏn looked unconvinced, but his wife's threat provoked the unbearably pitiable thought of her, heavily pregnant and picking rabbit food in her old school sports field, of all places. He put on his summer woodstripping hat and rubber shoes, handed a basket to his eldest child, who was just returning from school, and set off over the hill to M Girls' School in his everyday clothes.

At the sports field grass and clover were indeed confronting each other in equal numbers all over the place.

"No one will recognize me with this hat and no jacket . . . and even if they do, they'll just wonder what that Hyŏn guy is up to . . ."

Classes must have finished because the older girls were showing off their slender legs playing volleyball and riding bicycles around the field. Hyŏn felt as though he had ventured into somebody's garden and made a point of keeping his head down while he sat off to one side picking clover.

"Daddy?"

"What?"

His son was still standing, distracted by the girls riding their bicycles in front of the majestic school building, which towered up into the sky on the hill.

"Did mummy go to school here?"

"Yes . . . come on, pick this dark grass too . . ."

Two students appeared to have heard the conversation between father and son and walked over to them.

"Who's your mummy, little boy?"

His son sniffed and turned away. Hyŏn looked at him. It was the same look he would throw him at home, as if to say "Do not cause a scene." The boy quietly picked up his basket and began to pick clover.

"What are you picking this for?"

"It's for our bunny rabbits."

"Bunny rabbits! You have bunnies at home?"

"Yes."

The students also began to pull at the clover and fill up his son's basket.

"Hey, what are you two doing?"

Another group of students emerged from behind Hyŏn and crowded around. Hyŏn blushed, as if he was also part of the "you two."

"We're looking for four-leaved clover."

It turned out they were not gathering rabbit food at all but searching for their own good fortune.

"Me too, me too."

They plunged down into the clover like a flock of birds that had caught sight of something to eat. His head bent, Hyŏn went on picking in the opposite direction, all the while thinking of how his wife, too, must have once walked around the perimeter of this field with a copy of Browning's poems under her arm, yearning just as thirstily for the happiness promised by a four-leaved clover. The hero whom she had imagined appearing over a blue horizon, along with the fortune brought by four leaves, was surely not the man in a wood-stripping hat picking rabbit food here today. Just as he suppressed a bitter smile, something hit him on the buttocks. Laughter sounded out from across the broad field. A volleyball player standing at an angle from Hyŏn had missed the ball.

The next afternoon Hyŏn brought his eldest son to the sports field once more. The clover could probably be picked for five more days or so. But a harsh frost that night brought the clover to an early end. It was kimchi-making season, however, and Hyŏn's wife went from house to house collecting the discarded outer leaves of cabbage and radish. This could not continue for long. With no better idea other than trying to get rid of the rabbits one or two at a time, Hyŏn visited a doctor at the university hospital with whom he was not even particularly close. The man had been keeping rabbits for more than ten years, but these days taking on even just a couple more rabbits seemed to be a worry. On the way home Hyŏn stopped off at a bookstore. Books on rearing rabbits also contained information on how to kill them. They had only read the sections on how to rear rabbits in the book his wife had once borrowed.

Altogether there were six different ways to kill a rabbit: strangling, stabbing in the heart and bleeding to death, drowning, death by holding the ears and pulling one leg in a certain way, slicing the arteries and bleeding to death, and, finally, striking the skull between the ears three or four times with a hammer so that the whole body would tremble and the rabbit would die.

Hyŏn returned the dusty book to its place and quickly left the shop, casting a furtive glance at the owner on his way.

Back home he quickly changed and took out a rabbit. Heavy, soft and warm, with bright eyes and back legs kicking . . . now that they were old enough to breed, they no longer gave off the sense of being some kind of chemical concoction or delicate gourd flowers. They were beasts: slacken the grip momentarily, or even just pick one up a little awkwardly, and off it would leap into the hills.

Hyŏn gripped the chest and back legs firmly and walked over to the veranda. His daughter came outside shouting.

"Hey, daddy's got a bunny out!"

His two boys came running out.

"What are you doing, daddy?"

"Is he sick?"

"Can we play with him on the deck?"

"Isn't he pretty, daddy?"

His daughter pushed a piece of bread she had in her hands toward the rabbit's mouth. The rabbit twitched his whiskers and munched. Hyŏn thought of the six methods of killing a rabbit that he'd read about in the bookstore.

"What are you doing, daddy?"

"Go away, all of you."

Finally Hyŏn shouted at them. His wife came out of the kitchen. He thought of how she would soon give birth. A chill crept down his spine and he took the rabbit out the back. She followed and asked him what he was doing.

"Why are you following me around like one of the kids?"

She did not back off easily. Hyŏn put the rabbit back in its cage. No matter how he thought about it, he couldn't muster the confidence to strangle it: to tighten his hands on its throat as it struggled, and to keep the pressure up as he looked down at its rolling eyeballs and waited for its breath to stop. But for Hyŏn, who couldn't bear to watch someone being injected with a needle, it felt even more impossible to feel through the soft fur toward the heart in which to plunge a gimlet; or to plunge it into water when it hadn't even been caught first in a trap like a mouse; or to hold onto its ears and legs and pull them apart until its spine broke; or to cut the arteries in that throat, which reminded him of his children's, warm and bouncing up and down; or to sit behind it and beat its brains out with a hammer as it tried to look back. Each thought sent a shiver down Hyŏn's spine, and for the sake of the fetus now curled up inside his wife's stomach in the exact shape of a rabbit, he felt he must be punished for even contemplating such acts.

Once kimchi-making season was over, rabbit food grew even more precious, and they were paying out one won forty or fifty chon every day to buy bean curd and cabbage. Even people were struggling to eat like that. If this continued for just three or four months, they wouldn't be able to recuperate any more than the money they had spent on food, even if they managed to sell all fifty rabbits at once. And three or four months later the rabbits wouldn't be their only problem. What with the four or five hundred won they had gone through on account of the rabbits, and then the kimchi making and two cartloads of firewood, there would only be three or four ten-won notes left in his severance envelope.

"What will we live on?"

A while earlier, Hyŏn had received a request to write a short story for some magazine. Three or four reminders had already arrived. A measly ten won was not that important, but as he had found it impossible to find the peace of mind to write even a short story, it would be good to just sit somewhere in front of a piece of paper and write. One day he decided to write the story of those "damn rabbits" and stoked up a fire to warm the floor with the firewood. He was hesitating over how to begin, when he heard his wife call out to him.

"Where are you?"

He looked out to see her face as white as paper and her two hands covered in blood.

"What!"

"Could you fetch some water for me?"

"What's all this blood?"

She forced a smile onto her expressionless face. Her blood-drenched hands were trembling. She had taken a knife and somehow caught and skinned two rabbits. His hair stood on end.

"Who told you to do that?"

"We've got to do something, haven't we? There's another baby coming, isn't there? Please, fetch me some water to wash my hands."

She held out two hands covered in rabbit fur and fresh blood. Hyŏn suddenly recalled an old image of her, placing newspaper over a dead chicken's eyes before she could wield the knife. A sharp pain hit between his eyes and everything went dark.

Those ten bloody fingers were asking him for more than just water. He sat down, staring at the distant mountain ridge. White clouds hovered overhead.

—Shōwa 16 January 11
Translated from *Munjang*, February 1941

H an felt anxious. It wasn't any kind of identifiable illness, nor was it anything a dose of boar's blood might help. Back in the days when he used to be busy, there was a phrase that he had repeated like a mantra: "If only I could get away from work and quietly write what I want to write, read what I want to read." Now that there was nothing left for him to take care of, suddenly he yearned for those editorial rooms and classrooms, as if they had amounted to more than mere busyness.

Feeling at peace was not a matter of resting the body. For a while, he had closed the door and attempted to relax. Sitting beside the sliding panel doors, he would gaze upon the mountain birds perched on the bare branches of the cherry tree outside and try to enjoy the sound of icy snow falling upon the dead leaves, which rolled around his shaded yard. But instead of reaching a state of calm, his nerves had taken a turn for the worse, and now he felt more on edge than ever. This hunting trip had been arranged for a walk in the mountains, designed to soften those taunt nerves.

He was full of excitement. He was glad to be meeting his old school friend Yun, whom he hadn't seen in a while. He was grateful for the warmth apparent in Yun's letter of invitation, which explained that all was set for the lunar new year. Just the thought of the scenes to come brought forth the pleasurable wild passions that lay deep within him: he would walk a country path once again, run across a rugged peak, and gaze up at tall trees whose branches stretched out powerfully according to the will of the gods; pheasants would drop from the sky, rushing deer and wild boar would fall, and blood would gush over the white snow like a hot spring; and then afterward, legs would roast in their skin over an open log fire. It seemed that no matter how cultured man had become, a savage yearning always lurked somewhere in a corner of his heart.

When he disembarked from the train at Wŏlchŏngni, he found Yun waiting with two gunmen, as promised. Yun grasped Han's hand and eyed him with suspicion, "How would I ever have recognized you?"

Han, too, had to look his friend in the face for a while.

"I suppose fifteen years is a long time!"

They walked out of the waiting room to smoke a cigarette while Han met the gunmen, and then they all crossed over the railway tracks into a fairly wide country road heading to the northwest. The older gunman said that he wouldn't bother even loading his gun for pheasant season, but the younger one countered that they should at least prepare something for dinner and loaded up his gun before heading off after the dog, Tomu, who was already running down the side of the road, wagging his tail. What used to be wasteland had been developed by the Irrigation Association with the result that the road was fairly wide and even for at least ten ri, and not so much as a quail flew up into the air. During this while, Yun entertained Han with impressionistic yet sincere stories of what might be called a scribe's view of life and the world. The bottom line was that the common people were foolish, and those who might guide them with moral principles were far away, while those who would do otherwise were far too close and numerous. As a result, it was not easy for people to find happiness. When Yun had first graduated, he had felt a sort of righteous indignation on their behalf, but that had melted away like a snowflake in a red-hot brazier. At some point, he confessed, after living amongst the profiteers in the area for a couple of years, he had grown wise to reality, and because of this he could still feed his family even if he closed his office and took a trip like this for three or four days. He repeatedly sighed while complaining that the townspeople were too superficially clever and the villagers too ignorant and blind.

Slowly they approached some mountain slopes covered with a coating of fine snow. After they had passed through a hamlet, fields replaced the rice paddies, and the path took on more of a country feel. Tomu's tail was now erect, and he ran off into a field of cropped beanstalks. To the human eye there's nothing to be seen, but the dog puts his nose to the ground and spins around in circles, chasing some kind of scent. The young gunman holds his gun close and follows. The rest of the group watches on from the path. About fifty or sixty feet into the field, something flutters in a dip out of sight, and a pheasant flies up, looking as if it might have been embroidered on a purse. Before it can even spread its wings fully, white smoke radiates from the muzzle of the rifle, a shot rings out, and in an instant the pheasant drops to the ground like a dead weight. Han ran to retrieve it but was beaten by Tomu. He tried to coax the dog toward him, but it shot back to its master like an arrow from a bow. Once it had handed over the pheasant, it jumped up and down, rubbing its master's legs and barking. It didn't seem like a simple case of loyalty to its master, rather this was a dog with a keen sense of self-interest, which made it want to make its efforts known to all.

The pheasant looked as serene as a picture, apart from a few drops of blood visible beneath its shoulder. There was a kind of senseless futility to the way in which a momentary pop of gun-shot had extinguished this thing, which had once flown so pow-erfully through the air as if breaking through waves, and which had throbbed with life like a spark or gushing spring. At any rate, with this one pheasant, the atmosphere of the hunt turned extravagant.

The imposing mountains still hovered in the distance, and the group had to walk at least another fifteen ri to the vil-lage that would be their base of operations. The street was of a fair size, with a barbershop, an inn, and even a police substation. They untied their simple bags in a warm, reed-matted room before plucking the pheasant to make noodles. Perhaps because it had grown up wild on the mountain slopes, this pheasant tasted nothing like Han had ever tasted before, even after taking his extreme hunger into account.

By the time they had finished lunch, no more than a slither of sunlight the size of a deer's tail remained on the mountain peaks. Five ri further up was a mountain village full of experi-enced beaters, and beyond that vast hunting grounds with count-less mountain valleys full of deer, wild boar, and occasionally even bears, so that they would be able to hunt in a new valley each day for the next five to six days.

The old gunman went alone up to the village to assemble the beaters, while Han, Yun, and the young gunman stayed behind on the street. They set off in search of the pheasants that would come down at sunset. Sure enough, Tomu flushed out more birds than in the daytime. Whenever a bird or two flew up, at least one would drop with the sound of the gun. But when there was a flock of ten or more, one would be sure to scare first, prompting the others to fly off before the gunman and his dog had even reached shooting range. By the time they returned to the street, it was dusk, and a gentle snow was falling. They shook the snow off their shoes and entered the brightly lit room with at least five glossy hen pheasants in their hands. It was then that Han found himself missing several friends whom he had left behind in the city. He washed his feet and dried them in front of a bush clover fire, having removed the stone cover from the brazier, and then they all ate roast pheasant for dinner before calling in the young men from the house to play cards with noodles as a wager. At midnight they had a simple but tasty snack of pheasant and buckwheat with a cold radish soup that made their teeth tingle, and then they stayed up past two o'clock sharing stories of goblins that had appeared on midnight trips to eat noodles or go fishing, or on the way home from visiting girls in nearby villages.

The next morning they woke up with eyes blurry, heads muddy, and stomachs churning as if from a hangover. Han found this rather comforting. When he heard that a pair of pheasants fetched four won, he almost regretted not having bought a large field in a village like this and acquired his own gun license.

Naturally they ate breakfast late. It was a perfect day for hunting: the ground was covered by a layer of snow barely a footprint deep, and a gentle wind blew.

They reached the upper village around ten o'clock. The old gunman was angry, complaining in a harsh voice that he had been waiting out in the road with four beaters since seven o'clock.

They headed straight into the mountains. The beaters spread out evenly from the foot to the top of the slopes, while Yun, Han, and the gunmen walked along the mountain crest and took up position at narrow necks two valleys further in: the old gunman sat at the most critical point, the younger gunman at the next one, and Yun and Han at another narrow spot where an animal might just try to escape if things did not go according to plan. In the case that an animal seemed to be coming their way, they were to try to send it back into the other narrow necks by shouting.

It was almost an hour before the hooting sound of the beaters came into earshot. They were moving up and over the mountain, thrashing branches of oak and hooting to each other up and down the slopes. But apart from a few mountain pigeons, no animal appeared. The gunmen moved into a fairly small pine grove on the next mountain slope and began to look for paw prints. The old gunman soon discovered the prints of a fairly large deer. After taking a careful look, he declared that it must have passed through that very morning. They crossed another peak. Suddenly Tomu began to bark loud and long. Dammit! The old gunman groaned with frustration. The dog had gone too far ahead and flushed it out. It looked like a deer calf, but its slender neck and legs were already bobbing up and down as it leapt across the next mountain slope. The old man grumbled about bringing a pheasant-hunting dog along on a large-beast hunt. No matter how his master called, the dog kept chasing after the deer.

"That deer will go at least a hundred ri today."

They gave up on the calf and set about beating their way through another valley. Still no luck. On the next mountaintop they lit a fire and ate lunch. Han was still full, but his legs ached. It was most pleasant to smoke a cigarette while sitting tall on the mountain divide, gazing far across to mountain peak after mountain peak and down below at the sturdy branches of huge oak trees nearby.

The beaters took out their hemp wrapping cloths and heartily gulped down lunches made up of yellow millet with bites of kimchi. It was enjoyable to pass one of life's moments sitting around a bonfire with these simple men. Once their empty wrapping cloths had been pushed back into the rear of their pants, out came their pipes. Just then, one of the gunmen shouted out. A beater had picked up a gun and was fingering it.

"Are you worried he doesn't know how to use a gun?"

"Of course, he doesn't."

"But he shot a deer once."

"A deer?"

The beater in question blushed and walked up to the fire, his thick lips shimmered with saliva and puckered into a smile. He stood out from the other beaters because of the navy blue Western-style jacket he wore on top of a *chŏgŏri* jacket, although the broad stitches on its seams were worn and faded, and because of his slightly bent *toriuchi* hunting cap and the *chikatabi* socks he wore on his feet. He looked the most foolish of them all: his face appeared large and round from every angle and there was plenty of white in his constantly twitching eyes.

"And when did you ever shoot a gun?" asked the old gunman.

"Why? D'you think bullets won't fly if I pull the trigger?"

He was bragging somewhat.

"Dammit, who said the bullet won't fly? I just asked when?"

He laughed like a child. And then quickly became excited.

"D'you want to hear how I nearly shot somebody?"

"All right, let's hear it."

"Ah, I almost had to wear the fetters, you know . . ."

"It was down in that oak tree hollow, right?"

"That's right! I'd been watching a pheasant and kept on shooting at it, before I remembered I'd seen a couple of men there earlier burning wood for charcoal, didn't I? But when I stopped and looked, I couldn't see either of 'em! They must have gone down when I hit 'em, mustn't they? I tried running for home, when what happens but one of the men comes striding down with a bunch of axes in his arms? My legs were shaking so much I couldn't move . . . dammit, I thought, my time's up, but if I'm going to die at the hands of an axe-man, I might as well try to shoot first, so I pick up my gun. He looked like he'd scream, so I had to try to aim right. I did the best I could and held onto the gun real tight, and waited for him to get close. He'd a thick, black beard and didn't he look fierce! And he just kept on coming, so

I pulled the trigger. Bang! There's a boom in my ear, but there's no bullet, not even a trace of smoke, and in the meantime the axeman just keeps on coming until he's right in front of me! What d'you know, I was so confused I'd pulled the trigger without putting in any bullets, so of course nothing came out! Well, by this time he was about to chop my head off with an axe! That's what I thought, and everything went black for a moment, but then I managed to pull myself together and, wouldn't you know it, he's already walked a cow's length past me down the hill? I look again and there's a stone in his hand . . . he was only going down to the stream to sharpen his axe . . . ha ha ha . . ."

A roar of laughter burst out around the mountaintop.

"But where did you get the gun?"

His cousin had once been the mayor of the township and owned a gun. The cousin still lived in the next village and harvested around a hundred sacks of rice each year.

In the end they came back down the mountain that afternoon without having fired a single shot. The following day they did manage to flush out one deer and a wild boar, but the beaters either pushed too far ahead or left too big a gap between themselves, so neither animal could be driven into a narrowing.

On the fourth day, Yun went out in the morning and returned with a couple of pheasants. Han, meanwhile, stayed down in the village, he felt exhausted and excused himself by saying that he wanted to eat noodles for lunch.

The other hunters had still not returned by the time the dinner trays were brought out. Han and Yun finished eating and decided to take a stroll outside. Just then, a loud shot rang out from a valley in the mountains, which encircled them like a black folding screen. Another shot followed. Han's curiosity was piqued, but there was nothing to do other than wait. The hunters finally reappeared more than two hours later. They had caught a wild boar the size of a bull. They had cut down some oak branches to use as carrying poles, but it had been no easy job dragging the boar back down the mountain. If it had rolled to one side and into a ditch, they would have struggled to drag it back out again. When they had barely made it to the top of the village, all the beaters scattered, exhausted from hunger. Yun suggested they go up that night while the blood was still fresh, but Han could still feel the effects of his dinner and didn't feel like going out into the dark, cold night. Moreover, he was not one of those so-called blood-drinkers who go hunting in order to drink boar's blood, which, according to the gunman, tasted little different fresh from when heated up anyway. In the end they decided to go up before breakfast the following day.

At sunrise they washed quickly and went up to the village above. The villagers had already gathered, forming a mass of white. One of the beaters stepped out from the midst and said, "There's been an incident."

"What happened?"

"Some bastard cut the belly during the night and drained the blood. He didn't even manage to get the gallbladder out without bursting it, and on top of that, he took several pounds of flesh too!"

A closer look revealed things to be just as he had said. From the color to the texture of its fur, the collapsed heap looked more like the trunk of a tree some several hundred years old than an animal. The thief had hacked out some flesh from the hind legs in addition to cutting the stomach. It was the old gunman who had shot the boar, but now the blood had completely drained from his lips as well.

"It must have been someone who lives here."

He asked where the ward head lived.

"What are you going to do?"

"Don't worry. Just leave it to me."

The old gunman asked the ward head to gather all the young men from the village in his outer room. There were only about seven or eight men in all, which included the four beaters and, of course, the man in the navy blue jacket who had shot at the charcoal burner on his way to sharpen his axe. The old gunman waited for them all to sit down in the small room before speaking in a strong voice that seemed to defy the fact he had already lost some of his molars.

"This deed was perpetrated by one person, not two, and so I am sorry to have called you all in here, but please understand that this is unavoidable and bear with me . . . there is only one way to proceed. Sir, please have a bowl of water heated up. . . . Whoever did this was greedy for meat . . . at first he wanted the gall bladder, but once he'd punctured it in the dark, he thought he might as well take some flesh. . . . In any event, he must have cooked that meat for breakfast. I can't turn all of your stomachs inside out like socks. . . . But if you each put your hands into warm water, we'll soon know who's been touching meat . . ."

Everyone looked at each other's hands at once. They each had two. And those hands were all rough with bumpy knuckles. They were innocent hands, which simply did as they were told, irrespective of good and bad. They did not live by artifice but by their strength, and were more rough even than the feet of city people. This was the first time in their lives that these simple hands had suffered such merciless humiliation. A part of Han began to despise the gunman. He hoped that not one of these hands would release the oil of guilt into the water. But before the bowl of warm water had even appeared, there was one pair of hands attracting glares from several people. Those hands belonged to the navy blue jacket. At first they were knotted together, then they tried lying flat under the knees, then they scratched at the waist, before finally they pulled out a pipe and stuffed it with tobacco, by this time trembling visibly. The ever-attentive old gunman quickly proffered the brazier, which was at his side. The neck that craned to light the pipe was more than merely awkward; the bowl of the pipe shook as it touched the flames.

The old gunman suddenly raised his voice, "Are you trying to light a pipe or not?"

The man in the jacket grew all flustered as he tried to pick the pipe back out of the brazier, where it had fallen from his mouth. The old gunman glared at him, his sunken eyes by now so sharp they seemed almost to scratch. The jacket's face burned even brighter than the brazier. The old gunman pushed the inner door open and shouted out, "Sir? We won't be needing that water any more."

And then he turned to the men, "While one of you stays behind, let everyone who is innocent leave."

Eventually there was just the man in the Western jacket remaining, unable to stand or even raise his head. The old gunman suddenly lashed out at his ear.

In due course the ward head appeared, apologized for the unfortunate incident, which had occurred in his jurisdiction, and said he would consider whatever punishment was deemed appropriate. The old gunman laid out his calculations all too quickly.

"Would anything less than five bowls of blood have come out of that pig? Even if we only allow for five bowls, that's fifty won, and then there's the gall bladder, which he himself said just last night was worth at least forty won. So that's ninety won, and then he made such a mess cutting up the hind legs that the skin is useless now, isn't it? So that's ten won for the skin, which brings us to one hundred won. And now that this has happened, how can we feel like hunting today? We've lost a whole day as well."

"You have suffered great losses! But how could the likes of him get even ten won together? He has a cousin just over the way. I'll go confer with him and see to it that you are not too disappointed. Please wait for me down below and please don't tell the police."

At the mention of the police the old gunman added that he would make a formal complaint if there were no news by three o'clock and ended with a threat: "How many years do bastards like that have to eat prison food before they can even pretend to be human?"

In the end the old man cut three chunks of meat off the boar and came back down to the street. Everyone was hungry from walking ten ri before breakfast, but no one felt like eating meat. Han and Yun left the affair in the old man's hands and went out pheasant hunting until dusk with the young gunman, but by the time they had returned, events had taken an even more unfortunate turn. The Western jacket's cousin had offered thirty won in compensation, but since this was unlikely to be enough to satisfy the old gunman and rumors had probably already reached the substation, he also urged his cousin to go straight to the police, take a beating until he could stand no more, and then apologize and beg them to clear up the incident with that thirty won, which was all the money he had. But the Western jacket, with thirty won in its pockets, did not appear either at the substation or before the old gunman. A rumor had even spread that it had been spotted well into the night at Wŏlchŏngni station, buying a train ticket.

And so the hunt came to an end.

H an was woken by the noise in the carriage as his train passed through Ch'ang-dong. He was approaching Seoul and his home. Yet he did not feel any kind of joy. He thought to himself how wide the world must seem to the man in the Western jacket, who could run away with just thirty won.

First published in 1942. Translated from Yi T'aejun, *Toldari* (Pangmun sŏgwan, 1943)

For some reason Maehŏn ended up embarking upon his long-planned trip to Kyŏngju in the dog days of summer. Several friends had offered to accompany him in the fall, but even if he could wait until then, he was not so interested in waiting for his friends.

By nature, he found it hard to adapt to others. No matter how familiar the friend, he was always more comfortable alone. If he were to travel one hundred ri by himself, he would feel he had gone further than if he traveled one thousand ri in boisterous company. And so, when the opportunity arose, he set off in spite of the heat.

Whereas Puyŏ had been the ancient capital of Paekche, Kyŏngju was the ancient capital of Silla: this was the extent of his knowledge of the town. Even when buying his ticket at the bureau, he had not asked for any leaflets or information. He had switched to a pair of comfortable shoes and taken out his hiking cane, not even bothering to pack a bag. Rather than discover somewhere new, he was in the mood to escape his cares for even a little while; he wanted to simplify his daily life and return to solitude, and there didn't seem much need to stuff belongings into a bag. Upon his return he would no doubt be pressed to write several travel pieces, but he didn't pack even one sheet of manuscript paper. He did not want to clear his head so much as to unwind it. Perhaps he was already exhausted in every possible way. It was enough to make sure he had plenty of money in his pocket.

Because it was the height of summer in both the north and the south, there were none of the seasonal disputes commonly on view in spring or autumn during the course of the journey. Moreover, he had already ridden the Seoul-Pusan line several times, so dusk settled outside the window without much interest. It was still dark when he switched trains at Taegu, but several stations further down the line unfamiliar scenes began to reveal themselves outside the window. The green fields remained the same, but the sight of glittering dew gave the impression of morning. The names of passing stations, such as Panyawŏl, "Midnight-moon," emitted a whiff of poetry, while the sight of rods hanging over misty riverbanks, belonging to fishermen even more diligent than farmers, presented a rustic scene. Just as he was wondering whether to lower the blind to block out the strengthening sunrays, the train pulled into Kyŏngju.

A stone pagoda stood to the right-hand side as he came out of the station, which bore the contours of a Korean house. The sun was already beginning to burn, as if it were not in the east at all. The cracked and crumbling pagoda was yellowed and bumpy, like the spine of some beast extracted from a layer of earth tens of thousands of years old rather than something made from stone. Surrounded by mountains and stretching out quietly, the streets seemed too fragmented for a town.

Maehŏn didn't have to drag his hiking cane far before he entered a pleasantly low inn. He ate breakfast on the veranda without even securing a room, smoked a cigarette, and then set off for the museum.

There was an elegant garden that would have been pleasant for a walk had it been just a little larger. The shards and stone burial figures were most attractive. Their impression was altogether unlike that of the pagoda in front of the station; here daily life seemed to radiate even from the porcelain, as if they were Yi dynasty pieces. Standing under a luxuriantly leafy quince tree, the stone lanterns didn't seem like remnants of a past age, and as for the well stones, carved with generous and sturdy lines unlike the tottering earthenware of the Silla period, well, even the dirt from wear glistened on them, as if that very morning red hands had washed rice and rinsed greens at their side.

Inside the exhibition rooms, the crowns were merely strangely interesting, while the bell of Pongdŏk Temple made the greatest impression on him. From a distance, it was majestic; up close, of unbelievably fine detail. In front of this bell, with its harmonious combination of majesty and detail, he felt the same awe that he had felt when reading that literary masterpiece *War and Peace*. And yet, if one were to pull back the pounder and strike the bell, he had the feeling that the resulting sound would be more sorrowful than majestic, more sad even than its own legend.

By the time he walked back out onto the street he felt thirsty and was searching for a shaved ice shop when an antiques shop caught his eye. Although not particularly fond of Silla earthenware, his love for old things could hardly allow him to pass by such a place. Piles of roof tiles and end tiles were spread out alongside earthenware, and photographs and picture postcards of the area in antique frames. There was not much of note amongst the tiles. Of the earthenware, several had simple but quite unusual incisions that were hard to find in Seoul. He began to pick some out as if by habit, even though he did not want to carry them around, but soon the shop grew stiflingly hot. He asked a boy wearing a *jitsumi* shirt, who had come to his side, for some water. The boy rushed inside. But it was a girl who returned in his place, carrying a bowl of water on a tray. Maehŏn was taken aback by her pretty features. Her eyes were clear and rather narrow and, together with her round chin, left a quiet and dignified impression.

"That water's nice and cool!"

"I drew it fresh from the well."

Upon hearing her dignified voice, he noticed her chest and height were not those of a child. Her simple dress, with its pattern of green leaves printed sparsely onto a white background, made her legs seem too long for her body. She was a young woman, whose arms and legs were a little sunburnt but otherwise perfectly formed and evoked a sense of the refined city in their movement. Maehŏn was pleased. Although she was probably young enough to be one of his daughter's friends, he realized that for city people a whiff of urbanity could produce the same pleasant sense of meeting someone from a shared hometown. She was probably a student at one of the technical schools who had returned home for the holidays, he thought.

He put down the now almost empty bowl of water and picked up the earthenware he had been fingering before; he blew the dust from the object, which was neither a kettle nor a jar.

"Don't you have something a little more unusual?"

"Unusual?"

"Something a little interesting . . ."

"Unusual and interesting . . . wouldn't it be better to choose something of which you'll never tire, even if it's ordinary?"

Maehŏn was at a loss for words, and looked again at the young woman's face. Her words were full of such fine pregnancy. An ordinariness that will not tire the affections no matter how long you gaze upon it; this could well describe her own face and its tranquil expression, which seemed to invite unlimited affection.

"What type of piece would that be? Please choose something for me."

Obliging, she hesitated over several pieces before picking out something that would be called a ritual vessel if it were a Yi dynasty piece, with a high base and a rather wide top in the shape of a lotus leaf.

"With some fruit on top that would make a fine still life!"

"It would be even more still left as it is."

Her words were simple but contained a certain depth. Maehŏn wondered whether all girls with parents who deal in antiques were this cultivated, and suddenly felt it would be a shame to pay right then. He wanted to talk with this cultivated girl some more. But there was nowhere to sit and it was unbearably muggy, and so he left after asking her to recommend an inn.

After lunch he set off to visit the astronomical observatory and the stone icehouse, before walking along the Half Moon Fortress walls, past Rooster Forest, and alongside the Mosquito River toward the Five Burial Mounds.

This took him quite some distance. Only after he had reached the Onyang road did he see a thick pine grove across the bridge, which looked like an ancient royal burial ground.

The narrow signposted road was dark, covered as it was by pine trees. After a steady walk, which left him dripping in sweat, the pines drew back on both sides, and a cozy opening appeared. What seemed more like longish grass mounds than earthen graves gently rose into the air, drawing lines that seemed to have been painted with a soft brush. There were five burial mounds in this one spot, starting with Pak Hyŏkkŏse, the founder of the Silla dynasty. The strange scene appeared more surreal the longer he looked. But as he drew nearer, a wall blocked his view, so high that he could not see over even when standing on tiptoe. He tried walking further along the wall. A gate was locked. He continued walking around the wall, barely able to glimpse the upper contours of the burial mounds. From each new angle the lines of different heights and widths produced a slightly different sense of rhythm and harmony. He had almost completed a full circle. The ground was slightly elevated at this point, making it the best place to stand on tiptoe. Maehŏn pressed down on his cane and stood as high on his toes as possible to try to see inside. But it wasn't very comfortable, and he could not stand like that for long. He took out his handkerchief and wiped the sweat from his face, when suddenly a voice resounded through the air, "Why don't you take a look from up here?"

Surprised, he turned and looked up toward the middle of a fairly tall pine tree. His hair stood on end.

"Come up here. You can get the best view from here."

For just a moment he was happy to recognize the voice. Then he wondered whether this was a hallucination occurring in an all-too-lonely place, and found himself unable to move. The young woman looking down, not from ground level but from the top of a tree the height of at least several men, was clearly the girl from the antiques shop, to whom he'd been strangely attracted from first sight.

"What are you doing here?"

"I always come here."

"How did you climb up so high?"

"Please come up here. I can move up to a higher branch."

She had left her blue parasol and white canvas shoes in a heap beneath the tree. Maehŏn walked up to them. He picked up her shoes and set them straight. There was a faint trace of sweat clearly visible on the insoles. Suppressing an eerie feeling that was rising ever more strongly in his heart, he hung the jacket he had been carrying on a low branch, took off his shoes, and slowly crawled up the tree as she directed. The girl moved up to a higher branch.

"You'll fall off! Just sit back down. . . . I'll be fine here."

"It's all right. Come up higher. You'll get a better view."

Finally, he reached the branch where she had been sitting before.

"Ah! From up here the balance of the mounds is more . . ."

"More what?. . . Try to describe it."

He could see that her feet were dangling so close they might step on his head.

"Describe it?"

"Isn't it quite nihilistic?"

"Nihilistic!"

The beauty of the five mounds struck its most effective pose when viewed from the middle branches of this pine tree that the girl had discovered. As he looks down, he is struck by a sense of quiet comfort. These graves seem too simple to be called royal burial mounds; they are mere mounds of earth. And their lines are too attractive to be called graves. They rise up and sink back down into the earth like rainbows, as if flowing through endless space. The sound of the cicadas only heightens the silence. He doesn't know whether he should cry or sigh as he gazes in silence; he can feel himself falling into a stupor. There could be no more appropriate adjective than nihilistic, just as the girl said.

"Are all the royal mounds here like this?"

"I've been to Kwaerŭng and the King Muyŏl mound, but they are nothing like this."

"So, you come here often?"

"Yes. This is my favorite place in Kyŏngju. I was here yesterday as well."

"Aren't you frightened on your own?"

"What kind of feeling could there be without fear?"

Despite his best efforts, he could not see her face. Whether it was maturity or overcultivation, there was something in her spirit that overwhelmed her body.

"Are you from Kyŏngju?"

"I've lived here just a few years."

"Ah, did you say you come from Seoul?"

When she did not answer, Maehŏn decided it would not do to probe more deeply and changed the subject. "But why is a young woman like you visiting old burial mounds so frequently to enjoy their nihilism?"

She did not answer this either.

"I'm sorry. I disturbed you while you were quietly resting here alone."

"I was reading a book."

"A book?"

"Yes."

Maehŏn lit a cigarette. Soon he heard the sound of pages turning above him. He felt it had been a good decision to come to Kyŏngju. The mysterious lines of those mounds brought a strange sense of repose.

The sun began to cast a shadow on the first mound. The cicadas' cries seemed to be growing longer.

By the time he had finished his third cigarette, the mounds had completely disappeared into shadow.

"Did you have a good rest?"

The girl broke the silence.

"Oh, a very good rest. If I hadn't met you here, I would have missed this sight."

"My legs are beginning to ache."

Maehŏn climbed down from the tree, only to be surprised by the book that the girl was carrying as she too descended. It was none other than his own collection of essays, which he had published the previous spring. Although pleased, he also felt uneasy. The book contained quite a few of his early impressionistic essays, which could only be sneered at by one sophisticated enough to talk about nihilism in this way.

"The stream over there is really clear."

"Is it all right if I walk with you?"

"Please do. There's probably no time for you to go to the Stone Abalone Pavilion now."

Carrying the book under her arm, she seemed even more urbane in the way she walked. With her short upper body and long legs, she would look good in Western clothes. After a while he dared a question,

"Is that book any good?"

"There are several good pieces in it."

"Have you read anything else by him?"

"I suppose he writes fiction as well? I hardly ever read fiction."

"Why not?"

"Well . . . I haven't read much fiction, but it's usually too didactic for me."

"And that book isn't?"

"Some of the essays are. But I feel I could grow quite close to this writer. There's something lonely about him."

"Don't you think he praises loneliness too much?"

"Have you read this book?"

She showed it to him. He did not reveal his identity, but just answered, "Yes."

"Sometimes when he tries so hard to praise loneliness, he ends up turning it into mere words, don't you think?"

He blushed. She continued, "I think that his sense of loneliness is more subtly revealed in the essays that aren't supposed to be about loneliness."

"You are quite sensitive! If the author knew he had a reader like you, he would be very happy."

"So, what do you do, sir?"

"Me?"

Suddenly they were struck by a dazzling sun. The pine grove had come to an end by the side of a river. As if forgetting their conversation, the girl set off running across the burning sand, without opening her parasol or looking back even once. Maehŏn hardly knew what to do and retreated into the shade of the pines. And then gradually, he began to wonder if this was really happening and could not believe his own eyes. The girl, who was certainly no child and who in sophistication seemed to have reached a higher level than most adults, stopped in front of a pool not far away and cast off her clothes quite unreservedly. For one moment her naked body stands tall on the glittering sand with the distant green mountains as a background; she must be a fairy that has jumped out from those mysterious curves of the Five Burial Mounds! Then, splash splash . . . and the water leaps up, glittering gold in the slanting sunlight. She sinks happily down. Finally her upper torso reappears, "Aren't you hot?"

She shouts out. This is clearly a human voice. Maehŏn recalled the saying that genius and foolishness coincide, but he could not look down upon this girl as foolish. By the time he had shuffled down to the next pool and back, having washed the sweat from his face, she was dressed and sauntering along barefoot, parasol in hand and softly singing some song.

Maehŏn tried not to interfere with her mood. He did not want to spoil her innocence; he would rather take inspiration from her completely natural behavior, which enabled her to be absolutely solitary whenever she wanted, even if someone were beside her. They each walked beneath the bridge on the main road as if alone.

"Oh, it's nice and cool under this bridge."

"Yes, it's quite refreshing!"

"It'll cool down on the main road in a while."

As she spoke, she sat down on the grass and dangled her feet in the water. Maehŏn sat down beside her in the same position. Bicycles, buses, and people were passing over the bridge.

"Excuse me, but what school did you attend?"

"Me?"

A rare smile came to her lips.

"It might seem like I'm boasting about my age, but I have a daughter in middle school. Please don't misunderstand my casual form of address."

"Oh, I don't worry about such things. You can even order me around if you like."

"It's embarrassing to have to say so, but actually I wrote that book. I wasn't trying to deceive you a while ago, it's just that I was embarrassed to admit it."

"Really? Are you Maehŏn?"

"That's my pen name."

"Well I never would have guessed!"

"Thank you for reading my work so carefully."

"If I'd known that, I would not have spoken so carelessly earlier."

"How were you careless? You were very honest."

"Well I never . . .!"

She did not seem to believe in chance. Her serene eyes drew into sharp focus. It was he who turned toward her first with a look of growing excitement.

"You are very different from how I had imagined."

"In what way?"

"Perhaps you shouldn't show yourself. You're no match for your essays."

"My essays . . ."

"You seem to be a very practical kind of person."

He laughed. "Practical . . . well, I make my living by writing. But my writing is also part of me, and so I'm happy that you like it."

Deep down he felt a little jealous of his own writing.

Something had happened recently. A photograph taken when he was a student in Tokyo had appeared on some book cover. At first, he did not recognize himself. Was I that young? Did I really seem that passionate to others? He recalled now how at first he'd been amazed, but then wanted to tear the photograph into pieces once he had taken a look at himself in the mirror.

The water flowed slowly and silently past the burial mounds and on downstream. Sand from the riverbed also floated down and rubbed at his feet. He felt sad. In his face he could see that a romantic spirit one hundred times more lively than that in his writing had been stolen by the years, and those years could never be retraced but only flowed ever onward like this water.

"I dropped out of Doshisha University."

"Why? You were in the English Department?"

"Yes. My mother passed away, and I wanted to be in Kyŏngju more than Kyoto."

"When was that?"

"The second anniversary just passed this spring."

"And is your father at the shop?"

"He's at Panyawŏl. We have an orchard, and it's coming into maturity this year. So I'm taking care of the shop."

"By running around like this?"

"One of my young relatives works there. When she died, my mother requested that I should be allowed to do whatever I like. I received the most precious inheritance in the world, you see. But my mother always understood me from when I was a very small child."

"You lost a most wonderful mother."

"I try not to feel too alone. When you think about it, is there anyone who isn't alone?"

"Excuse me, but what's your name?"

"You see!"

"What?"

"That's the practical side of your nature . . . you say 'excuse me' a lot, and you introduce yourself by name. I'm right, aren't I?"

Maehŏn felt a little uneasy. But as that uneasiness lifted he could feel his own long-lost innocence reviving throughout his body.

The girl swiveled around, pulling her feet out of the water. Maehŏn was instantly attracted to those ten wriggling toes trying to shake the water off onto the green grass. Even though everything about this young girl's appearance seemed younger than her spirit, these toes looked younger still. He burnt with the simple desire to touch them, as he would pinch a baby's cheeks. He quickly took hold of her two feet. In an instant, one hand had taken out his handkerchief. He dried between each of her toes, before placing each foot back into its shoe, from which he'd shaken the sand, and fastening it close. Later, he was surprised at how naturally his hands had acted. She too acted as if it were nothing.

When they climbed back up onto the main road, Maehŏn lit a cigarette, and the girl walked along, humming a simple tune that children sing. They each walked along with their own thoughts, as if they were each alone again.

"Sir, would you like to go to Pulguk Temple tomorrow?"

"Will you show me around?"

"If you will agree to go in this heat."

"Then, let's go!"

They separated in front of his inn after discussing what train to take the next day.

It was late in the evening by the time he had taken a bath and eaten dinner, and he felt tired enough to lie down. But when he did so, he could not fall asleep.

Somehow it seemed as if the girl would visit him after dinner. The sound of mosquitoes nearby and frogs croaking in the distance made the silence of the night seem more intense; there were no people around. He thought the girl might be waiting for him to take a walk to the shop. Even so he could not bring himself to sit up, despite smoking almost a whole pack of Haet'ae cigarettes. He hadn't felt anything when he was moving around, but once he'd laid down it was hard to raise himself again. At times like these when he was at home, his wife would ask, "Why are you getting lazier and lazier?" But for several years now he had been quietly realizing that this was not laziness.

"Everything comes down to youth!"

Maehŏn rested his two parched hands on his stomach and tried to submit peacefully to the shapeless force that was pressing down on his joints more with each passing year.

The following day, the girl was already there waiting in time for the first train. The same dress, the same white shoes without socks, the same parasol. As soon as Maehŏn saw her, he ran toward her. He was really pleased to see her. He felt fresh, as if the morning was returning to his life as well. *Youth! Youth is a virtue all of its own!* They were only traveling one stop, but Maehŏn bought second-class tickets. This was more for the feeling of the purchase than for the journey itself.

The second-class car of the local morning train was empty. The girl chose a window seat. Maehŏn didn't have the courage to sit knee to knee with her in such an empty car and chose a seat facing her.

"That's Anapchi Pond."

"That's another royal burial mound."

Maehŏn was more captivated by her lips and teeth, which glistened like autumn fruit as if she had eaten an oily breakfast, and by her bangs, which blew gently up and down as if alive. But the carriage did not only head into the sun and breeze. It also turned corners, throwing her face into shadow. That face had been lit up and plunged into darkness three or four times by the time they arrived at Pulguk Temple.

The narrow hired bus was packed to bursting with people. In such cramped conditions the girl needed more room than Maehŏn.

"I'm all right, really. Please make yourself more comfortable, sir."

He cringed each time the bus jumped on the journey up the ten-ri hill, as if he were riding a horse.

"What do you think? Isn't it better than in the photographs?"

They had only taken a few steps since getting off the bus before they stopped. The scene was ripe with a bucolic lyricism that made it seem unlike a temple. It was as if dancers might appear at any moment and glide down the floating stone staircases, known as the Green Cloud Bridge and White Cloud Bridge.

"When I come here, my favorite thing is to walk up and down those staircases! I wonder what Silla women wore on their feet?"

Maehŏn followed the girl up the White Cloud Bridge, and then the Green Cloud Bridge, before walking through the Sunset Gate. The graceful altar of the Hall of Great Virtue was in the characteristic Silla style, made of stone and about the height of a man; to the east was the Jeweled Pagoda and to the west the Shakamuni Pagoda. Above and beyond the pagoda's religious significance, Maehŏn thought that it must be the greatest work of art upon which a person could ever gaze. Its harmonious combination of space and solidity could hardly be matched in its natural majesty by any Greek statue.

"You see all these cornerstones left here and there? Apparently there used to be more than two thousand buildings inside this temple!"

"They must have stood side by side, row upon row."

"Everything went up in flames at once, it must have been a blazing sea of fire, mustn't it? Just imagine, only these two pagodas survived that sea of fire. How heroic, how tragic!"

With these words, the pagodas looked even more majestic. The gentle curves of the Jeweled Pagoda attained the pinnacle of feminine beauty—they seemed to have been melted into shape rather than chiseled from stone—whereas the Shakamuni Pagoda was simple apart from its elaborately woven hair, and left a powerful impression as if one hundred Deva kings had been gathered together in it. It was the apex of masculine beauty and formed a perfect contrast with the Jeweled Pagoda.

Maehŏn and the girl sat side by side all morning on the Pavilion of Floating Shadows watching the clouds pass over the pagodas, as leisurely as if they were clouds themselves.

They ate lunch at the hotel. Cool-looking easy chairs were placed in groups in the hallway, as if it were an observation deck. The girl led Maehŏn toward the chairs with the best view over the Pond of Shadows. They leant far back, he holding a cigarette, and she a fan on which were printed the symbols of yin and yang, and they gazed into the distance. It must have been some tens of ri through the hazy air to where the dark green mountaintops formed a circle, layer upon layer, and at their feet lay a valley that glittered like a mirror.

"So that's the Pond of Shadows!"

"Yes. Where Asanyŏ drowned herself . . . I love to sit here and look down upon it!"

The scene evoked the same kind of eternal nihilism as the Five Burial Mounds. On closer inspection there were small hills, woods, twisting roads, winding streams, small villages in the folds of each mountain, rice paddies, and dry fields, and above them all floated the clouds, which cast shadows on the villages and the streams . . . but at a casual glance there was merely the green earth and the misty air, and nothing else.

Maehŏn threw his cigarette to one side and yawned slowly. Soon they were both fast asleep.

Maehŏn was the first to wake from the heat of the sun on his legs. His entire body was damp with sweat. Drops of perspiration had formed on the girl's forehead. He took his handkerchief and tried to lightly dab her face as carefully as possible. She gently snored away, unaware. With each breath her rounded breasts rose and fell. He took her fan and quietly waved some air onto her, all the while trying to match his breath with hers.

He was surprised at how much more quickly she drew breath. For every five of his breaths, she took six. He was struck by the loneliness felt upon losing a travel companion, and once more wiped the perspiration rising on her forehead. The sun was now encroaching upon more of her face. Her lips moved, she swallowed and then opened her eyes.

"Oh, I slept so soundly, not even a dream!"

"That's good."

"I wonder if that's how death is."

"I wonder!"

The two of them walked back down to the stream and refreshed themselves with water. The sun was turning red and beginning to set on the mountaintops. The girl bought a fan with a photograph of Pulguk Temple on it from a shop in front of the hotel. And then she bought a ticket to go back on the evening train.

"You don't want to go to the Stone Grotto?"

"I'd better take the evening train home."

He did not ask any further. There was more than an hour left before the train would leave. They walked up White Cloud Bridge and Green Cloud Bridge again, and further up the hill behind the temple, passing behind the Jeweled Pagoda. The seasonal rains had left holes in the grassy path in places, but otherwise it was a pleasant walk up through a pine grove. When they reached the top, clouds had cloaked the sun and burned the color of a red rose. They sat on the grass, facing the evening sun. With each moment, the Pond of Shadows was tinged with a deeper shade of red. A fortuitous air seemed to wind around the mountaintops, and from somewhere a gentle breeze blew in. The girl opened her fan. The evening sun cast a bewitching dye over both the fan and her face.

"Sir?"

"Yes?"

"Would you please write something on this?"

He gently took her fan. He took out his fountain pen and gazed at the evening sun, deep in thought for a while. Then he wrote a verse by the ancient poet Li Yishan:

夕陽無限好
只是近黃昏

It was a lament that the evening sun is beautiful beyond limit, but dusk comes all too soon. He had thought of this verse as he felt the sun set on his own life. This brilliant girl took the fan and quietly drew it toward her eyes, which she then closed.

"I will write to you."

The sunset did not last much longer. Although they stood up quickly, it was already dusk as they walked back down the path. Maehŏn accompanied her to the station and sent his precious companion away in the dark on the evening train.

He stayed at Pulguk Temple for four days. But he never went up to the Stone Grotto. Each day he sat in the hotel hallway, looked out over the Pond of Shadows and wearily faced the evening sun.

A few days after he returned home, a letter arrived from the girl. Autumn in Kyŏngju is beautiful, she wrote, and particularly the Five Royal Burial Mounds and the view of the Pond of Shadows from the hotel at Pulguk Temple. If he were to visit in the autumn, she would accompany him to Pulguk Temple and stay there a few days. Her name was signed at the bottom, T'aok, Jewel on a Cliff.

"T'aok!"

He replied immediately. He wrote that he had vowed upon his return to make another trip in the autumn and that in the end he had decided to save the Stone Grotto until T'aok could accompany him. Together with the letter, he sent a limited edition copy of his collection of essays.

Another letter arrived from T'aok. She thanked him for the book and for saving the Stone Grotto, and added that she was eagerly awaiting his autumn trip to Kyŏngju.

Autumn came. In truth, it came all too soon for Maehŏn. And while he hesitated, it seemed to go far too quickly as well. Yet it was not any particular work schedule that restricted his movements. He had no choice but to send a letter postponing the trip until the following autumn along with the lament, "Living a simple life is also a kind of blessing, but I don't seem to have been allowed that."

Sometimes he missed T'aok. Not Kyŏngju, but T'aok. Then he would wonder why he was waiting for autumn.

Several times he left his house in the morning after saying, "It looks as if I have to go down to the countryside today." But once he had left and thought some more, he would feel embarrassed that he was going just to meet T'aok.

Am I in love with T'aok?

He would shuffle back to his house, teasing himself that by now he was probably taking four breaths for every six of hers. He would sit for a long time and stare at the Silla earthenware on the table, the one about which she had said, "It would be even more still left as is."

And yet, for old and young alike a life crisis seems to hit the most often in spring. Unable to quietly endure, he finally went down to Kyŏngju before the azaleas had dropped their blossoms. T'aok was pleased to see him. But from the moment he saw her again, he did not know how to control the instant change in his heart, was this wonder or disillusionment? She seemed completely different. The T'aok in Kyŏngju was someone he could have waited until autumn to meet. It was as if the one who had twisted him up inside more with each passing day had been a temptress he himself had produced, whereas when he stood in front of the real T'aok, all his depraved thoughts disappeared in an instant.

"You seem to be quite the romantic, sir!"

She said this, quite politely and with an expression as serene as still water. His own faltering stability was washed clean by that calm water. As if waking from a nightmare, he told himself, "It's really better this way."

They went first to the Five Burial Mounds. She climbed up the pine tree, and he followed her. The nihilistic atmosphere of the mounds was no different in spring from summer.

That same day they went to Pulguk Temple. The long staircases of the Green Cloud Bridge and the White Cloud Bridge possessed the same lyricism, as if a dancing girl would appear and slide down them. The pine leaves were a fresher green, but the Jeweled Pagoda and Shakamuni Pagoda struck the same pose in exactly the same color.

Oh, you two sphinxes! Will you stand there forever?

He grew a little melancholy.

By the time they reached the hotel, the Pond of Shadows was already buried in the thick dusk. They ate dinner by lamplight, retelling old legends and talking about literature and art, about the rise and fall of nations, and sometimes stopping to listen to the deepening night and wonder where in the world that same moon must be shining dimly. In the end it was Maehŏn who struggled to stay awake and ended up snoring.

On the following day they went up to the Stone Grotto. The grotto was a purely man-made temple, which did not seem to converse with nature. It was art at its ecstatic height. As T'aok said, they could only wonder at being able to feel the beauty of muscles and silks rendered in stone. She said she wanted to tear the baby finger from the right hand, where it lay in the Buddha's lap, and take it home. At first, Maehŏn thought it would suffice to merely look at the grotto and understand the concept. But the weight of such vital beauty confused him unbearably. He began to examine the grotto from the point of view of its structure. Soon he was exhausted.

He went outside for a rest, and then began to examine the Buddha statues. It seemed merely frivolous to praise the statue of the Buddha at the front. As he looked at the eleven-faced bodhisattva that stood behind the Buddha, he realized that without a grasp of religion or philosophy it would be impossible to make manifest such sublime beauty, which exceeded that of any beautiful woman. He called to T'aok. They stood side by side before the bodhisattva. He stroked the bodhisattva's plump hand, and then with the same fingers stroked T'aok's equally plump hand. When he encountered his own depraved desire in that instant, still tenacious at the age of nearly fifty, when one is supposed to understand heaven's meaning, T'aok, whom he had forgotten momentarily, had become his own sublime, eternal woman.

"T'aok!"

The cave was filled with solemn silence.

They spent four days together at Pulguk Temple.

For those four days, he thought of T'aok as a piece of Yi dynasty white porcelain. Ostentatious pots fight for a spot, are jealous of their master's eye, and grow more rowdy and tiresome the longer they are around, but Yi dynasty white porcelain are completely different. Unnoticeable at busy times, they are waiting to one side when it grows quiet. They are vessels from eternity that provide quiet comfort and refreshment and never exhaust.

When he returned to Seoul, Maehŏn sent T'aok an Yi dynasty white porcelain brush rack, which he had stood on his stationery chest and treasured night and day. Autumn came for real, followed by spring and another autumn; all that while he continued his innocent correspondence with T'aok.

Maehŏn agreed with a certain publisher to put out a volume of his writing. It was supposed to appear before the end of autumn, but by early winter he still had not handed over the manuscript. After one month crouched in front of his desk, not only did his sides and shoulders ache, but he began to feel dizzy for the first time. When he had to heat his room as the days grew colder, his dry skin began to contract, and even his heart seemed to be fighting a losing battle. He was not going to be able to finish the manuscript at home, and so he removed himself to the hot springs at Haeŭndae.

It was not far from Kyŏngju, and he contacted T'aok upon his arrival. He asked her not to visit until he was done with the manuscript, but she appeared suddenly without waiting to be asked.

She was in full bloom. She wore a light-green patterned *chŏgori* jacket, and her face looked like a lotus bloom rising out of a lotus pond. While Maehŏn was aging, youth seemed to have reached its peak in T'aok. It was only to be expected. In conversation she spoke more plainly than in her letters, but Maehŏn inhaled deeply on the warmth emitted by her blossoming youth.

"Were you always this pretty T'aok?"

"Whatever did you used to think of me!"

"I've grown old, haven't I?"

"Isn't age in the mind?"

"I wonder."

When T'aok returned from the public bath, she quietly took away his pen, the steam still rising from her hand. Maehŏn closed his dizzy eyes for a while before he was able to get up and walk down to the beach with her.

There was a cold wind blowing by the water. Waves were rolling in too. Maehŏn pulled up his coat collar and huddled down into his jacket, while T'aok ran ahead of him, wearing nothing more than a loosely tied men's *chŏgori* jacket.

"Come on."

He had been to this beach several times, but this was the first time he tried running along it.

"Sir?"

"Mm?"

She was staring out at the water.

"Sir?"

"What?"

"Do you like the sound of the waves?"

"Of course!"

"Doesn't it remind you of Tagore's meditation upon hearing waves?"

"I'm a bit too cold to remember Tagore at the moment."

"If we were to travel around all the coasts in the world, I wonder how much the sound of the waves, and the weather too, would change according to the shape of the coast, the sand, or even whether the water is clean or murky. Where would the waves sound the best?"

"That's quite some meditation!"

"The sound of the waves never stops!"

"Aren't your legs cold?"

At the sight of her long, slender legs wearing tight, thin silk socks beneath a black serge skirt, which was flapping in the wind, Maehŏn felt himself newly aware of her sensuality.

It happened that evening. Once a shivering Maehŏn had returned from the beach and drank three or four cups of rice wine at the warm dining table, his whole body was overcome with drowsiness. Sitting back from the table, he had barely exchanged a few words with T'aok before he suddenly dozed off. When he opened his eyes again in surprise, he had no idea how long or short a time had passed, but saw T'aok staring at the ceiling forlornly. He was embarrassed and rolled his eyes vigorously as if nothing had happened, but deep down he felt really sad. A sharp loneliness pierced his parched breast, almost as if he were jealous that her spirit had been conversing with someone else while he had been asleep.

"I fell asleep, didn't I?"

"You've been working too hard for a while now. You mustn't overdo it."

"I was hardly overdoing it . . . so I heard that some Koryŏ porcelain has turned up near Kyŏngju?"

"Did they say Kyŏngju? It was at Kimhae. It looks like the stuff made at Mt. Kyeryong, but every now and then something turns up that is much simpler."

"Similar to the stuff at Muan . . . now that . . ."

Again he nodded off.

"Sir?"

". . ."

"Sir?"

"Now that . . . that isn't Koryŏ . . ."

"Why don't you go to bed early?"

She opened the sliding door and went into the next room. Maehŏn dozed, still sat in his chair. When he woke up some time later, the alcohol had worn off and he felt quite cold. He went to the baths. By the time he had warmed up his body for an hour or so, he felt so refreshed it seemed a shame to go to sleep. Recent experience suggested that if he had slept for a short while early in the evening, he would not be able sleep even if he went to bed. He lit a cigarette and picked up his pen.

But time never passes as quickly as when holding a pen. Sometime later, when his body had cooled down so much that his hands felt chilled, the sliding door quietly opened. T'aok appeared, stroking her disheveled hair with one hand and clutching her sleeping gown with the other.

"Do you know what time it is?"

Only then did he look at his watch. It was almost two o'clock.

"Didn't I say that you shouldn't overdo it?"

He put down his pen and stood up, stretching. T'aok's sleepy face was the pearly red color of a peach flower, all the way down to her softly rounded chin.

"You should go to sleep."

"I will."

She went back to her room and returned holding her pillow. Then she switched it with Maehŏn's pillow.

"Please sleep in my room."

"Why?"

"Don't worry about that."

"Why?"

"Please don't worry."

And she laid down in Maehŏn's bed.

He did not ask again. Secretly kissing the kind heart that had offered him her warm bed, he softly buried himself in that heat from her body, which was even more fragrant than the spring waters themselves.

He had no idea how long he had slept, but it was the first time that he had woken late since coming to Haeŭndae. When he opened his eyes, the sunlight was glaring through the gaps in the ceiling. He felt around the bed for his watch and fumbled instead upon a piece of paper. It was T'aok's handwriting.

> Sir, I have to go. Recently I got engaged. I wanted to tell you this last night as we talked, but there was no opportunity. He is arriving on the morning boat from Tokyo today. I want to meet him in Pusan, and so I have to leave before you wake up. You'll forgive me, won't you? I hope you will not work hard but have a good rest and return to Seoul with a wonderful, completed manuscript. Sir, you'll wish us well for the future, won't you?

He stood up abruptly. The letter was not the only thing by his bed. She had cleaned his ashtray and placed it on his desk beside his cigarettes and matches before leaving.

He closed his eyes and sat with his head in his hands for a while, and then read her letter again. He pulled the sliding doors open. The room was empty. A cold air wafted out. He picked up his cigarettes. He only managed to get up when he had smoked all the remaining cigarettes, more than half a pack.

"She's gone!"

He could not settle the whole day. He tried drinking. He kept on smoking. In the evening he went down to the beach, even though the wind was even colder than the day before.

The waves sounded the same as the previous night. It was just as she had said, it seemed as if their sound would last forever.

The evening sun over the ocean was beautiful. But it changed with every instant. Dusk was falling far too quickly.

—*On the Twenty-seventh Day of the First Month of*
the Year of the Water Horse

First published in 1942. Translated from Yi T'aejun,
Toldari (Pangmun sŏgwan, 1943)

UNCONDITIONED

At first I used to go along for the joy of catching fish, then gradually fishing itself became the attraction, but it seems to me that fishing begins long before taking up a spot by the water. Whether it's time spent mending a broken line or tidying up a net or basket beneath a lamp in the evening in order to set off at daybreak on the following morning, lying beside fellow fishers and entertaining each other with past tales of broken lines, or even writing this story now—all of these too are a kind of fishing.

I have tried fishing on a boat, once at Songjŏn and once at Inch'ŏn. To speak of ocean fishing on that basis alone is not terribly reasonable, but it did seem to be the case that fishing at sea is a little too tumultuous and close to labor; in fact, it might well exert an occupational effect on days when the catch is higher than average.

For its purity, serenity, and lack of burden, there's no doubt that freshwater fishing is the best.

The first time that I tried freshwater fishing in Seoul was at the Chungnang Stream outside of Tongdaemun. Here the water runs off the paddy fields and apparently meets the sewerage water coming from the direction of Hoegiri with the result that the smell is quite fetid. The most commonly caught fish were catfish, and all kinds of people were up to all kinds of things, from scoop-netting to fishing with multiple hooks on a line, and even bathing.

Next I tried the reservoir at Sorae. You have to take the Kyŏngin line to Sosa, where you can transfer to Taeyari if there happens to be a bus waiting, if not, then you have to walk a long ten-ri road. There are many shallow fields of wild rice, and you have to sit on mounds of stones in places where the water is deep, so the ground isn't great, and people get too hot. But occasionally you can catch a carp the size of your fist, and so on public holidays up to thirty or forty people gather there.

I learned much later that there are three or four good ponds in the village of Sut'aek, which is over the Manguri Hill, not so far from Seoul. The water is deep enough to earn one of those usual legends of a serpent emerging to swallow a calf, and indeed, the water did reach halfway up my two-and-a-half-k'an fishing line.

If a good place to sit is at least as important as the fish, there's a wonderful wide-open view of the distant mountains from some well-chosen spots here, in addition to clear water. Occasionally, a carp would appear that was even larger than those at Sorae, and it was not uncommon for a really large fish to break the line, or even swim off dragging a fishing rod in its wake while someone looked the other way. The sight of silver scales leaping out of the water and snowy white herons dozing at leisure made for a perfect waterside scene.

And yet, so very many people began to gather at these ponds. It became a race from the moment of stepping off the bus. It's not so much greed as human nature to want to sit where the most fish bite, but no one looks good when old people run a distance that takes even a young person fifteen minutes, or they start off running but then fall by the wayside, or even push aside other old people who can't run any more, just so that they can run on ahead along the narrow bank between the paddy fields.

"Are they taking the bait?"

There's little sign of the cultivated habit of passing by others quietly. Neither is anyone particularly honest with their answers when in fact many fish are biting. If the float doesn't move for a mere hour, then already sighs are heard. After two hours, people move to another spot. That's when they start to curse already. If the dragon king were to show up at their side, he would surely clobber them. Nothing is spared as they sprinkle sesame dregs and paste as bait, as if to attract all the fish in the pond to their line. When those sitting nearby can't stand it any more, a competition to throw the most bait arises. And so the fish fill up their stomachs without any need to fight each other for a hook. But what I hate the most of all are those who get excited about big fish. They go around noisily splashing the water with these things called *nange*, from which lead weights the size of walnuts hang down, as if to chase everyone else away. People seem to bring with them all the shamelessness, obstinacy, and envy that are rife in town.

Is there nowhere I can escape these people, even if it's further away?

Finally, I thought of a place that I had forgotten for some decades, and a faint memory gradually began to grow more distinct. This was a mountain village in the region of Tongju in Kangwŏn Province, where the hamlet went by the name of Dragon Pond because there was so much water, even though it was in the mountains. I had often gone there as a child to visit my mother's family.

My mother's father loved to fish. He made his own fishing rod and used handmade fishing line. This was different from the fishing gear we buy today. Because bamboo was hard to come across in that village, he had someone traveling to Seoul buy him a bamboo stalk and a piece of split bamboo of similar length; the two pieces were longer than an arm-span and about twice the diameter of a pipe stem, so that when cut, the ends were as thick as the cap for a letter-writing brush. He used fire to straighten out the stem and bore holes into the joints, just as when making a pipe stem. He shaved and engraved some cow horn, which he mounted as a handle, and then he wound silk thread around the end and sealed it with beeswax to be sure that it would not come undone. From the split bamboo he fashioned a rod to insert in the stem. To begin with, he straightened out any crooked parts and then tidied the split bamboo, using first a knife and then a fragment of porcelain. He would oil the bamboo to avoid any cracking or taking in of water, before finally attaching a stone to the end and leaving it to hang for several months. This rod could be inserted all the way into the stem upside down, or attached the right way up it would stretch out like a pheasant plume on a flagpole with no sag in the center at all. I remember holding my grandfather's rod several times as a child, and it was nowhere near as heavy as those fishing rods we buy today. For the fishing line, three rolls of silk were dyed using oak before being wound around a piece of slate, oiled, and then boiled in a rice pot. It was no small amount of work. One of the farmhands' children would be made to bend the hook, and the barb would be large enough that a fish could not easily escape; the snell was braided from white horsehair, which would be transparent once in the water and not catch the fish's eye. For the rainy season my grandfather wove a fishing basket by hand using broom cypress, and I remember that there were several lines of small letters engraved on its base—something in classical Chinese, although I'm not sure what.

This grandfather would only fish sitting down, in the style that we call "sinking." I accompanied him several times to a place called the Calf's Dying Spot. Here the slightly cloudy water of the brook flowing down past the village met with the cold, clear waters of the Hannae Stream, which came down from a valley deep on Kŭmhak Mountain, forming several ponds along the way with names like Seven Pine Pavilion and Gentleman's Pond. Even during a drought the waterbed could not be seen beneath the rock cliff. Both cloudy and freshwater fish would gather at Calf's Dying Spot, whose name derived from a tale that a serpent had once emerged and swallowed a calf here. Among the fish were bright-yellow carp, the so-called sorceress carp with its brilliant rainbow colors, the long-nosed barbel with sapphire-like scales, and even the strong-boned black perch, king of freshwater fish. If it was raining or the water was muddy following rainfall, we could catch carp, barbels, and catfish with worms as bait, but once the water cleared up we took mineral bait and fished in the rapids for long-nosed barbels and perch. The surrounding silence seemed infinite, with no sound apart from the crying of the cicadas and water rushing in the rapids below. If I appeared to be growing bored, my grandfather would leave his line in the water and take me to the hut in his melon field. There we picked white melons in the dirt, covered in morning dew. White and round with green lines in every groove, you could tell they were ripe if they were reddish when you removed the stem. Their fragrance and sweet flavor is reminiscent of the more recent "melons," but their soft, delicious taste is incomparable.

Yet, I used to prefer to trail after my uncles rather than my grandfather. My uncles found sinking boring and would take nets to places like Gentleman's Pond or, if they fished, they preferred to play in the rapids. The rods were lighter than those used for sinking, and the hooks were small too, just enough to fit one fly. For a float we would choose the inner part of some kind of wood, which was much thinner than a kaoliang stalk. We would walk into the rapids and let the fishing hook flow with the stream. The fish in the rapids are quite nimble, and the float plays along like one of the fish to attract no suspicion. Because the water flows downstream and the fish must be dragged back up against the flow of the water, the pressure exerted on the rod is at least twice that in other types of fishing. After the rainy season, sometimes a luxurious *mumang* carp might emerge from the water. A little like a sweetfish, this one has a black back, while its body is green with splashes of red. There's even a trace of yellow on its stomach, making this the most pleasant fish to be found in the rapids. During a drought, it's more likely the plain and oily *kalberi* and *nalberi* that will bite. On the less than five-ri stretch down from Gentleman's Pond to the True Pond, it's not uncommon to fill two nets. Anything big enough to bite is at least the size of a span of the hand, and the bigger fish are sometimes almost as large as one foot.

When we went up to Gentleman's Pond, we didn't take the basket made from broom cypress. Instead we took the woven baskets that were used for gathering corn or cucumbers. We would spread our baskets all around a large rock before grinding a stone noisily on the top of the rock, then different kinds of perches and nalberi a foot long would rush out and into our baskets. At Gentleman's Pond the water was clear and the riverbank tidy, so many people came there to fish. A long time ago, a gentleman was sitting on a rock here reading when the wind blew his book away and he fell into the water and drowned trying to retrieve it, hence the name Gentleman's Pond. The place was also famous for goblins, and we children were too scared to go there alone, even in the daytime. And yet, it didn't seem at all dark. The rock cliff had nut pines along its ridge and, with the green dragon to the left and white tiger to the right, it always received the warm southerly rays, and there were endless pebbles and water, which didn't start to flow away no matter how you swam about in it. Beautiful, smiling wild lilies were spread across the cliff, and Kŭmhak Mountain, its head in the clouds, always looked like a hermit dozing during meditation. Whenever I think of Dragon Pond I find myself yearning for Gentleman's Pond.

After we moved to Seoul I saw less and less of my mother's family, as I was busy moving around within the city—first because of my studies and then later because of work—and then a few years later, my grandfather passed onto the jeweled pavilion while I was in Edo, and my uncles scattered, leaving behind the Dragon Pond their family had lived next to for generations to head for Manchuria and other places in the northern territories, and so my connection to that place grew gradually more faint.

And yet, as I began to visit the water once more to fish, the first place to come to mind while I sat by the waterside was that Dragon Pond. I took pleasure in it all by myself, almost as a kind of legend because the road was so remote and no one was likely to recognize me even if I were to go there. Whenever I visited various fishing sites and found the mass of people dizzying, or when a pleasurable excursion ended sometimes even in curses, the urge arose to lower my fishing rod just one more time in Gentleman's Pond or that Calf's Dying Spot, where the only sound to be heard was from the cicadas, and the wild lilies smiled, and that desire grew ever more urgent until finally last summer I made a resolution, prepared my traveling clothes several days in advance, and chose a day with a cool breeze to set off on a dawn train to visit Dragon Pond, my heart aflutter, as if I was on the way to visit a loved one.

Ah! Perhaps it was because two or more of those decades had passed during which the mountains and rivers are said to change, but does that mean we can't even trust the mountains and rivers over time? A young girl was rinsing her rags beneath the "big stone bridge" in the middle of the village, but there was no more than a small gully, a muddy puddle, no longer a stream! In the past even in winter you could strike the ice with a rice-cake mallet and a carp the size of your hand would be floating underneath, just like that. I asked why the water in the brook had decreased so much, but this turned out to be futile, because the little girl washing her rags had never seen the brook as it used to be. It was the height of the farming season, and the village was quiet, completely deserted. Even if I were to meet somebody, we wouldn't recognize each other, and so I simply gazed in the direction of the upper village, where my mother's family used to live, before heading toward the Calf's Dying Spot with a plan to do some fishing first of all.

I walked as far as should have been necessary. But when I reached the point where the Calf's Dying Spot should have been, I was still completely lost and hesitated a while. The whole area seemed to have been filled in and the mountain razed, to be replaced by a red muddy track going up the slope. I asked a farmer doing some weeding, and he said that I was in the right place. The pond where the calf had supposedly died had disappeared some time ago now, and a track had been created in its stead to take trucks in and out of a mining operation, which had started up in the valley on the other side of the hill. I looked more closely to see just a trickle of water flowing down a narrow gully. I turned back to the farmer and asked some more: the source of water for the brook out front had been taken away by the Irrigation Association's reservoir, and the water trickling down here came from paddy fields and the like; even the Hannae Stream, which had once flowed through Gentleman's Pond, had run dry, having been turned into catchment for the townspeople's drinking-water supply. When I asked whether the water in Gentleman's Pond had dried up too, he replied, "Water? It's just a dry riverbed." All had come to nothing. Since I had come this far, I sweated my way up to Gentleman's Pond in the hope of retracing old memories, but the nut pine wood on the ridge had been cut down to skeletal form, leaving the ridge white and covered in gourd-bowl-shaped graves; it looked like a public burial ground. Have that many people from here died since then? There should be water, but there was none. Only when I went closer could I hear a water-like sound. It seemed rather strange though, because it seemed to stop and start rather than flow continuously. It turned out to be the sound of someone else walking on the gravel. I looked up to see an old lady as white as a ghost, rising up from beneath the rock cliff at Gentleman's Pond. A shiver went down my spine, and I stood still.

What could it be? She climbed falteringly up to the gravel patch, where she bent right over. She was picking up pebbles and collecting them in her skirt. After gathering pebbles for a while, she straightened her back, turned around, and walked back down to the foot of the rock cliff with faltering steps. Although I couldn't see any water, I could hear it. The sound I'd heard earlier was that of pebbles being poured into water. The old lady's head, with hair sticking up like green onion roots, rose up the bank again. She climbed up to the gravel with the same faltering steps, placed pebbles into her skirt, and then went back down again. I was at a loss as to what was going on. There were several different legends about goblins at Gentleman's Pond, but this was daytime and a clear day at that; it was beyond common sense to think that I was seeing a goblin. Yet if she were human, then not only did a white-haired old lady seem out of place here, but her actions—picking up stones in order to fill in the water—were beyond my comprehension. I looked around and saw people scattered around the mountain fields weeding. I summoned my courage and made sure to step noisily on the gravel while I walked toward the old lady, who was climbing back up from the foot of the rock cliff, having made yet another splash in the water.

"Hello?"

The old lady looked straight ahead with tired, murky eyes, gasping.

"Why are you putting stones in the water?"

No answer. She bent over to pick up more stones and went back down to the water. When she came back up, I asked again, louder this time.

"Are you trying to fill in all of the water?"

Only then did the old lady nod.

"Why?"

She was silent once more but continued her work.

This place had once been a deep and wide pond, second only to the Calf's Dying Spot, but with the gravel leveled, the flow of water had been completely cut off. This strange old lady was diligently trying to fill in the few yards of water remaining beneath the rock cliff.

Only Kŭmhak Mountain remained unchanged from of old. White clouds clustered around its peak while it dozed peacefully. I managed to find a few wild lilies blooming bright red on the rock cliff. Thinking of Mencius's words, that to climb a tree to look for fish could cause no harm, I put down my fishing gear and sat for a while in the sweltering sun until there was nothing left to do but return to the village. The old lady was still carrying her stones to the water with true devotion and took no break despite being drenched in sweat.

I did manage to find a hut in a melon field. Recently it's impossible to find anything other than the yellow Kinmaka melons. The white, persimmon-red, and black melons of old seem to have become extinct. Perhaps they didn't suit the age of enlightenment either, because they did not bear fruit as prolifically as the Kinmaka, and now they're hard to find.

So even melons can become classics! I ate a Kinmaka that was just a little more fresh than those I buy in the street of Chongno while the owner of the melon field hut solved the riddle of the white-haired old lady at Gentleman's Pond for me.

She was neither a goblin nor a senile old woman, but simply a tragic mother. Her youngest son had become depressed about his handicapped body and drowned himself at Gentleman's Pond. She had a water exorcism performed to try at least to recover his spirit, yet what had emerged most unexpectedly was not the spirit of her son but that of a slave girl from the inner village, who had drowned herself some decades earlier. Because people say that spirits only emerge from the water if someone else goes in to take their place, her son's spirit could not be retrieved without another drowning, no matter how many exorcisms were performed. While alive her son had hovered in corners because of his handicap, and now in death she was unable to guide her son's spirit out of these dark waters at the bottom of an isolated cliff and pray for him to enter the eternal heaven; unable to bear this thought, she had thrown herself into the water several times only to be repeatedly rescued by her eldest son, thus failing to become the water spirit who might take the younger son's place. When the waters had finally begun to dry up at Gentleman's Pond, and only more pebbles were washed down with each rainy season, she had thought heaven was not ignoring her after all, and everyday she would come out to work on filling up the little water that remained. What an unbelievable, yet all so sincere, human story!

I climbed up to the upper village to take a look at my mother's family home. A middle-aged woman carried a small child, who must have been her grandson, on her back and was chasing chickens away from the straw mat in the yard. When I asked if I might take a look at the men's quarters since I was passing by, she said that her son was out somewhere but I should go inside and make myself comfortable.

As I entered the yard to the men's quarters my memories were dazzling, but nothing looked familiar at all. The veranda was nowhere near as high as it had seemed when I had gazed up at it as a child. Where sliding doors had once been hung on three sides, there were now glass windows. There was no sign of the plate once affixed to the front of the quarters, carrying the words

"Thoughts by a Moat Pavilion," nor of the carp-shaped bell that had once hung from the eaves. The sliding doors were closed. I walked around the veranda toward the lotus pond. There was not a single lotus to be found, only clumps of sweet flag and frogs leaping into the water, caught by surprise. This was the lotus pond where the frogs had once croaked so loudly at night that my grandfather would order a servant to throw stones into the water to silence them while he slept. Across from the pond the thatched hut remained. My grandfather had complained that the large men's quarters looked empty and desolate and so had a veranda built onto the small room in the hut, where he ate his meals in the three winter months. The new owner did not appear to be taking care of this hut, because water full of rotting straw was dripping down the walls and pillars. Above the sliding doors between the veranda and the room, I could make out the traces of several lines of writing. The paper was very faded. I was delighted to see what I thought must be the only brushstrokes of our grandfather remaining in this house and took a closer look; the thick strokes in the style of Yan Zhenqing seemed somehow fitting to my grandfather.

I end the day sitting among the luxuriant trees, keep myself tidy by washing in the pure waters of the stream, eat fine herbs that are picked in the mountains and fish caught in the river. With no set time to rise or sleep, I simply follow what feels comfortable . . .

The bottom of the paper had faded and fallen away, so I could not read any more. It was a fine piece of writing, lacking any trace of the vulgar world and fitting to that thatched hut. Later, when I returned home and looked it up, I realized it was a piece by Han Tuizhi. Yet although the words belonged to someone else, they well described my grandfather's life at one point.

"With no set time to rise or sleep, I simply follow what feels comfortable . . ."[1]

Sitting down on the veranda, I gazed up at the clouds surrounding Kŭmhak Mountain's peak and murmured to myself. "If the lord of this thatched hut were still alive today, what would he think of the Calf's Dying Spot and Gentleman's Pond?

He lived well and died well!

Perhaps nature, too, comes and goes with its lord!

It was a futile dream to think that I would be able to take this most vulgarly painted fishing rod, bought in the market, and find the true happiness that exists only in legend now that there is no such thing as a life with no set time to rise or sleep!"

I guessed there must be some members of my mother's family remaining in some of the houses in this village, but I bowed my head and walked back down the road and beyond, still thinking of the sadness of that old mother so devoted to trying to rescue her son's spirit by filling up the water.

Living submerged by the current of the age is like a spirit living beneath the water. They say that even the mulberry fields turn into blue ocean, but it's simply that all things follow the movement of the general current, and it's not possible to fill the ocean back up by moving pebbles.

—*The Third Month of the Year of the Water Horse*
First published in 1942. Translated from Yi T'aejun,
Toldari (Pangmun sŏgwan, 1943)

UNCONDITIONED

1. The first version of this story, published in 1942, ended here. This final section was added when the story was republished in a 1943 short-story collection.

BEFORE AND AFTER LIBERATION

A WRITER'S NOTES

A pparently it was now called a "notice" rather than a "summons," on account of the latter causing too much excitement, but there was no equivalent change in the unpleasant feeling brought on by the piece of paper that ordered Hyŏn to appear at the main police station, which the local policeman had arrogantly tossed down as if performing some irritating errand. A notice was no different from a summons in that it only created added anxiety for the already timid Hyŏn, even though he acted as if nothing was out of the ordinary in front of his wife's blanching face. Despite this, he would rather deal with the notice immediately than wait until the following morning, since he would neither be able to focus nor eat properly for the rest of the day, and inevitably bad dreams would disturb his sleep.

Hyŏn subscribed to no particular ideology and had no previous convictions. Yet it appeared that he had now risen to the status of a quasi surveillance subject, judging from the fact that he was being asked to come and go from time to time on suspicion that he might be providing some kind of ideological leadership to young people—perhaps some rural youths had been caught in the wake of some incident, and his writings had come to light in the resulting house searches, a letter or two might have been discovered, or his name mentioned under questioning about contacts in Seoul. He supposed that were the situation serious enough to warrant imprisonment, they would have taken him away by now rather than send a notice or summons, but still he was constantly anxious and, this time, even quietly rather worried. Though he was a mere novelist, more than a few young men had visited him in their search for a possible solution to their contradictory dilemma: the Special Student and General Volunteer Systems offered the prospect not only of meaningless death, but also meaningless murder, for while their own deaths would benefit the enemy Japan, they would have to kill the friendly troops of China, Britain, the United States, and even the Soviet Union, who constituted the only hope for their own people. Hyŏn had met young men who had suffered severe nervous breakdowns in the course of a mere day or two, and one young man who had sent a suicide note the week following a visit. Hyŏn was no student-soldier, but when he pondered the future in the face of such extreme national suffering, even he could hardly control his sadness at belonging to such an unfortunate brotherhood. When he met complete strangers, he occasionally suspected they might be spies trying to probe his views, but then he would reproach himself for harboring such unforgiveable suspicions and in his excitement blurt out all his thoughts at first meeting. Sitting in his quiet study afterward, his face still flush with excitement, he would grow uneasy about what had just occurred until, realizing that he had already gone so far, he would feel the urge to make a more rewarding mistake in the face of the imminent end of the nation. Yet he was neither prepared nor strong enough to crack open the shell of his long-encrusted character and leave it behind. He could only summon a bitter smile at his own worthlessness as he repeated a phrase from a short story he had recently written.

"Living submerged by the current of the age is like a spirit living beneath the water. They say that even the mulberry fields turn into blue ocean, but it's simply that all things follow the movement of the general current, and it's not possible to fill the ocean back up by moving pebbles."

"You keep saying it won't be long now, but if those stubborn Special Forces or Volunteer Forces, or whatever they're called, resist until the very end with their one-man boats, then surely even America with all its riches can't build as many ships as there are Japanese soldiers. We're just waiting for Japan to lose . . . but it's like trying to pluck a star from the sky!"

After yet another sleepless night, Hyŏn's wife urged him to sell their house and move to the countryside. She wanted to go to a remote village far away from the authorities, where they could grow their own food and live in peace for once before they died. Hyŏn had thought of this too, but escape overseas was no longer an option, and, as long as they were under a Japanese sky, where would they find a village from the age of the sage kings Yao and Shun, one where the officials were nowhere to be seen and even the dogs were quiet at night? Yet, neither could they hold out forever in Seoul just because there was no paradisiacal peach valley, especially as Hyŏn—who would rather stop writing entirely than produce propaganda or write in Japanese—had been struggling to support them for a while now. All they had left was their house, and if they were to touch that, then the best plan would undoubtedly be to use it as security for a few fields in the countryside, rather than let it go for the measly price of a skewer of dried persimmons. And yet, it was no easier to replace the shell of their life than to break open the shell of Hyŏn's character.

"Let's just wait a bit longer."

This was how Hyŏn had seen off his family's complaints about his uselessness for more than a year now.

At Tongdaemun Station, Detective Tsuruda from the Higher Police had been assigned responsibility for Hyŏn, but he did not leave a particularly severe impression. As long as the chief was not present, he would greet Hyŏn first in Korean, saying, "I'm sorry to ask you to come in again today, it's really nothing special." Today, however, the chief leant back in his chair, eyes deep set and forehead round like a gourd bowl; Tsuruda ignored Hyŏn's fairly lengthy bow of greeting and merely glanced toward a chair placed to one side.

Hyŏn quietly took a seat, nervously fingering his hat, which differed conspicuously from their wartime National Defense caps. It was a while before the detective stopped writing and asked Hyŏn what he had been up to recently. When Hyŏn replied that he was doing nothing in particular, the detective pressed him on his future plans. "Well," Hyŏn hesitated, forcing a friendly smile, at which the detective glanced back at his chief. The chief was busy pressing his seal onto some documents. Only then did Tsuruda take out some covered papers and look through them while keeping them out of view, and then he asked, "Why are you doing nothing to help with the current situation?"

"What could someone like me do?"

"How about you stop thinking like that and just do something? To tell the truth, we've received an urgent directive from the provincial police department asking us to report back on several persons including yourself . . . what you have done to cooperate with the current situation, what you are currently doing, and what kinds of possibilities there are for your cooperation in the future. We also need to know your source of income and so on."

"I see."

Hyŏn watched Tsuruda's face nervously.

"So, what should I report back? How about changing your name? That would be easy."

Hyŏn did not know how to answer this, as Tsuruda seemed to think he hadn't adopted a Japanese-style name because of the paperwork involved.

"I'm just a low-ranking policeman, so what do I know? But it seems to me that no one will be allowed to stand on the sidelines from now on."

"You're probably right. . . . In any case, I had been about to do something soon. Please report back that everything will be fine."

Hyŏn was just relieved that this summons did not mean he would be imprisoned as feared, and with this vague reply uttered after some hesitation, he left, stopping by a certain publisher on his way home. He could no longer refuse the request to translate the *Record of the Greater East Asia War*, which was not so much a commission from the publisher as a directive from the Central Police Bureau, directed through the editor; that editor had suggested it would be wise to make a gesture of sincerity soon, because the army was causing a fuss about Hyŏn being the only one to speak in Korean at the last Writers Lecture on the Current Situation, where he had read just one verse from the *Tale of Ch'unhyang* at that.

When Hyŏn tossed down the pile of Japanese newspaper clippings in his study, which his wife had taken especial care to tidy that day out of sympathy for her husband and his perturbed state of mind, he had never before felt that study to be so dirty.

For more than forty years lived in humiliation since coming of age we've never known the pleasures of love, the glories of youth, nor the honor of art. What am I doing, touching this record of war with my own hands when it doesn't even record Japan's defeat but supports its cause?

Hyŏn really did want to live. Or rather, he wanted life to be bearable. Apparently one poet who had believed that socialism would bring about the overthrow of the Nazis—enemies not only of his homeland but of all humanity and culture—had watched Molotov shake Hitler's hand and sign the Non-Aggression Pact between the Soviet Union and Germany, and committed suicide in despair at the simplicity of thought.

That poet had passed judgment too rashly. Aren't Germany and the Soviet Union at war now? America, Britain, and China are all at war with Japan. I must believe in the victory of the Allied Forces! I must believe in justice and the laws of history! If justice and the laws of history betray the human race, there will still be time to fall into despair later!

Hyŏn did not sell his house. A second front was yet to open up in Europe, and Japan was still holding Rabaul out in the Pacific. Thinking that this might last another two to three years, Hyŏn put his house down as security to borrow the largest amount possible and left Seoul. He moved his family to a mountain village in Kangwŏn Province, where they knew a village doctor. It was an old, secluded village, eighty ri by bus from the railway line, and although a county magistrate had once lived there, only a township office and police substation remained. Hyŏn's chief goal was to avoid conscription, and he presumed that the doctor would have connections amongst the officials, as in other villages, but he had also chosen that place with the problem of food in mind, because it was located in a grain-producing region and he would be able to wait out the months fishing in the upper reaches of the Imjin River, which flowed nearby.

Upon arrival, however, he discovered that none of these suppositions could be relied upon. The township office was under the charge of a model mayor, who had at least ten certificates of commendation hung on his office wall and exhibited all the contradictions of an age when receiving a commendation earned an equal amount of resentment from the people. The polite and upright doctor had soon clashed with the mayor and been sent to Seoul for six months of training; he could no longer guarantee Hyŏn avoiding conscription. Hyŏn's only other acquaintance ran the village Confucian school and had been introduced to him by the doctor. An old-fashioned gentleman who still wore his hair in a topknot and only surfaced in the villagers' memories twice a year, at the time of the spring and autumn rites, "Headmaster Kim" was in reality just as impractical as Hyŏn and struggled to feed his family, let alone his friends.

Even the fishing site that had at first seemed so close could only be reached by an almost ten-ri walk, which was too exhausting for frequent visits and took Hyŏn right past the substation of all places, so that if he wanted to go unseen by the station sergeant and constable, he had to climb over a hill with no paths. One day he was turning the corner of the post office when he caught sight of the Korean constable Kanemura. Startled, he quickly hid his fishing gear behind his back as he retreated back into the shadows and watched on while the villagers seemed to examine a pile of bark they had gathered together with the township clerks. Kanemura was stripped to his vest on top but still wore his gaiters and sword as he strutted up and down before the group, whip in hand. It did not appear as if the inspection would come to a quick conclusion, and so Hyŏn turned around, having decided to climb over the hill to the rear yet again.

He had just reached the more gently curved middle slopes, after pushing through the undergrowth in the pathless woods and wandering for a while on a steep incline, slippery from the rain, when suddenly towering over him at close quarters there appeared a figure as black as a bear; it was the station sergeant. Hyŏn would not have been more startled had he encountered a real mountain beast, and he dropped his fishing gear on the spot.

"And where are you going?"

The sergeant shot him a fierce glance.

"I just thought I'd get some fresh air."

Hyŏn quickly removed his wood-stripping hat in greeting, but the sergeant had already turned away. Hyŏn could see the mayor standing in the sergeant's line of sight and a rope marking out a rectangular shape the size of a large tennis court on the south facing slope; judging from their conversation, they were selecting a site for a Shinto shrine. Hyŏn froze, not knowing what to do. He did not have the courage to pick up his fishing rod nor to continue past the shrine site, which would involve him climbing over at least two ropes. To make matters worse, the sergeant and the mayor were whispering to each other and glanced in his direction from time to time. If there had been any flowers around he might have even pretended to be picking them, but not a single pink was to be seen. Finally, he took advantage of a moment when the sergeant and mayor were both looking in the other direction to quickly pick up the evidence of his own negligence toward the current situation with hands that felt as if they had been handcuffed, and then he rushed back down the hill to his home.

"Dad, why aren't you fishing?"

Before he could even think of a reply, the boy from next door, who must have followed him, answered, "Your dad was caught by the sergeant."

On days that he could not go fishing, Hyŏn would either read or visit Headmaster Kim, who would invariably come calling if it seemed that Hyŏn might not be at the river. The more time that Hyŏn spent, indeed was honored to spend, with the old man, the more the latter's integrity became apparent; he was the only true gentleman in the village worthy of deep respect. Hyŏn sometimes felt as if the phrase "as pure as jade" had been coined with men like Kim in mind. Since the collapse of the Chosŏn dynasty, Kim had avoided traveling of his own free will to the capital, where the Government General was installed, although he had been imprisoned there during the March First Uprising. Needless to say, he had refused to change his name to the Japanese style, and from the day of his release from jail was back in his topknot and horsehair hat. Both his and Hyŏn's only regrets were mutual: that with several decades separating them in age, Hyŏn's classical Chinese was not good enough to appreciate the poems that the old man wrote, and the old man, in turn, was unable to discuss the new literature, in which he had no interest. Yet as members of the same unhappy race, fumbling through the endless darkness toward a faint ray of light, no words were necessary for the feelers of their desperate hearts to clasp onto each other, and they had already grown quite intimate after only a couple of meetings.

One evening the old man arrived with tears welling up in eyes that glistened brightly from the midst of wrinkled skin. Hyŏn lit a precious candle.

"I caned my grown-up nephew in the street today."

Kim's hands were still trembling. This nephew worked as a town clerk, while his brother-in-law, the young lad who had married Kim's niece, had fled to the village after being drafted to Japan. When the mayor discovered the lad was hiding out at his in-laws, he had instructed the nephew to bring him in. In the meantime, the young lad had sensed what was going on and fled into the hills. But his brother-in-law had those hills surrounded by the Civil Defense Forces and turned him over to the substation like a trapped rabbit.

"What kind of a heartless brother-in-law does that!"

Hyŏn sighed along with him.

"Apparently if he didn't catch the lad, they had threatened to send him instead, but even so, how could he go and round up the Civil Defense Forces to trap a brother-in-law who'd fled to his own house, and even beat him with stones on top of everything else? Today's youngsters have no principles!"

"But these days parents don't dare take their children to task in public."

"I was so angry I didn't know what to do! So what if he'd just left the office and we were in the street! I beat him until the stem of my pipe broke. That asshole knew why I was doing it, and so did some of those watching, and that's a good thing."

It had not been a good day for Hyŏn either. A telegram had arrived summoning him to a rally organized by the Patriotic Writers Association in Seoul. It was unlikely that this long telegram had gone unnoticed at the substation, as the police were the first to know if even a postcard arrived for him. Now that the fate of the Japanese Empire hung in the balance, it wouldn't just be at the substation that people would want to know whether he would forsake his daily fishing and respond or not; when Hyŏn's daughter had gone to post a letter that evening, even the Japanese postmaster, who was also the head of the Anti-Communist Watch, had asked whether her father was going to Seoul the next day.

At first Kim told Hyŏn not to attend the rally. This had made Hyŏn rather afraid of what might happen if he failed to appear. A second telegram urging him to reply either way had arrived the following day, and a third the day after. When he heard this, Kim rushed over to see Hyŏn.

"What use will an old man like me be when the new world dawns? But you, young Hyŏn, should do what it takes to survive and do your part when the time comes. So don't be too stubborn over things that aren't very important. Just do whatever it takes to avoid conscription."

Next, Kanemura showed up and asked when Hyŏn was leaving: there were only two days left, and Hyŏn would need a travel permit before his departure; and if he wasn't planning to travel, then why was he not attending the rally; and, by the way, if he were to go to Seoul, would he mind taking Kanemura's fob to be repaired.

"I just want to live!"

Hyŏn let out a silent scream before leaving a day early for Seoul and the Patriotic Writers Association in heavy rain, Kanemura's watch in hand.

There was a reason Hyŏn had been sent three telegrams. Recently some executives from the Patriotic Writers Association had arranged an evening meeting with the Head of Information for seven or eight midrank writers who were not exactly enthusiastic about cooperating with the current situation. As Hyŏn had been the only absentee, it would look good for him, and also prove the sincerity of the executives, if he were to assume a special role at the rally. He was asked to offer some words on behalf of the fiction section. He grumbled for a while but could hardly resist, having already shown up, and the next day he followed the others into the rally hall. The scene in the assembly hall at the Municipal Center took his breath away. Never had there been such a breathtaking display since literary circles had formed in Korea: ceremonial cordons were draped over the standard imperial wartime uniforms, and swords glittered beside the uniforms and ceremonial wear of the higher ranks of the Korea-based Army and the ministers from the Government General, and then, there were the writers from Japan and from Manchukuo. Hyŏn wore flannel trousers under his jacket, which was still rather muddy from his fishing trips in the countryside; he would have been hard pushed to justify his sartorial insensitivity to the current situation as he wore neither gaiters nor the khaki of the wartime uniform. But Hyŏn had no way to suddenly disguise his clothes and, in any event, as he watched the proceedings unfold, he gradually found himself interested in the great gathering. His eyes and ears seemed to have grown more simple while gazing at carp and listening to orioles in the countryside, and now the barbarity of the fascist state's cultural policies was ever more apparent to him. One minister even repeated Hitler's words, that anything that could not be used as an instrument of war—whether literature or art—must be relentlessly eradicated, because culture could always be quickly revived when necessary. All the producers of culture present—whether poets, critics, or novelists—did not merely applaud the military speeches but competed with each other to be first to stand up, and then not in support of a dying culture but in order to expend their saliva lapping up the vulgar tastes of bureaucrats and soldiers. Yet, what struck Hyŏn as even more pathetic were the congratulatory remarks offered up in clumsy Japanese by the pale, thin writers from Manchukuo. Their faces looked so small and sad as they contorted into unnatural positions in order to speak a foreign language with which they were not familiar. The Korean writers were for the most part fluent in Japanese. Why, when it should be more pleasant to watch something fluent than clumsy, did that fluency seem more ugly here? Somehow even dogs and pigs seemed more honorable with their inability to speak any language other than their own. When a weaker nation begins to learn a stronger nation's language, so begins the tragic submission. Nevertheless, the congratulatory remarks and statements offered by the Japanese writers did not look or feel particularly natural or right either. Hyŏn had a hard time understanding the behavior of the Japanese writers. At one time some among them had spoken out, such as Yanagi Muneyoshi, who had said, "My fellow countrymen, let's abandon militarism. It's no honor for Japan to abuse those weaker than itself. If we push our violation of ethics to the extreme, then the whole world will become Japan's enemy, and it will be Japan, not Korea, that ends up ruined." Even when Hitler had sent the homeless Jews into exile and burnt books of philosophy and literature in the name of rules and regulations, like the first emperor of Qin, hadn't there been men of culture in Japan who had resolved to resist? What were they doing now, remaining as silent as mice? Was there not freedom and responsibility enough for them to voice their opinions and true love for their homeland and compatriots, more so even than in Korea and Manchukuo? Instead, pseudo-believers had sprung up all over, attempting to stifle the instinct—if there was any sincere conscience at all left in people of culture—to at least disagree with what was going on, even if they were unable to comfort the Koreans and Manchus or resolve their discontent. And even if they could not protect the culture and arts of Korea, which might be considered one origin for their own culture, to go so far as to become the agents of a barbaric bureaucracy and take the lead in the slaughter of the Korean language, with their nationalistic plays and meaningless theories of the common descent of Japan and Korea, seemed to suggest the last half century of Japanese culture amounted to nothing at all. Of course, those people of culture with a conscience must certainly be encountering a lot of trouble. But wasn't it all just too calm and quiet? A round of applause suddenly jolted Hyŏn from his train of thought, and he realized that he would soon have to take to the podium and contract his own facial muscles to excrete foul content in Japanese, even more tragically than those writers from Manchukuo, and just as he had been sitting there criticizing Japan's cultural figures. He could only ask himself, "Just who are you then? What are you doing sitting here?" It was all a horrific nightmare. He braced himself as if to jump up, but instead he barely managed to rise from his seat, as if he really were in a dream where no matter how hard he tried to move he just remained sitting down. Unlike in the dream, however, his feet began to move as soon as he stood up. Forgetting his hat on his seat, he quietly slipped out of the hall, where every stare threatened to ensnare him.

What will happen? Soon the chairman Kayama will introduce me. In front of all these breathtaking, high-ranking officials and army officers, the executives of the Patriotic Writers Association will have to look for me and call out my name, which is not even Japanese!

He hears someone coming down from upstairs. Hyŏn slips into the toilets. There is the slap, slap sound of a sword approaching. Whoever it is also seems to be heading toward the toilets. It could well be that lieutenant colonel, a compatriot no less, who had once threatened our writers in the dining hall of this same Municipal Center with the words, "This sword will show no forgiveness to the throats of those who are not loyal imperial subjects." Hyŏn quickly enters one of the stalls. It takes quite some time before the protagonist with the sword finishes urinating and goes out again. Immediately new footsteps enter. There is no reason anyone might glance inside the stall, but Hyŏn freezes, just like the time he had bumped into the station sergeant on the hill as he was heading off to fish. The toilets are flush operated but still reek a humid and toxic smell. Hyŏn takes out a cigarette to smoke. It's hard to suppress a wry smile as he considers the fact that the toilet stall is not the kind of place you wish to stay once your business is done; even in a prison or police cell it would not be this narrow nor the air this foul. Up on the third floor way above, applause rings out. And then, silence. After a while Hyŏn leaves the building. Deciding to let things be, he flees bareheaded to a friend's house in Sŏngbuk-dong, far from the city center.

As it turned out, Hyŏn did not go unrewarded for his trip to Seoul. Now that Hyŏn had helped him fix his watch, Kanemura had become quite genial, where before he had been stiff and refused to properly acknowledge greetings, and the postmaster, station sergeant, and mayor all seemed to have a higher opinion of Hyŏn now that he had received three telegrams from the organizers of the writers rally, to the point where they would greet him of their own accord, and Hyŏn could walk around without hiding his fishing gear from their view.

For Hyŏn, fishing was truly a kind of oriental pastime; perhaps this was because he still used oriental gear and methods. Sometimes when it was so quiet that he yearned for the float to quiver, he would doze off with his mind in the river, and when he occasionally felt like mumbling a verse in his croaky voice, a short sijo or a Chinese poem would seem more fitting than one of the new-style poems.

In a small hamlet at the foot of a mountain,
A bell hangs from an official's pavilion.
He peruses books in the midst of birdsong,
Hears petitions before falling blossom,
With a salary so small, he's but a poor servant,
But a body so free, he's a walking wizard.
Having newly joined a fishing party,
Half the month is spent down by the river.

Since moving to the countryside Hyŏn had taken to humming this poem whenever the fancy took him. One day, during a discussion about writing with Headmaster Kim, the subject of old steles had arisen, and, afterward, having nothing better to do, they had walked down to the entrance of the village to look at the steles commemorating county magistrates. Hyŏn was pleasantly surprised to discover that the very first stele commemorated the poet Taesan Kangjin, who was known as the inheritor of the tradition of the four great poets from the late Chosŏn era and who had once stayed here as a county magistrate. On his way home Hyŏn had stopped by Kim's house and borrowed the two volumes of Taesan's collected writings only to discover that most of his midcareer works had been written in this very mountain hamlet and that hardly a known place was missing from the title lines of the poet-magistrate's poems: there was Full View Mountain where Hyŏn would sometimes climb, his fishing haunt Nine Dragon Pond, and the hamlet of so-called Closed Doors where the loyal Koryŏ minister Hŏ had lived in seclusion after the fall of the dynasty. Taesan seemed satisfied with a post in the mountains and had early on admired the style of Tang poet Han

Yu, who had once written to a friend, "Go make your home amidst the mountains and rivers, And read in the woods of pine and cinnamon." Whether reading in the midst of birdsong or settling the people's disagreements before scattering blossom, this poem sang the praises of a leisurely life on a small salary and of spending half of each month in the company of fellow fishermen by the river. If an official's life were always like this, there would have been no need for the Jin poet Tao Yuanming to resign his official post at Pengze. A post that allowed one to sing to the wind and the moon could provide a life as literary as that earned by deciding to cast off official clothing and return to the fields and gardens.

He peruses books in the midst of birdsong, hears petitions before falling blossom! It's our contemporary politicians' misfortune not to be able to experience such graceful governance. But will such a world ever come again? It's surely a misfortune for contemporary writers that we cannot spend our time singing to the wind and the moon. But will there ever come a time when literature can consist of singing to the wind and the moon once more? Then again, perhaps there's no need for such a world, which might not provide either the life or glory to which our contemporary politicians and artists aspire?

Even though Hyŏn tended to recite Taesan's poem from time to time as a kind of habit, this was something akin to the pleasure of fondling an antique from dynastic times, and he did not feel that it held any connection to his current literary life.

But what is the literary road that I have traveled? Has my work really been so different from the leisurely literature of feudal times?

Such thoughts had bothered Hyŏn even before he had read the works of poets from previous ages, such as Kang Taesan, and even before he had more time to examine himself now that he had stopped writing and taken refuge in the village. To this date his literary oeuvre had mostly focused on the personal realm. It was not so much that he had limited himself to the personal things that he enjoyed, but that in feeling the suffering of the nation more sharply than the issue of class he had felt some resistance toward the Left with their predilection for that very issue of class. Nevertheless, when it came to direct confrontation with Japanese imperial policies toward the Korean people, the literary ranks in Korea as a whole, including Hyŏn, were far too weak and isolated internationally. Occasionally the pressures of reality would set light to a rage inside of him, but under the extreme censorship regime he had no choice but to submit; the only path that seemed open led to a world of resignation.

So, what am I to write now? Japan will surely lose. I must prepare myself! But what if Japan does not lose? Literature and culture are not the most serious problems in Korea. The Korean language is becoming so distant that this will lead ultimately to the annihilation not just of the language but of the very character of the nation. Will history really allow this terrifying plot of Japanese militarism to succeed?

Hyŏn kept insisting to his wife and Kim that it would take a year from now at the most, but when alone with his own thoughts he was unsettled by the vague nature of the information they were receiving. Yet his fears of what would happen were the fascist states to win would soon disappear. The ousting of Mussolini, the opening up of a second front, the fall of Saipan . . . even the little reported by the Japanese newspapers seemed to suggest the course of the war had already been decided.

Hyŏn still could not pick up his pen. He could not find the peace of mind to read other people's works, let alone write his own. He could sit on the riverbank and recite "He peruses books in the midst of birdsong, Hears petitions before falling blossom," but the great works of European literature would simply not enter his head, and he remained stalled on the final volume of *War and Peace*, which he had been rereading for more than a year now. No sooner did he step into the house than he had to worry about rice, firewood, and the holes appearing in the floor, about the inconvenience of the kitchen, the lack of shoes, clothes, and medicine, and, later on, that the money borrowed on their house, which they thought would last three years, had all been spent in less than a year. It was not even certain that he was safe from conscription, since a new law forming a National Volunteer Force had been decreed, which targeted all men up to the age of sixty. One day he was called to the substation. Instead of receiving a notice, this time a boy had simply shown up at his house with the news, but this did nothing to decrease the anxiety and unpleasantness. At least he did not have to wait until the next day to ease that anxiety, as he had in Seoul, but could run over there immediately to find out what was going on.

The station was packed full of people from the village to the point where he could not even get through the door. At first he watched on quietly, thinking his own case must be in some way connected. It turned out the villagers had come to appeal to the township for food rations: after all, what were they supposed to live on when they received no rations as farmers but all the wheat and barley they harvested was taken away, right down to the very seeds; and despite all the talk of increasing production and fulfilling quotas, how could they farm without eating themselves, and how could they deliver grape vines, pine knots, and oak bark if they could not feed themselves? The station sergeant merely snickered in response, but adopted a more dignified expression when he caught sight of Hyŏn and came outside.

"You didn't go fishing today?'

"No, I didn't."

"You were exempted from serving in the Civil Defense Forces and Anti-Communist Watch so that you could write for the country, but unfortunately rumors are circulating that all you do is go fishing. I was at the head office yesterday and they kept pressing me to tell them who it is that they can see from the bus, the man who has so much free time that all he does is fish. Now let me suggest that you refrain from fishing again until our Japanese Empire has attained its final victory."

Hyŏn had no option but to apologize, "Oh, is that so? I'm sorry."

"And haven't you missed all of our sending off parties, when our soldiers leave for the front?"

"I'm sorry. I'll be sure to attend in the future."

Hyŏn felt depression setting in.

Now that the first rains had passed, the fish would be fattening up and on the move. This ban was being enforced at exactly the best time of year to be by the river. He packed up his fishing gear and put it away on the shelf, and from then on meeting with Kim became the order of his day. Talk would naturally turn to the current situation—with Germany already destroyed and Japan facing the enemy as close to home as Okinawa, they were inclined to be optimistic and dream of the day when Korea would gain independence.

"Did you say the country is going to be called Koryŏ?"

Hyŏn had once told Kim what he'd heard in Seoul.

"That's what they say, the Republic of Koryŏ."

"And why would they choose Koryŏ?"

"Apparently Koryŏ is better known than Chosŏn or Taehan overseas. What name would you choose, Headmaster?"

"I'm not so bothered about the name, I just want independence as soon as possible. But since you ask, I would prefer Taehan, Great Han."

"Taehan! But wasn't that name used only briefly at the end of the Yi dynasty, when the country was on the brink of ruin?"

"Yes, I know. But it was the court that chose that name, just like Silla or Koryŏ."

"But what does that mean when we're no longer living in the age of the Yi kings? Of course, the court or the king always chose the country's name, according to their rise and fall just as you say, but our nation has been called Chosŏn—"Morning Beauty"—from the beginning of time, hasn't it?"

"Well, that's true. In the Chronicles we see Old Chosŏn and Wiman Chosŏn, so the name Chosŏn pops up all over the place, but still, I think . . ."

Kim had been lying down and smoking his pipe, but now he sat up.

"I think I would like to return to the name we used before, to Great Han, and to serve King Yŏngch'in, and I would like him to marry a Korean woman so that I could live under the Chŏnju Yi dynasty once again."

"Do you really miss the previous dynasty that much?"

"It's not simply that I miss it. And it's not just that ordinary people like us should only serve one king. I'd like to show those foreigners that we can revive Great Han and get our own back on them."

"So you'd like to be Governor General in Japan?"

They laughed merrily.

"Well, whether it's the Republic of Koryŏ or whatever it is, do we have an army? Have we been recognized by the Allies?"

"I don't know whether it's true or not, but they say that war has been declared on Japan and that there's an army of more than three hundred thousand soldiers altogether, led by Kim Il Sung, Kim Wŏnbong, and Yi Ch'ŏngch'ŏn."

"Three hundred thousand! Now that's a proper army! In the old days a hundred thousand was considered a lot! It will be quite some spectacle when independence comes and our government returns to the country! It's been worth living this long after all."

Kim lit up his pipe again. In the smoke that wafted up before him he pictured the fine men of our government in their splendid uniforms, escorted by a grand army of three hundred thousand men. Tears soon welled up in his eyes, and he let out a sigh that could only suggest the depth of emotion in his heart.

Not long after, Kim was called to the substation. It turned out that the magistrate had called the district police asking for Kim to go to the county office. The following day Kim had made the seventy-ri journey by bus. The magistrate had greeted him warmly and treated him to dinner at his official residence before speaking as follows.

"Why didn't you attend the Provincial Confucian Scholars Assembly in Ch'unch'ŏn last month?"

"Is that why you asked me to come here?"

"No. There is something else that I have to say."

"Then, please say it."

"This is more important than an assembly that's already been and gone . . . as both you and I well know, Headmaster Kim, the current situation will not allow anyone to stand on the sidelines. I am sorry to say this to someone of your years, but sometimes you seem just a little too old-fashioned and that goes against the current trend. Don't they say that even a sage should follow the customs of the times?"

"And so?"

"The county will be organizing some classes in the national language and the imperial spirit before the upcoming National Confucian Assembly. I'm sorry to say this, but please shave your head before coming to the classes and get yourself a wartime uniform, as you will need it when you attend the assembly."

"Is that all you have to say?"

"That's it."

"Mr. Satō, as you well know I am a Confucian scholar. What kind of Confucian scholar fails to uphold the words of the sages, who clearly stated that our whole bodies are received from our parents? What kind of Confucian Assembly would that be? I did not take on the role of headmaster of the village school for the title only. I accepted the position because of my duty as a student of the sages and because there was no one else there who could perform the spring and autumn rites properly. Telling me to cut my hair, to learn Japanese when I've already lost all my teeth, to change the color of my clothes, you might just as well tell me to give up my position, and I do understand that is what you are saying."

Kim had left shortly after, but within four days he was called to the substation again. There had been another phone call from the district office, but this time telling him to go to the police station. He dropped by Hyŏn's house on his way.

"Hyŏn? It looks as if those bastards are going to try to force me."

"Mmm. They're getting desperate in their final days, so please just try to avoid any kind of confrontation."

"What if I don't go?"

"That's no good. At the moment they have no excuse to detain you, but if they were to throw you in prison and shave your head for defying official orders, it would be like 1919 all over again."

"You're right. You're absolutely right, Hyŏn."

The next day Kim left for the district office; three days later he still had not returned. The following day was August 15.

As there was no radio, and even the newspapers took two or three days to reach this place, Hyŏn passed the whole day without hearing about the history-making "August 15." He suspected something was up on the following day, when he received a telegram from a friend in Seoul telling him to hurry to the capital, but when he went to the substation to obtain a travel permit and try to figure out what was going on, the constable and station sergeant acted as if nothing unusual had happened. Even when he delicately asked Kanemura why Kim had not returned, he received the following reply:

"Stubborn old men like him should be left to sweat it out a bit!"

"So does that mean he's been detained?"

"Well, I don't know anything about that. Don't go around spreading needless rumors."

It seemed as if nothing had changed at all.

Hurry to the capital, what could it mean?

Hyŏn wondered as he waited for the bus, which arrived earlier than usual that day. He boarded, noting yet again the absence of any sign of Kim.

None of the other passengers looked familiar to him. Most of them were wearing the wartime uniform, and no one showed any sign that something unusual might have happened. After about forty ri they met the bus coming from the opposite direction. Hyŏn's driver held up his hand and the two buses stopped alongside each other.

"What's going on?"

"What do you mean?"

"Haven't the newspapers made it to Ch'ŏlwŏn?"

"Well, yesterday's broadcast was correct."

"We could hardly hear because of the interference. But they say it's unconditional surrender?"

At this point Hyŏn jumped up from his cramped seat.

"What did you say?"

"They're saying the war is over."

"What? The war?"

"It's over now."

"Over! How?"

"Well I don't know, that's why I'm asking."

"Japan has finally lost. When you get to Ch'ŏlwŏn you can read about it in the papers."

With this, the other driver moved on. Hyŏn fell back into his seat as his driver suddenly pressed a foot down on the accelerator.

So I was right! What was meant to come has come! This tedious affair . . .

Hyŏn's nose twitched, and he blinked as he looked around the bus. None of the passengers appeared to be Japanese, and yet nobody seemed interested.

"Did you all hear what the drivers just said?"

They looked around at each other, but no one replied.

"If Japan has lost the war, then can you imagine what this means for our country?"

Only then came a reply, from an older man wearing Korean clothing at that.

"Well, whatever it means, we can't do much about it, can we? What kind of a world do you think this is, to talk about something we don't know is certain?"

The driver had been cheerily chatting away up to this point, but now his tired, wrinkled face and sunken eyes were focused on driving the bus as he spoke, "That's right. It's too scary to even ask whether it's true or not."

Hyŏn's head sank. The sad sight of his spiritless countrymen made him want to cry more than celebrate Korea's independence.

Am I dreaming?

When he reached Ch'ŏlwŏn and read the *Keijō Daily*, he discovered it was not a dream. He immediately began to visit everyone he knew, grasping them firmly by the hand and even crying with them out loud. He gazed up at the clear sky dotted with clusters of clouds, looking just like gourd flowers, and he looked at the grain growing profusely from the earth and at the lush green shade of the trees, and he wanted to bow before each and every one, to jump and to shout out with joy.

At dawn on the seventeenth Hyŏn squeezed into the crowded back of a truck, full of people instead of its usual grit, and traveled up to Seoul, all the while debating who should be president and who head of the army, and shouting himself hoarse with cheers for independence at each stop, where the T'aegŭkki flags would be flapping amidst a flurry of excitement and he became increasingly anxious that he wouldn't make it in time for the National Construction Rally, which was due to start at ten that morning.

Yet, what was going on when he reached Ch'ŏngnyangni? Against all expectations, in Seoul people were calm and hardly a flag was to be seen. He went into the city only to find the venomous Japanese soldiers still posted at strategic points on every street, ready to react at any moment with their sharp weapons, and the tone of the *Keijō Daily* measured as always.

He rushed to see the friend who had sent the telegram. Before they had even finished shaking hands, Hyŏn asked where the rally was to take place, but his friend didn't know. When Hyŏn asked where the main figures of the government were, who had supposedly arrived earlier by airplane, again his friend couldn't answer. But when Hyŏn asked whether Japan had really surrendered, the friend said that was true at least. Exhausted, Hyŏn collapsed in a chair and tried to clear his mind for the first time in some hours. Then his friend recounted the gist of events in Seoul over the two days that had passed since August 15.

Hyŏn was frustrated by the state of affairs in Seoul. The city seemed to be in disorder, and people were behaving rashly: the Government General and Japanese army still held power over the Korean people, and though the Provisional Government had either returned from overseas that morning or might arrive in the evening, in the meantime others were impatiently pushing their own plans for rebuilding the country without consultation. In the cultural realm too, various groups were rushing around and hastily hoisting placards as if this were their chance to reap advantage from the confusion, when Hyŏn, for one, could hardly tell dream from reality and most of the other writers and artists had yet to return from the countryside. Hyŏn was even more concerned to hear that most of those rushing to raise banners and organize groups were the leftist writers of old; he sensed a danger that with the leftists now able to do as they please and dominate not only literary society but the country as a whole, the nation could collapse in self-destructive strife. The danger seemed so real that Hyŏn decided this was no time to sit still and visited the newly formed Central Council for the Building of Korean Culture. A few of his close friends from the Group of Nine and the journal *Writing* were involved, but the main roles were taken by former leftist writers and critics. When he arrived, they were in the midst of rewriting the proclamation that was to form the council's basis. Hyŏn cautiously read through the first draft. He then read it a second and a third time. He was on the lookout for signs of hypocrisy in their expression or actions, but found himself quietly surprised.

Have they really prepared this sincerely for the situation here in Korea?

He found that he agreed with them on all points in both their attitude and declarations. Their first slogans called for the "Liberation of Korean culture, Building of Korean culture, and a Unified Cultural Front." They vowed to "work toward order in every field and unified communication in the current cultural realm until such time as our future government can establish cultural and artistic policies and the institutions to carry them out." Above all, Hyŏn felt the urgency of establishing principles for the nation's future based on unified action between Left and Right, and he had been worried that the leftist writers would disrupt any such attempt. In fact, he had even harbored feelings of hatred toward them, but this had turned out to be his own unfounded fear. It was too soon for more concrete plans, but simply the fact that they were not making class revolution a priority suggested not so much hesitation or caution as a considerable degree of self-criticism and deep consideration of the relationship between Korea and international players; without such consideration the leftists would not have been able to satisfy themselves with such a simple attitude and principles. Hyŏn was relieved and happy to add his signature to their proclamation.

However, he was not to remain relaxed for long. All the fluttering banners and songs reaching the street from the council building were phrased along the lines of "Power to the people." This might well hold a certain truth, but it was just all too soon for the ears of the common people. They had yearned so heavily for a country, for Great Han, and for a government and heroes, all of which had hovered enchantingly like a mirage over the ocean, and now they even rejected the rights that were their due, so captivated had they been by these dazzling fantasies and emotions. On more than one occasion it seemed to Hyŏn that the shouts of "Power to the people" originated in a habitual communism rather than democracy, and even though "to the people" did not sound either particularly new or dangerous in the current situation, especially when he recalled how those like Hugo had already shouted "to the people not the subjects" in a previous age, he was still cautious, and the majority of his friends and seniors who truly cared about him were quietly rather worried about his joining such ranks. On top of this, in all objectivity, the political situation was growing more complicated by the day. The Provisional Government barely made an appearance even as individuals, let alone in the grand fashion for which the people had so yearned; and while rumor had it that in the North the Soviet army had thoroughly expunged the Japanese troops and begun a total purge of the foreign enemy, which revealed a true understanding of the deep enmity that pierced Koreans to the bone; the U.S. army, on the other hand, had ignored the people's expectations and even distributed cordial leaflets to the Japanese, which allowed the Government General and the Japanese army to adopt a position that seemed to say, "Look at this, Japan is still a partner of the United States, countries like yours count for nothing." Meanwhile, on the Korean side there appeared first the People's Republic, an organization that would surely clash with foreign powers in the future, and eventually the Proletarian Arts Federation, which was made up of leftist writers only and clearly opposed to the Central Council for the Building of Korean Culture.

At first Hyŏn and others with the Central Council had tried to dismiss the Proletarian Federation, saying that "neither this age nor history would allow for its separate existence," but they all knew that this one immediate problem would need to be solved if they were sincere about a united cultural front. What Hyŏn found even more unpleasant was the fact that the basic principles in the Proletarian Federation's proclamation barely differed from those of the Central Council, with the result that he could not help but feel that the leftist writers of old did not want to join the literature section, for which he was responsible, simply because they had opposed each other in the past. One day, a few friends on the Right had quietly pulled him aside, as if they had been expecting the appearance of the Proletarian Federation all along.

"It's not that we are unaware of your true intentions. But you won't survive there in the end. It will all come to nothing. In the final instance, some of them are on the Proletarian Federation's side and not yours. If you're going to be left behind in the end anyway, why not get out now and join with us? What's the point of facing the embarrassment of such an awkward situation?"

Hyŏn left them, having acknowledged only that there was room for more reflection at this point. The very next day a demonstration led by a popular leftist organization passed through the street of Chongno. Red flags fluttered all over, but none of the other Allies' flags could be seen. In the procession people were singing "The Red Flag." The crowds in the street did not warm to the demonstration. It was only from the building of the Central Council that passionate applause and cheers for the demonstrators could be heard, and then a fairly high-ranking council member went to the pile of Allied flags, which had been prepared to welcome the Allied troops upon their arrival, untied the Soviet flags only, and carried an armful up to the fourth floor, from where he sprinkled them over the procession. The whole street turned red. Hyŏn immediately leapt up to stop him. He also blocked the way when the man tried to go back down to get more flags.

"Please, just calm down."

"What is there to be calm about?"

Their eyes met like daggers. To make matters worse, the young writers standing to one side all looked at Hyŏn with disgust and stamped their feet to applaud and cheer the leftist demonstration when they were no longer able to throw down more red flags. Once the procession had passed, no one would go anywhere near Hyŏn. He left the building feeling terribly isolated. But he also felt confident that he would be able to gather an equal number of supporters for a cultural or literary group, were he to split from this group.

But . . .

But . . .

He mulled over events until dawn. The next day he didn't go to the council building.

Should I work only with those who share my views? But what would such self-centered action achieve in the face of this enormous new reality? The freedom and independence of the new Korea must also be the freedom and independence of the masses. My conscience tells me that instead of failing to understand their passion for a mass movement, I should learn from it, encourage it, and try to support it with whatever little power I have. I merely want to point out that at this moment in Korea handing out only red flags is no mass movement and that those who support the red flag do not make up the entire masses. If they can't understand my feelings, or if they misinterpret what I'm saying as simply the words of a reactionary, then how can I work with them?

The next day, too, Hyŏn did not feel like going to the council building and was puttering about at home alone when the flag thrower came to see him.

"Hyŏn, you weren't pleased the other day, were you?"

"No, I wasn't."

"Hyŏn, let me be honest with you. For how long have our dreams been haunted by the fantasy of a red demonstration? When I saw it actually happening in front of me, I got overexcited and lost all sense of reason. I'm embarrassed now. I was rash. If it hadn't been for you, our imprudence would have had far wider repercussions. For every ten of us who think the same way, we absolutely need one of you."

His voice trembled as he finished his speech. They quietly smoked a cigarette together, and then got up and headed to the council in silence.

After the red flag demonstration, the people, including students, intellectuals, and ordinary citizens, clearly began to divide into camps to the Left and the Right. In the evening, Hyŏn's friends would take him aside to a quiet place. Once again they would plead with him to withdraw from the Central Council, and he would explain at length that, contrary to what they thought, the Central Council was not leaning to any one side. Then, one day, he received a phone call at the council from the friends he had met the previous evening.

"You are either lying or being used, which is what we think is going on. If you want proof, just take a look at the enormous banner that has appeared on the front of that building this morning."

The caller hung up before Hyŏn could even respond, leaving an unpleasant aftertaste. Hyŏn did not bother asking the people around him. He ran all the way down the stairs to the street and looked up at the front of the four-story building. His surprise was immense. "Absolute Support for the People's Republic of Korea"—a huge canvas banner extended all the way from the roof down to the second floor, covered entirely by specially written characters, which were larger than those of any previous phrase or slogan. He'd missed it when he entered the building earlier. All the people packed to bursting on the traffic island and the crowds swarming past the Hwasin department store . . . everyone's heads were tilted back to look up. Suspicion and unease were written all over their faces. It took Hyŏn about ten minutes to climb back up to the fourth floor. His disappointment was immense at having been betrayed yet again. Neither the president nor the secretary of the council had made an appearance. When the secretary of the literature section entered moments later, Hyŏn took him by the hand and all but dragged him up to the roof.

"Who did this?"

"What is it?"

He too had entered the building with his head down because of the drizzle, and had clearly not taken part in any planning for the banner.

"Did you really not know either?"

"No, really! Who on earth did this?"

"If neither you nor I knew, and we're both here in the building, then the council members who've not arrived yet can't know either. This is dictatorship. All the talk of a united cultural front is just lies as long as this goes on. I don't want to believe anything they say any more. I want you to know that I'm leaving."

Hyŏn turned around, and the secretary blocked his way, flustered.

"Why don't we find out what really happened first?"

"What's there to find out?"

"Don't rush to judgment."

"There's no harm in rushing with them. I really didn't expect that they would promote a mass movement with so little thought."

"Still, wait a bit. A split today would be suicidal for our cultural figures."

Hyŏn's voice rose of its own accord, "Then, why are you doing this?"

"Truly, I didn't know. But if we don't expose and correct these kinds of mistakes, then who will?"

Tears welled up in the secretary's eyes. He ran to the banner, now heavy with rain, and started to haul it up with all his strength, as if he were reeling in an anchor that fell back half as much again with each pull. By now tears had risen to Hyŏn's eyes as well.

That's right! The problem is not whether I'm being subjected to ridicule, used, or made to look an idiot. Worrying about such things just shows my own lack of sincerity.

Hyŏn rushed to help the secretary pull in the heavy banner.

Later they found out that neither the president nor the secretary of the council knew about the banner. What had happened was that a member of the secretary's team had heard an announcement about the People's Republic and was aware that sentiment within the building veered toward that name; at the same time, the propaganda team in the Art Department had asked whether there were any work orders and so, thinking that such a banner would be necessary eventually, the secretary's team member had come up with the wording on his own; and then because the propaganda team had thought the phrase simple but important, they had written it across an entire piece of canvas and come in before breakfast to hang the banner, since their responsibility extended to hanging all banners once dry. The council had to spend the next three months explaining a simple banner that had been hung for just three hours from eight until eleven in the morning, and received quite some criticism as a result.

Yet, this had also provided the motivation for them all to become more sincere in their self-reflection and appraisal of the political situation and in working together with the Proletarian Federation.

B y this time the U.S. army had arrived, and the Japanese army had withdrawn its gun muzzles from our streets, but the United States had proclaimed its own military government, just as the leaflets distributed earlier had foretold. Anyone was allowed to form a political party, with the result that some fifty to sixty parties had been thrown together overnight. While Dr. Syngman Rhee had appeared amidst wild cheers from the people and declared that all Koreans must stick together no matter what, the national traitors and profiteers had spotted the gaps in our midst and they also stuck together and resumed their activities once more—such as the president of the Japanese-era air company who returned as vice president of the newly formed national airline. The ultimate effect was the opposite of that the doctor had imagined: the people's minds were not one, but scattered, and doubt began to rule over faith. There was nowhere else for the people's hopes and expectations to gather other than around the erstwhile members of the Provisional Government, now reduced in status to individuals; the people had yearned for them and fantasized about them for so long that they had even forgotten their own rights. Yet were the members of the Provisional Government really fated to behave a certain way, whether as individuals or a group? During its long exile, the Provisional Government did not have its own people, and now that its members had returned home they did not seem to feel the slightest need to stand up on oil canisters in front of places like the Hwasin department store and talk with the common people. The split with the People's Republic grew deeper, and, day-by-day, the thirty-eighth parallel choked the country around the waist ever more strongly; robberies increased while prices rose, and just as the people's nerves had further weakened from the extended excitement, the question of trusteeship arose.

Nobody could maintain their calm. Voices rose up all over the place in opposition to trusteeship. Even Hyŏn gave a speech voicing his opposition, together with some friends, and a transcript appeared in the newspaper.

Yet Hyŏn, and indeed the friends who had given speeches alongside him that day, were less committed in actuality, and they soon came to regret their actions. Gradually they realized that the problem of trusteeship was not such a simple affair, just as the Communist Party had been first to point out. Although they were grateful for the party's detailed observations and accurate judgment of the situation, because it was the Communist Party that had come out in support of the tristate talks, Hyŏn and his friends had been misunderstood by some and even used as material for political infighting, and thus misfortune had followed upon misfortune.

"We were too rash on the trusteeship question!"

"That was some mistake!"

"Mistake? But given the Korean people's current state of mind it wasn't really such a huge mistake. It's good to express our national pride to some extent."

"It's one thing to express your pride when you know what you're talking about, but mindlessly sounding off on the basis of ignorance is another thing entirely, isn't it?"

"That's right! Since it's clear that we Koreans are quick to rush in but lack political insight, what's the use of talking about pride?"

"But can anyone do anything without making mistakes? Even Lenin said that without mistakes we can do no work, so only someone who does no work can never make a mistake. Now that we ourselves are more aware, we just need to educate others more effectively about the delicate state of the international situation."

Hyŏn was talking with others in the building when an old man appeared, looking incongruous in a horsehair hat.

"Oh!"

Hyŏn jumped up to greet him. It was Kim, who had flashed in and out of Hyŏn's thoughts from time to time since Liberation and had now appeared in Seoul.

"Headmaster Kim!"

"Mr. Hyŏn!"

"How are you?"

"I'm doing so well I came to take a look at Seoul."

In fact he looked tired and weak, having probably walked and traveled by freight truck over the thirty-eighth parallel from the North.

"When did you arrive?"

"Yesterday."

"And where are you staying?"

"Well, I dropped by Ch'ŏlwŏn on the way to check up on your family. They said they really want to move back here."

Hyŏn's family had only made it to Ch'ŏlwŏn so far and had not been able to return to Seoul.

"As long as they're all right, that's all that matters."

"And because this isn't really your home yet, I found somewhere to stay before coming to see you today. You must all be working hard?"

"Not really. I've been wanting to see you more than anyone, and thinking about how happy you must be. But you must have had a really hard time when you went to the district office back then?"

"They almost cut off my topknot, but luckily I avoided that."

"I'm so glad."

It was lunchtime, so Hyŏn led the way to a quiet restaurant where they could catch up.

"Hyŏn, they say that you've changed a lot?"

"Me?"

"Rumor is that you've really changed."

"Well . . ."

Hyŏn was a little sad to hear this. It was not the first or even second time that this had happened. Already several times since Liberation, and especially since a clear divide had opened up between the politically conservative and progressive groups, a word or two had sufficed for a respectful distance to insert itself between him and someone he knew; even some of those he had considered reliable comrades in a time of need seemed like different people altogether since Liberation, and occasionally this distance would even insert itself into their friendship.

"Hyŏn?"

"Yes?"

"Do you remember how much the Korean people thirsted for independence? How desperately we waited for the return of the Provisional Government?"

"I do."

"Then, how have you come to switch over to the Communist Party?"

"Are people saying that I've joined the Communist Party?"

"That's the rumor. And that, whatever you think you're doing, you are being used."

"Is that what you think as well, Headmaster?"

"Well, it may well be that you've done so of your own accord, but I don't think you're the kind of person to be easily fooled by others."

"Thank you for that. And you are right about me changing. But before Liberation I didn't have any position clear enough to be able to say whether I've changed or not, and I think that was because most of my friends were too passive in their approach to life. Now that we've been liberated I cannot agree with continuing to live like that and not working."

"What's happened to everyone's sense of propriety? In the past they said that a gentleman should withdraw himself during suspicious times."

"I don't believe in that. It's not wise at a time like this, don't they also say it's foolish not to try to straighten a crooked hat under a plum tree? A passive life means you think of no one but yourself. We're living in a most urgent time for the nation, and we must continue to work in spite of all suspicion and even danger."

"A person has to conduct himself according to his position. What have we ever achieved? There can be nothing wrong in remaining loyal to those who spent their entire lives overseas fighting for our nation."

"I do understand how you feel, Headmaster. And I am as grateful and as moved by those people as anyone else. But Korea's current situation is not so simple, either at home or abroad. Since you brought up the question of proper conduct, just think about what happened during the reign of Kwanghae. We received aid from Ming during the Imjin wars, but then when Ming was threatened by Nurhaci, they asked us for extra troops, didn't they?"

"And that was when the debate on proper conduct began in our country."

"The Imjin wars had just ended, and Korea lacked the resources to help Ming, but some of the ministers said that, according to the rules of proper conduct, we could not stand by and do nothing, even if it meant Chosŏn would fall alongside Ming. They became known as the proper conduct faction. The others, who became known as the faction for the people, said that more suffering should not be brought upon the people without allowing them time to catch their breath after being pressed by enemy forces for so long, even if this would lead to the fall of the country and the deposal of the king. And King Kwanghae eventually did lose the throne after advocating for the people, didn't he? Kwanghae demanded that the people should not be made to suffer in the games of kings and countries, to the point that he had to leave the throne behind like a pair of old shoes, but I think he was a truly great leader for that, far superior to those ministers who sought only the proper conduct of the powerful no matter the consequences for the people. What's more, why should the rules of loyalty and proper conduct apply only to those who've returned from overseas?"

"But they endured a lonely existence overseas for more than twenty-seven years, fighting far away for the restoration of our homeland, didn't they?"

"I certainly don't want to make light of their suffering. Everyone who continued to fight for us with such sincerity, whether here or overseas, deserves our equal respect, but when it comes to suffering and bloody battles, I do think that the suffering was far more severe for those who shed actual blood under harsh punishment and lost hands and feet to the cold when they were dragged off to police cells and prisons here for resisting. And their torment was not only physical. I believe that the most admirable statesmen were those who continued the struggle within our country and refused to give in, despite all the psychological torment of numerous threats and the temptation of bribes."

"So you really are siding with the communists, Hyŏn!"

"Who said that the communists were the only ones who fought at home? I think it was wise of the Communist Party to quickly announce their recent change in policy from class revolution to capitalist democratic revolution, and above all, I am relieved for our country because it should in principle no longer be possible for the polarization between Left and Right to worsen, and we should therefore be able to reduce the conflicts and strife among us."

"I don't really understand what you are talking about, but I blame the Communist Party."

"Please, let's have another drink."

"What does an old man like me know . . ."

Kim could not hold his drink well. His face flushed a drunken pink, and soon this turned to anger.

"How could old men like me not rest our dreams on them? If only the Communist Party would shut up we would soon be independent and the members of the Provisional Government would be able to assume their rightful places, be rewarded for all their suffering, and govern us well, isn't that the case? The question of trusteeship arose only because we were all fighting each other. If that's not the case, then what is?"

Kim argued that Korea's independence was being hindered by the Soviet Union abroad and by the Communist Party at home. Hyŏn realized that he himself did not possess the skills to enlighten someone who had no historical or international viewpoint but simply believed that Liberation had come as a result of the struggle for independence, and so he just smiled and urged Kim to eat more.

Kim came to see Hyŏn again the next day, and the following day Hyŏn visited Kim at his lodgings. That day Kim asked, "How can you and your friends take such pleasure in trusteeship?"

"We're not enjoying it."

"Then, does that mean you end up supporting something you don't like just because the Provisional Government is against it, and you want to oppose whatever the Provisional Government is doing?"

"Isn't that a little too harsh, Headmaster?"

"No, there's no reason for an old man like me to be bought out by the three foreign powers and silently dragged into support for trusteeship, is there?"

"That's going a bit too far! You think, then, that I've sold out just because I have longer to live?"

Kim did not answer, but his disapproval was clear. Hyŏn tried to argue his position as best he could, while trying not to get overexcited: that Korea's independence could hardly escape international control when Liberation had come about through the influence of international affairs and not on our own strength; that support for the tristate talks did not mean he was asking for or was satisfied with trusteeship, but that the independence and neutrality of Korea in the international realm needed to be publicly guaranteed, because Korea was precisely where the vanguard of the capitalist United States and the socialist Soviet

Union powers met; thus a hasty independence in name only, with the Soviet Union, the United States, and China all beginning their own underground diplomacy with a Korea that was both politically and economically weak, would surely be the road to disaster and internecine battles of the kind that had characterized the late Chosŏn era, when the king had taken up abode in the Russian legation; that was why there was little choice but to choose the path that would guarantee internationally this long overdue freedom until full independence; that given that the Yi Royal House and Great Han had not obtained victory through a war of independence, to talk of Great Han this and Great Han that, and to confuse the common people with nostalgic reminiscences of the autocratic age of empire was not a position that would lead the Korean people to happiness in reality; and that whatever one thought of the United States and Soviet Union rushing ahead with the division of Korea into North and South, they were the two most practical states in the world and so only a viewpoint and preparation of the most absolutely scientific and world historical nature, rather than impractical fantasies and sentiment, would help the Korean people to respond appropriately. Despite all this, the Kim whom Hyŏn himself had lauded as a man as pure as jade before Liberation, now seemed as obstinate as rock and made no attempt to understand what Hyŏn was trying to say, remaining displeased that a fellow Korean would criticize Great Han and stubbornly insisting upon his own interpretation that it was all a communist trick.

K im did not show his face for a while. Neither did Hyŏn feel like visiting Kim, though he was also busy to be sure.

The problem of trusteeship proved to be an all-too-harsh political test for the Korean people. Each demonstration against trusteeship was followed by a demonstration in support of the tristate talks. And so, the crowds clashed, and would-be leaders used this as bait for brutal political fights. In the end, it was the student conscript soldiers—some of those who had borne the cross of national suffering before Liberation but had managed to avoid death and return home—who now ended up bearing the cross of the unfortunate people's trials once more.

On yet another such depressing day Kim showed up at the council building. He was leaving for the countryside that day. When Hyŏn suggested they go out for lunch, he firmly declined, unlike in the old days, and would not even let Hyŏn escort him back down the stairs to the exit. He had apparently dropped by simply to say farewell in recognition of those days gone by and seemed to find Hyŏn's hospitality and greetings unnecessary.

"When will you come to Seoul again?"

"I've no wish to come back to Seoul like this. I will return to a quiet corner in the village and close the door."

He walked back down the stairs resolutely, without even taking a second look. Hyŏn stood still for a while, stunned, and then went up onto the roof for some fresh air. The dignified shape of Kim's white *turumagi* overcoat and black horsehair hat stood out all too clearly between the U.S. army jeeps, which wriggled like a swarm of whirligig beetles. Hyŏn suddenly recalled the late Qing scholar Wang Guowei. Hyŏn had heard him lecture on Ming drama during a visit to Japan when Wang still wore his hair braided in a pigtail, Qing style. All the Japanese students giggled, but when the stateless Hyŏn thought of Wang's loyalty to the former dynasty, tears of awe had welled up in his eyes. Afterward he heard that Wang had gone first to Shanghai and then to Beijing, but however much he wandered, the shadows of the old Qing dynasty for which he so yearned were growing ever fainter, until finally he had drowned himself in the Kunming Lake at the Summer Palace, his pigtail still intact, and reciting the verse, "The blue waters and green mountains remain the same, While the rain merely washes the moss on the rocks." Now that Hyŏn thought about it, what had broken the Qing was not enemy troops but the revolution in the name of the happiness and truth of the nation and the people. Wang surely deserved praise for consistently devoting himself to his monarch, but if he had directed his devotion and his life toward the revolution, then wouldn't that life have held even greater meaning, perhaps even attained the nobility of a greater truth? When Hyŏn gazed at the conspicuous rear view of Kim, who had endured abuse and contempt yet retained his topknot throughout the era of colonial occupation, and who had braved the thirty-eighth parallel to come up to the capital of Hanyang in search of Great Han but was now disappearing into the distance like a speck of dust into the grand current of world history, he could not help but recall Wang Guowei's tragic fate.

The wind was still chilly but somehow also soft, as if spring were already on the way. Hyŏn smoked a cigarette and went back down into the building. His friends had by now concluded the merger with the Proletarian Arts Federation and were busy making preparations for the upcoming National Writers Assembly.

—*March 23*

Translated from *Munhak*, July 1946

TIGER GRANDMA

The total count of households in this hamlet known as "Twenty Walls" exceeded that number by only one or two. It was a tiny mountain village where scarcity had long reigned over plenty. Being so far from the ocean, seafoods such as fresh fish or seaweed were indeed rare, but even grass-eating livestock was in such short supply that fights over oxen would invariably arise whenever the plowing season began, and if there was a gathering in someone's yard, then the shortage of straw and bamboo mats in the village would be sure to cause a commotion. But now a form of plenty had arisen in the village of Twenty Walls, where there were always more things that were scarce. This was people who could neither read nor write. On average, there were more than three and a half per household.

"They say that our village comes top for people who don't know the letter ㄱ even when they see a sickle!"

"Mm, well we have to have our share of something!"

"They used to say there were a couple more *kisaeng* than flies at the governor's office in Chinju, Kyŏngsang Province. Well here in Twenty Walls we've got more cannot recognize letters than can!"

"Oh, that's good, that's good! In other words, if we can't read letters we're more like *kisaeng* than flies!"

Ch'ŏngŭn's father and Mansŏk's grandfather were good at cracking jokes, but they too were among the illiterate ones who couldn't read the letter ㄱ even if they saw a sickle. With their gift of the gab, these stubborn, illiterate men were tough cases that brought sweat to the brows of the young members of the Children's Alliance and the still rather awkward speakers from the Federation of Democratic Youth, who were trying to encourage the study of hangul.

"Huh, you call me illiterate? What do you young pups know? I accept that my eyes can't see as well as your feet, but you want me to sit down in front of you and open up a book? I've picked up enough to know that a king is a teacher is a father. That means that a teacher is still a teacher, even if it's the old letters that he learned, and he should be looked up to as a father. What am I going to do learning all that ka, kya, kŏ, kyŏ nonsense and speaking to you like you're a teacher, which is no different from a father, eh? Making old people like us mouth that nonsense, it's too much . . ."

Ch'ŏngŭn's father gave the young people a good scolding, using a lot of difficult words even though he couldn't read a single letter. Mansŏk's grandfather jokingly made an excuse, "Why don't you leave us living corpses alone? What does it matter if we can read or not when we'll be on the way to the public cemetery tomorrow or the next day . . ."

A second visit to the old people provoked their ire. At a third visit they spat and raised their fists.

Younger people generally didn't grumble at a second visit. The young women quivered with joy, even while blushing at being called illiterate. It was not simply their true desire for the enlightenment promised by learning to read, but also the joy of the enormous change brought about by being able to wipe the water from their hands, put on dry clothes, and escape from a life in which they seemed to run round and round in circles like ants—even if that escape was just for a short while and if going to school meant only to the men's quarters or a large inner room belonging to some family they knew.

But this ant-like repetitive life did not easily open its doors for these young women and girls. They were all busy and tied down by things that would not let them go. No small number of them had no one else to care for their babies, and the new brides among them were daughters-in-law, who had to walk long distances to fetch water from the well and returned home later than everyone else in the evening. After the evening meal, cotton ginning and spinning awaited them, or they would have to tie up straw into sheaves to store in the bags their husbands had woven. The members of the Children's Alliance and the Federation of Democratic Youth knew that whatever kinds of strategies they employed, even if they were to encourage the women a thousand or ten thousand times, their efforts would come to nothing if they did not first create the conditions where the barriers to these women attending the hangul school were removed. And so, the twelve members of the Children's Alliance and six members of the Federation of Democratic Youth in Twenty Walls determined to relieve the women from their ant-like life.

To houses far from the well, they delivered water; for houses that kept oxen, they helped to divvy up the hay; in some houses they did the washing up, at some they ginned cotton, while at others they kept an eye on the children and on the house itself, if it were left empty. The passion of the Children's Alliance and Federation of Democratic Youth members not only moved those who couldn't read, but also brought the village to the attention of the township, the county, the party, and those responsible for various social groups. Once representatives from all these places had visited and added their strong encouragement to the remaining villagers who couldn't read, even Ch'ŏngŭn's father and Mansŏk's grandfather no longer felt able to kick up a fuss, and they tidied up their beards to put in an appearance at the hangul school. Of the seventy-nine villagers in Twenty Walls who couldn't read, seventy-six came out to the school, and as a result the remaining three became a conspicuous problem.

"If we can get those three to come out, then our illiteracy eradication rate will be one hundred percent, regardless of age!"

This became the desire of not only the members of the Children's Alliance and the Federation of Democratic Youth, but even Ch'ŏngŭn's father, who only yesterday had stubbornly clung to the idea that a king is a teacher is a father, but who now was busily reproaching Yŏngdol's grandmother.

"There's an old saying that even saints must follow the times. In other words, if you leave the group and work on your own, you'll get nothing done!"

The three who remained were: Noma's grandfather, now completely deaf; old Mr. Sŏ, whose consumption had deteriorated to the point that he could not stop hacking for even a moment once winter had arrived; and, finally, Yŏngdol's grandmother, the subject of the warning "Tiger Grandma's coming," which was enough to stop any child from crying, not just in Twenty Walls but in all the surrounding villages as well.

There was no doubt that Noma's deaf grandfather couldn't read, but as this was not a school for the blind and mute there was no reason to include him in the eradication count; as for Mr. Sŏ, there were plans to teach the old man separately in the summer when his stubborn cough would improve; and this left just Yŏngdol's grandmother, otherwise known as Tiger Grandma. If Tiger Grandma would come to the hangul school, the village of Twenty Walls would attain a perfect completion rate for the literacy campaign, but if this one Tiger Grandma were to remain illiterate, the damage would be the equivalent of ten or twenty other women not being able to read. This was because Tiger Grandma exerted more strength than ten or twenty women in the stubborn attachment to darkness and backwardness in the village.

Tiger Grandma turns sixty-five this year. Although the deep traces of a harsh life are etched all over her forehead and cheeks like a cobweb, her hair's still black, and her chin protrudes quite unusually so that it closes up over her mouth, from which only a couple of molars are missing. With high cheekbones and sunken eyes, when she's angry her neck seems to stretch so tall it's as if she's looking out over everybody. Her nose is as sharp as a knife with such a soaring bridge that some mischievous children even call her "Cluck-cluck nose Grandma." Her voice resounds like an enormous bell, she's strong by nature, and to cap it all, she became a widow before she reached thirty. The father of her only son, Yŏngdol, had, unlike his mother, been a weakling, more like a crushed chick.

His widow had struggled on alone as a desperately poor tenant farmer, taking any job that came along whether it meant working inside or outside, staying clean or getting dirty. Her character had been strengthened by a fierce sense of resistance to all harassment and intrusions, whether from landlords, officials, or even troublemakers, to the point where she'd acquired the nickname "Empty Cart," because her voice would start to rattle before she'd even listened to what was being said.

Whoever said a widow's house has three measures of sesame while a widower's house has three measures of lice might well have had Tiger Grandma in mind. Even young widowers with the strength of Xiang Yu will ignore a broken fence that could be fixed in a day and so allow dogs, pigs, and all sorts to trample in and out, let alone take care of chores such as washing, but this Tiger Grandma, who lived all by herself, was by far the most diligent person in the village when it came to repairing thatch or replacing fences. Her fields were better kept than anyone else's, and her firewood measured up to that found in houses with designated woodcutters and large mountain properties.

But this Tiger Grandma wasn't only passionate about her own home. She was always the first to turn out when the village well was cleaned, or there was snow to be removed from the lanes, or pig or cow muck to be cleaned up.

"Since when did anyone get by cuddling up next to a man and sleeping in until the sun hits their arse? To live means to get up early and move your arms and legs . . ."

No one complained when she showed up chattering at the crack of dawn in just about anyone's yard, because they knew that Tiger Grandma would clear the village lanes of snow, and that the cow and pig dung she shoveled would fall onto their fields of garlic and potatoes. To top it all, Tiger Grandma knew all about the superstitions that the women so enjoyed. As a mother who had raised her sickly only son alone and in poverty, there had been more than a few times when she had been left frustrated. She could neither consult books nor go to the hospital, since she was unable to read and had no money. When facing difficulties or despair the best she could do was to gather together all the stones she could find and pray, and then steam some grain and pray to the gods once again. At each new harvest, she would select five measures of the finest hulled millet and grind it into a small basket, which she had woven herself from rice straw and kept on the shelf in her best room. She would then insert a piece of folded white paper into the basket. She called this her *manguri*, or "Place to forget her worries," and would sit beneath it and pray if ever someone ill or unclean entered the house. Squatting down, she would rub her hands together and soon her head would start to shake of its own accord. This shaking of her head would begin whenever she rubbed her hands before the gods. If there was no improvement after praying to *manguri*, she would try praying in front of some water drawn from the well at dawn and placed in front of a heap of stones about half the height of a human being—she called this her Ursa Major Altar—and then later she would cook up some rice and greens and offer them to the crows and magpies in a corner of her yard and perform what was called a shaman's "scolding." If this produced no improvement, there was nothing else she could do. She would comfort herself with the thought that this must either be the result of a sin in a previous life, be the way of heaven, or simply just her fate.

If a woman in the village gives birth and cannot expel the afterbirth, it's invariably Tiger Grandma who comes down from the upper village. She takes a look at the young woman of course, but then declares this to be a trick played by a resentful spirit who died in childbirth, and she tells the family to prepare some white rice and seaweed soup. She brings this out to the side of the street and sprinkles it around, calling out, "Resentful spirits who died so unfairly? Eat your full share and back off now."

If a child catches malaria, the parents' first thought is to visit Tiger Grandma, because quinine costs money. Tiger Grandma doesn't hesitate one bit. She breaks off a branch from a peach tree that is reaching out toward the eastern sky, and then shakes her head and mumbles, all the while patting the sick child's quivering back.

On the first day of the New Year, Tiger Grandma rises before everyone else, comes outside, and looks toward the eastern sky. If the clouds are red, her prophecy is, "Drought this year," if white she says, "Floods this year," and if black, "This year's a bumper harvest." She looks at the first full moon of the year and once again makes her prophecies: this year's moon is white, so white-stemmed millet will grow well, or this year's moon is red, so better plant red-stemmed millet instead.

For people who are sick or have sick family members the question of whether they will get better or not is secondary; they can't help but be grateful to Tiger Grandma, who gives them something to do in their darkest hour. And for those with farming worries and no scientific knowledge to do anything more than look at the sky, they can't help but be drawn to these simple prophecies. To the villagers of Twenty Walls, Tiger Grandma was certainly imposing, but she was also an old woman who knew many things and for whom they were thankful. They could not begin to imagine this stubborn old woman meekly holding a notebook and pencil in order to learn the "ka kya kŏ kyŏ" alphabet. For her part, Tiger Grandma believed no one had the courage to challenge her, even though they might drag Ch'ŏngŭn's father and Mansŏk's grandfather out to school.

"What's that? Ibliterate? That means you can't read? Huh, it's a good job I've already lived through the first year of the rat once, because if I had to do it again there'd be nothing I hadn't heard! What's an old woman like me to do if I learn letters?"

"What do you mean? Hasn't Yŏngdol been pestering you to go to hangul school in every letter he writes, at least this will shut him up . . ."

"He seems to have gone out of his mind since he stepped up to his responsibilities!"

Yŏngdol was her eldest grandchild, who had joined the People's Army. Knowing his grandmother's temperament all too well, he had deliberately not pressed her from the beginning.

None of the members of the Children's Alliance or the Federation for Democratic Youth had the courage to go and plead with Tiger Grandma, and so they kept passing the responsibility around amongst each other until a few days after the hangul school had opened, when a young man named Sanggŭn finally went to see her. With his gentle eyes and amiable personality, he was recognized from previous experience for his great skills of persuasion.

Sanggŭn first took off his rubber shoes and replaced them with patched socks and tall straw sandals, which he'd made with his own hands. This was because Tiger Grandma prefers young men who do not smoke in front of their elders and who wear homemade shoes.

"Grandma, how have you been recently?"

Tiger Grandma was busy peeling berries from the cotton branches, which she'd pulled up by the roots and left on the sunny side of her privy roof.

"Come on in. Now that you're married, your heels are no longer sticking out of your socks. Is that your wife's needlework?"

"Yes. Which is better, her sewing skills or the shoes I made?"

"Your wife's pretty good with her fingers for her age. It's a shame to wear socks like that with them shoes you made!"

"Oh grandma! There's no winning when I talk with you!"

Sanggǔn stepped onto the edge of her straw mat, where he sat down and began to peel berries next to her.

"Grandma."

"What?"

"Have you had any letters from Yǒngdol lately?"

"I get them sometimes."

"You're talking about him as if he's a stranger?"

"Well, it's not the same, is it? He writes to his mum and dad, so why would he write to me?"

Right, thought Sanggǔn, and he didn't let this opportunity pass.

"Ah, but that's not fair is it, Grandma? If Yǒngdol writes a letter to you, I bet you want to reply to him, don't you?"

"How can I reply when I can't even read?"

"That's what I mean. That's why grandma should come and learn to write with the others."

"You mean I should put myself through all that trouble just for that grandson of mine?"

"But why do you think learning to write is trouble?"

"Don't say that to me. It's not just that it's trouble, it's that people look down on you."

"But who would look down on you for learning to write?"

"Ah, people look down on me just because I try to light my pipe from theirs, so you think they wouldn't look down on me if I tried to get something from inside of them?"

"Well, I suppose you might be looked down on for not knowing how to read and write, but I've never heard of anyone being looked down upon for trying to learn! The boys from the Children's Alliance will soon put a stop to that, so why don't you come along this evening grandma?"

"And who'll keep an eye on this house?"

"Do you think the Children's Alliance members won't look after it?"

"Uh, so they can eat up all the squash seeds I've got drying by the furnace?"

"Eat them? If any squash seeds disappear, then we'll collect more for you ourselves."

"So that's it! I wondered what you were doing up here in this part of the village, you came here to try to drag me off to school, you rascal!"

"Even if that were the case, you shouldn't be so surprised, should you? Just imagine, if Yŏngdol hears you're studying hangul, he'll dance for joy!"

"You rascals are all the same, ain't you? If I really wanted to learn, do you think I would wait around for someone to tell me? Ridiculous! I've never done anything because someone told me to! Do you think I'm going to change at this point in my life and do what someone tells me? You're telling me to learn to read? You've spouted your nonsense, now be off with you!"

Tiger Grandma turned away from Sanggŭn in a sulk.

At moments like this, to keep pushing the point would be like beating on an unhitched cart. Sanggŭn looks around to see if there's not something he could use to talk Tiger Grandma up. Just then, three or four hens come tottering out of the kitchen, chased by a cockerel.

"My, your hens are really plump!"

"Well, we're not buried in snow yet, so there's lots for them to eat, ain't there? Who's got thin chickens already?"

"Still, you take good care of your land and animals, grandma."

"That's true, even chicks from the same batch change depending on how you look after them. There's nothing gets done without hard work!"

Tiger Grandma shook her head.

"Grandma, you're our role model in the village when it comes to farming and looking after your house. If you were to become a role model in just one more way, the rumor might spread all the way to the center."

"What are you talking about?"

"If you were to send a handwritten letter to your grandson in the People's Army? Now, wouldn't that appear in the newspaper?"

"What, you're crazy! What are you talking about, putting an old woman like me in the newspaper? Haven't you said enough already?"

"I mean as praise. To praise you . . ."

"It doesn't matter if you're young or old, if the rumor comes out that you're a widow, nothing good will come of it! You can be like this or that, but best is to know nothing. Learning to read just makes you busy, what else is it good for?"

Sanggŭn looked up into the mountains behind them, smiled, and went back down to the main village.

Several days later, the chairman of the Township Farming Committee, who was known for his sweet-talking, went to visit Tiger Grandma.

"What's all this fuss because you can't drag me down there? Do you think I've nothing better to do than sit down with kids young enough to be my grandchildren, to recite "This is a cow, this is a chicken" and to repeat it all without even the excitement of a shaman's do? So I don't know how to read, but I don't owe you nothing! I've lived to sixty-five without owing anybody a letter, or even a prayer! I've done nothing wrong, so why the hell don't you stop bothering me, telling me what I don't know and all that!"

The chairman merely smacked his lips and went away again.

And so this Tiger Grandma emerged as an obstacle in the project to completely eradicate illiteracy in Twenty Walls, and because of this one woman remaining illiterate, all the women of the village, who were just barely beginning to walk toward the light and rid themselves of various superstitions, were unable to completely free themselves from their superstitious attachments. While they easily forgot the letters they had learnt while the hangul school was closed throughout spring, summer, and autumn, they continued to be influenced by Tiger Grandma and her mountain of superstitions in their daily lives. Many would ask Tiger Grandma to select an auspicious day when leveling the ground to repair a house, or ask her which days they should send their daughters-in-law to their parents or their daughters to their in-laws. Each time this happened Tiger Grandma would never fail to interject sarcastically and loudly, "Don't people who've learnt the letters know how to choose a day? What on earth's the point of learning those damn letters then?"

It seemed as if more than a couple of old people might refuse to attend the upcoming winter school as long as Tiger Grandma were left out and they could see her resist the pressure to learn to read. Those who had worked hard all the previous winter and just about managed to fumble their way through "This is a cow, that is a chicken," just as Tiger Grandma had complained, were supposed to move onto a real textbook this coming winter.

"What can we do to make sure that Tiger Grandma comes to the school?"

From early autumn this question became a major headache for all the members of the Federation of Democratic Youth and Children's Alliance in Twenty Walls, including Sanggŭn.

"I wish she'd move to a different village!" said one honest youth.

"If that old woman would just go deaf. Then no one could go hear her tell a fortune, could they!" added one quick-tempered youth in anger.

"But none of this talk is helping . . ."

This was the ever-hopeful Sanggŭn. Whenever leaders from the township or county or someone from the party's social groups showed up, he would always confer with them about the problem of Tiger Grandma. But they didn't have any good ideas either. Then one day Sanggŭn had to go to the county office on some errand and happened to mention the situation at the end of his conversation with the representative there, and that person's words gave him courage as well as a clue toward solving the problem. This is what the person said, "Korea's high illiteracy rate is one of the most toxic remnants left by Japanese imperial rule, so the project to eradicate illiteracy is an important step in cleaning up those toxic remnants of Japanese imperialism. To open the eyes of the likes of Tiger Grandma, who cannot read, means expunging the most deeply entrenched feudal remnants from our most conservative villages, but it also means to utilize in the best way possible the great dedication to the people of this grandmother, who likes to work. We have to rate highly the lifestyle of this grandmother who loves labor. She is a woman of good character with many positive qualities. A woman like her must have a strong sense of pride, so please try to influence her positively by stressing her strengths and ensuring she doesn't fall by the wayside."

Sanggŭn spent several days absorbed in thinking about the best way to properly utilize Tiger Grandma's pride for both her sake and that of the village.

On the day that the newly built adult schoolhouse was to be completed, Sanggŭn gathered together everyone involved and announced that he had come up with a plan to deal with

Tiger Grandma, who lived closer than anyone to the new schoolhouse. Of course, at first not everyone agreed with his plan, but eventually it was approved, in no small part due to Sanggŭn's firm belief that perseverance would open up a path and his willingness to accept full responsibility were they to fail.

Sanggŭn did not encounter too much difficulty in encouraging Tiger Grandma to attend the opening ceremony for the adult schoolhouse. Because the opening ceremony for this building was a big event and a happy occasion for the entire village, he said, they were inviting those village elders who had always worked the hardest for the village as honored guests. Worked the hardest for the village . . . at these words a flash of anger flickered in her sunken eyes.

"This is village business too, isn't it?"

"Um, it certainly is!"

In fact, whenever something went on in the village that demanded everyone rush in to make a fuss, Tiger Grandma would always be there; she was at the head of the line when rebuilding river banks, repairing wells, or fundraising, and precisely because she took the lead the project would be sure to progress quickly. Yet deep down she felt that she was more rightfully owed respect within Twenty Walls for chasing away the resentful spirits of those who died in childbirth from mothers who could not expel their afterbirth, and for ridding patients of malaria with peach branches, and for choosing the right day for all kinds of special occasions. It was with a feeling of pride for these acts that she took up her place amongst the honored guests at the adult schoolhouse, having taken out her most-prized, brand-new clothes, which though only made of cotton she was wearing for the first time since the land reform.

But on this day there was something of which Tiger Grandma was not so proud. She had not stepped to the forefront when it came to raising the funds to build this schoolhouse and had ultimately even shirked making a contribution of several measures of rice. Now she was full of regrets: if only she had known events would take this course, she would not have resented a sack of rice let alone a few measures!

On the morning of the first day of classes at the newly built schoolhouse, Sanggŭn visited Tiger Grandma once more. This time he was accompanied by five or six others, including the chair of the Farming Committee, the chair of the Cell Committee, and other members of the Federation of Democratic Youth; he hoped to make a more dignified impression, even though he planned to do most of the talking.

"Grandma, you owe us a favor!"

"Come in, come in. A favor? And why not two, if I can?"

They went inside and sat down, and then Sanggŭn began to speak in a more polite fashion.

"Grandma, we need your help this evening."

"What do you mean?"

"Grandma, we need you to do something for our village this evening."

The pupils seemed to rise out from Tiger Grandma's sunken eyes. There would surely be a momentary change, but would it be a spring breeze or a frost that would emerge from those eyes?

"This evening we will hang the bell at the school and ring it for the first time. Now could we leave that job to just anybody? We're here today because after a discussion we decided that one of our village elders should ring the bell, and we all decided that we should ask you."

"Really . . ."

They all looked at once at those eyes, which could easily have turned ferocious. But this was no frost for sure. She wriggled her protruding chin a couple of times and then burst out laughing.

"You hold a special position in our village, don't you grandma?"

"Well, I know this is Twenty Walls, but I don't see why you have to keep on annoying me like this. You want me to go to the school and ring the bell? You want me to make a fool of myself in your exorcism?"

"This is village business too, isn't it?"

Tiger Grandma struck a serious expression and replied.

"It certainly is!"

That evening Tiger Grandma not only rang the first bell at the adult schoolhouse, but she was also installed as the president of the Twenty Walls Adult Schoolhouse Support Committee.

"What do I know to be president? What's possessing me? What's gotten hold of you all?"

"Will the women in this village listen to anyone but you, grandma? We'll do all the work, all you have to do is show up at the school each evening as an elder looking after our school. Please just keep an eye on anyone who misses a lot of classes or who stops studying, and give them a talking to. This is village business too, isn't it?"

For once, Tiger Grandma did not say, "Um, it certainly is." All of the students—children, adults, and the older people—whispered to each other. In the confusion that followed some said Tiger Grandma, who couldn't recognize a single letter, was now the president or chair of some school society, and some children even said she was the headmistress. Tiger Grandma ran home, embarrassed to the hilt.

The teachers came to fetch her first one day and then a second, but from the third day Tiger Grandma was waiting out front of her own accord. And when the students started to call her "Grandma President of the Support Committee" no one objected. Here and there murmurs could be heard, however, including from the unforgiving Little Grandma, who coughed a couple of times and said to herself in a rather loud voice, "What, so you get to be president because of your age? Not because you've studied hard?"

Tiger Grandma ground her teeth when she heard this. She didn't think she would hear something like this from someone growing old in the same village. How could someone so well known for being a dunce, who had married into a family in the village and even had a grandson but still couldn't remember the memorial days for the ancestors in that house, how could someone like that complain about her own lack of learning just because they knew a few letters? If those letters had been stones, Tiger Grandma would have chewed them up and swallowed them on the spot, even if it meant breaking all her teeth. She took a gulp of saliva and responded.

"You're younger than me, aren't you? Let's see where we are a month from now. If I only study by looking over your shoulder, I'm not afraid of someone with your memory . . ."

A month later Tiger Grandma and Little Grandma were already worlds apart in their reading ability. When they were learning the row of letters beginning with *ch'a*, Little Grandma was told off several times for not knowing the letter *ch'ong*. Her daughter-in-law, who was sitting by her side and feeling sorry for her, gave her a hint, "*Ch'ong*, it's *ch'ong*. Think of *ch'ong*, the guns that soldiers carry around on their shoulders."

"That's right, it's the soldiers' gun *ch'ong*, that's how I remember it! *Ch'ong ch'ong* . . ."

But when the teacher quizzed her on the letter *ch'ong* the following evening, she started to feel dizzy. Her daughter-in-law couldn't bear to watch her blink and blink, and prodded her on in a low voice, "Have you forgotten about the soldiers?"

And Little Grandma went a step further from *ch'ong* to blurt out, "*Kkwang*, bang—that's what it is!"

The whole school erupted in laughter.

By this time Tiger Grandma, president of the Support Committee, had written the following letter to her grandson Yŏngdol, who was serving in the People's Army.

"Yŏngdol, are you all right? Are you keeping warm? Is your commanding officer well? You must listen to what he says. You must have seen our General Kim several times by now. Your grandma has been made President of the Adult School Support Committee. I'm very busy learning to write and taking care of school things. Your mother is also studying hard. I wondered what the point of learning to write was, but this is it. Your favorite millet has done well this year. When will you have a holiday? You must do your best for our country. Our cow has had a calf. I agreed to be president because they said there was no one else, but it's hard work looking after all these ignorant people. Everyone tries to talk at once, it's enough to hurt my ears. I have a mountain of things to say, but my eyes are beginning to blur, so I'll stop here."

This was the first letter that Tiger Grandma had written in her life, and that mountain of things to say included the story of Little Grandma reading the letter *ch'ong* as *kkwang*, but she hadn't yet worked out how to write such complicated sentences. She spat on the end of her pencil several times and stopped there.

—*January 12, 1949*

Translated from Yi T'aejun,

Ch'ŏt chŏnt'u (Munhwa chŏnsŏnsa, 1949)

DUST

1

It had been a long time since Mr. Han Moe had taken out his prized paper twine bag. Bluish mold spores had blossomed in the old dirt stains. The spores did not easily shake out from the gaps in the bag, which had been woven from old Korean paper. He tried flicking with his fingernails and even held the bag up to his lotus-bud-shaped beard to blow on it.

When leather goods had been banned toward the end of the colonial occupation, Mr. Sŏng, an antiquarian book broker, had carried around this bag, which he had woven from paper twine made by taking apart old histories and volumes of the *Comprehensive Mirror* that were worth next to nothing. With its simple but elegant style, it could not help but attract the attention of Mr. Han Moe, book collector, antiquarian, and lover of Korean things, who had even adopted an old vernacular word for mountain as his pen name. Though he would hesitate over a won or two when bargaining for books, he had offered a generous price for this bag and ended up able to buy it for less.

Han had no sons. The eldest of his daughters lived in Seoul, but the youngest, and his fondest, had moved down to Pyongyang upon marrying, and it was partly to be near her that Han had evacuated in the final years of the occupation. As he went back and forth selling his house in Seoul and buying a new one in Pyongyang, he proudly carried the bag with him, and when he had finally moved the several thousand old books that he had collected over more than three decades—enough to reach up to the rafters and make the proverbial ox sweat—it was into this bag that he had placed the inventory of his books and the checks for their carriage.

Over the five years that had passed since then, both before and after Liberation, this bag had done nothing but sprout mold spores each summer alongside his old books in the attic.

When Liberation came Han had wanted desperately to go to Seoul to see all his friends and his elder daughter's children, whom he had not seen in a while, and he had wanted to see the libraries belonging to Japanese scholars that were sure to pop up here and there at bargain prices. Yet being overcautious by nature, Han had not left Pyongyang.

In the aftermath of Liberation and before public order had been restored, burglaries and fires had occurred frequently here in Pyongyang too. It was fire that Han feared above all, more so than burglary. Since the end of the war he no longer had to worry about bombs, but his fear of fire remained unabated. In the absence of a separate library that might offer more protection, his books were piled up in the attic and in his own room; at night, the thought of a fire kept him awake to the point where, though no Buddhist, the whole world seemed like a burning house, and he could not relax for even one moment. From time to time, he would go out to the nearby Yŏn'gwang Pagoda for some fresh air but would always have to turn back several times to check with his own eyes that the hearth had been well and truly extinguished in both the inner room and the garden room, which he had rented out, and even then he would repeatedly entreat his wife to take care before finally setting out once more. Han had taught classical Chinese and calligraphy at the same middle school in Seoul for more than twenty years. He had been able to support his small family by taking in student boarders and devote his entire monthly salary to the collecting of old books.

Back then, the Japanese had yet to start acquiring Korean books, and with little competition he had been able to procure extremely rare editions from the Koryŏ and early Yi dynasties at cheap prices. Against all entreaties, he had stubbornly stayed away from books with pages missing and editions with missing volumes, and whenever faced with two identical books, he had invariably chosen the one with the most interesting history of ownership. Although not large in number, Han's book collection had caused many scholars and libraries to salivate for some years now, precisely because it contained so many rare and pristine books. He had been approached several times by the Government General Library and both the Kyŏngsŏng and Tokyo Imperial University libraries, as well as by some notable Japanese scholars, with generous offers to buy all or part of his collection. Yet he had refused all such offers, even though it meant having to live modestly, and he also did his best to avoid lending out his books for photoreproduction.

I would rather burn my entire collection than allow it to be used to support the distortion and defamation of Korean culture and history by the Japanese Empire! Whatever happens, one day our nation will rediscover our language and letters, and we will be able to freely research and appreciate our own culture and history! It's only because I believe that such a day will come that I can go without food and clothing to collect these books!

Such was Han's secret wish. Because of this wish, the August 15 Liberation had brought more joy to him than to most, and later, when the Kim Il Sung University had been established in northern Korea and scholars from there had come to him expressing their respect and requesting that he make his book collection public, he had been moved to tears and felt the most rewarding pride in this labor of the past three decades.

It was also true that Han had in the meantime been thinking even more ardently of Seoul. In Seoul there were more collectors of a like mind, who understood the special nature of the library he had worked so hard to build and who had envied it for quite some time. If only unification would bring about a stable nation in which interest and passion in culture could thrive, he hoped to reveal his rare collection with a public exhibition, which would have a great impact on the scholarly world, and he would then donate his books to the nation or some library, gathering respect and praise from friends and scholars alike.

Is this too much to wish for now that I have devoted half of my life to this collection at the expense of all other desires?

From time to time, Han would stroke his lotus-bud-shaped beard and conclude that this particular desire was only natural.

He had yet to reveal the inventory of his books to the scholars who had visited him from Kim Il Sung University. Yet he did not want to keep his secret collection to himself forever, but rather hoped to preserve expectations and the interest of the scholarly world in his rare editions until he could hold a public exhibition.

As Han packed everything required for the journey into his paper twine bag, now divested of its mold, he pictured the welcoming face of the good man Mr. Sŏng, the antiquarian book broker. The journey to the South that he had been planning ever since Liberation was about to begin.

Han believes in the political position of the North. But he does not want to believe that the situation in the South is really the way it appears in newspaper reports in the North. Why? Because he has not seen it with his own eyes.

In his sixty years Han has come to realize that few things in the world can be trusted. Even if other people are crossing a stone bridge, he has to first test it with his own hands before he will walk across. "They say that old house has several rooms full of rare books." "That's so-and-so's grandson's house and they've got all his valuable paintings and scrolls out. No one has touched them yet." Every time he heard such things, he would pay a visit only to struggle to find even one usable book among the thousand covered in dust, or be told he was the first to look and start diligently sorting through books, only to hear later that several people had been there before him and taken away the egg yolk, so to speak.

Everything turns out to be different from what people say! Now I have to see it with my own eyes first . . .

It would be fair to say that his suspicious nature had only been strengthened over the many years he had spent dealing with antiquarian book brokers.

What he had seen with his small but sharp eyes, though limited to an extremely small part of the world around him, had led him to recognize that the political line in the North was correct.

Han had let the garden room of his house to a father and son from another region. The father worked for the Industry Bureau as a department head, while the son attended Kim Il Sung University. Since a bureau amounted to a ministry, the father must be a fairly high-ranking executive, and yet he lived a simple life, walking everywhere, leaving the house early and returning late at night to eat a few spoonfuls of cold rice. The son worked hard too, studying and cooking the father's meals himself in the absence of a housekeeper. In the old days, university students had worn uniforms made of serge—a light serge in the summer and a heavier weave in the winter—their trousers were braided, and their books were thick with gold lettering on leather covers.

But this university student in the garden room wore a wrinkled cotton twill uniform with, at best, sports shoes on his feet. When he went out, he wore his cap on any which way, sometimes crooked or slipping down at the front, and he never took off his uniform, no matter whether he was shoveling coal, cooking the dinner, or cleaning their room. Most of his books were copies produced without much care; their cheap ink and yellowed printing paper emitted a piercing smell. His friends would sometimes visit wearing similar attire, and there would be loud debates, regardless of the time of day or whether someone was trying to sleep elsewhere in the house. They wasted no time on idle gossip, but sprinkled their arguments with philosophical terms, such as "historical materialism" and "dialectics," and even more fierce sounding words such as "mercilessly" and "pulverize other lands." The room was no more quiet when the father returned late at night, because he too would take part in the boisterous talk of historical materialism and "showing no mercy."

The university holidays had begun recently, and the son had been mobilized to work each day at the borough office in advance of the upcoming elections for the Supreme People's Assembly. Even though he worked all day at the borough office, he always came home to eat lunch. This was not because he ate particularly well at home. Lunch would be plain cold rice at best. Nevertheless, both father and son would return home from work and school without any complaints, and their happy faces seemed full of hope for the future.

This university student was strong in body too. When reading something in Russian, he would stretch out a clench-fisted arm as if to exercise, and when trying to memorize some mathematical or chemical formula, he would stride up and down the yard as if brimming with energy. Some days he would even trim green onions and bean sprouts while reading out loud about the "art of surveying" and the "theory of dynamics" from a book propped open, one of those whose ink smell offended Han's nose.

At first, this all looked rather strange to Han. Ridiculous even. After a while though, he could no longer dismiss it as lacking in dignity. Gradually the son's behavior grew to seem substantial and mature, almost fitting. Just as his hard lump of a body now appeared upright and dignified, even in that crumpled and ill-fitting uniform barely worthy of the name, so the record of some eternal truth seemed to glow in every sentence that he read, even in those textbooks lacking leather covers and gold lettering, and that sparkling truth seemed to allow this university student to see through the universe with great insight. Han came to feel a kind of awe.

Then he witnessed a striking incident involving Taesŏng, his housekeeper's son, who was only in the third year at People's School.

Taesŏng could not be more than twelve years old, but sometimes he would joke around with the university student in the garden room and sing "The Song of General Kim Il Sung" in a voice as strong as a crackling stream. One day Han had secretly observed the boy holding a study session with his classmates in his room. At the start of the session, the five boys, all of Taesŏng's age, held their own meeting. One lad stood up and began to argue so vigorously that the veins in his throat were clearly visible.

"Yesterday was not the first time that comrade Ungi did this. It's already the third time this month that he's been late, we absolutely cannot allow this to continue. Comrade Ungi must pay more attention and try to eliminate this backwardness, which brings disgrace upon our entire class, and he must not be late again. Comrade Ungi should do a self-criticism and swear before all of us that he will not be late again."

Even before the child had sat down, another one jumped up and repeated the same content in even stronger terms, before sitting down again. Next up must have been the backward element Ungi himself, who stood up and slowly opened his mouth to speak, after wiping away his tears with the back of his hand.

"I confess my mistakes in all honesty in front of my comrades . . . we don't have no clock at home and some days when I think I'm late, I run to school but it's still early, and some days I think there's still plenty of time, but it turns out I'm already late. . . . I will pay more attention in future to be on time and try to remove the disgrace that I have brought on our class."

The two other boys clapped loudly. But just as all seemed to be over, Taesŏng, who had not clapped even once, wiped his nose and stood up. He clenched his two fists and began to speak with such vigor that the veins on his neck protruded too.

"I cannot agree with my comrades' discussion or comrade Ungi's self-criticism. It's easy to say he's done something bad, or I've made a mistake, but will this solve the problem? Will paying more attention help him know the time when there's no clock at home? Just telling him to pay more attention is not much of a discussion, and saying I will pay more attention is not much of a self-criticism either. We need to help create the conditions in which comrade Ungi will not be late again. This is what I conclude. Comrade Ungi needs to make the effort to talk to his parents and ask them to buy a clock quickly, and until comrade Ungi gets a clock, the four of us need to take turns to stop by comrade Ungi's house in the morning and go to school with him. What do you think of this, comrades?"

All of them, besides Ungi, agreed with this.

Han's jaw had locked open as he watched, but now he walked up to the door of their room. He wanted to praise them, but was so dumbfounded and awestruck by their smartness that no words came out of his mouth. While he stood there with a blank expression, one lad closed the sliding paper door in front of him.

"They seem like bright kids . . ."

With that, Han had no choice but to turn around.

On his occasional trips to Pyongyang, Han noticed many things had completely changed. The narrow lanes through which a handcart could barely pass were now roads as wide as a sports field, and such-and-such a hospital and such-and-such a news-paper building some four or five stories high had popped up all over the place, like mushrooms sprouting overnight. Places that had once been filled with mountains of rubbish had now become parks, where fountains spurted out water. Trees the size of houses had been planted to produce a luxuriant, cool shade, as if in the woods even during the boiling-hot dog days of summer.

"I wonder if I should buy one of those trees?"

Many people were anxious. Yet for the most part they had endured quite well. Some people even joked about the situation.

"Why shouldn't we live when we've been ordered to?"

In fact, nothing seemed impossible in the face of the com-mands of the people's sovereignty:

1. A strong practical politics where public and private are clearly divided,
2. A politics run by patriotic, self-sacrificing executives,
3. A politics where laborers and farmers are respected as people,
4. A politics where all receive equal education regardless of ancestry.

But . . .

From what he had seen with his own eyes in the three years since Liberation, Han agreed with these conclusions about pol-itics in the North, but he could not avoid this final "but."

He did not try to explain this "but" to anyone. And yet,

"Hearing something over and over is not equal to seeing just once. Not until I've been to the South and seen with my own eyes . . ."

This is what he told himself after hearing from several friends who had returned, and then, when the August 25 elections for the Unified Supreme People's Assembly were announced, this "but" had started to play more insistently on his mind.

Moreover, he wanted to be in the South just once for the anniversary of Liberation. He had already celebrated the anniversary twice in the North, but he felt that he would only experience the full emotional impact of Liberation as a national event if he could spend the anniversary in the South, even just once. By this time, order had been restored to Pyongyang, and his fears of a burglary or fire had eased.

All right, this is my chance to just do it! Forget about the thirty-eighth parallel, even if I won't be able to escape that damn unified election . . .

And so, Mr. Han Moe had taken out the old paper twine bag that had lain forgotten for five years and shaken off the rainy season mold.

2

The train arrived in Haeju on time, but quite late at night. When Han came out of the station, he stood in the street for a while and looked around; the town had changed considerably since Liberation.

He could not help but recall how life had been before. When exiting a station, the first thing to catch the eye would invariably be a police box lit by a red light, where a policeman wearing a long sword would stop all the Koreans and grill them like criminals for no reason at all, and if absolutely no fault could be found, they would be made to read the Imperial Oath and free to go only if their Japanese pronunciation was judged acceptable. The fact that nobody paid any attention to him in his current solitude left a profound impression of the nature of liberation and freedom.

He began to walk in the direction of Suyang Hill. From time to time, he hesitated and looked around, wondering which way to go. It was at one of those moments that a safety patrolman appeared before him.

"Excuse me. Is this the way to Okkye-dong?"

"You can get there this way, but who are you looking for?"

"A Mr. Yun Myŏnu, who lives at the entrance to Okkye-dong."

Yun Myŏnu was originally from Haeju and a relative of Han's son-in-law in Pyongyang. Yun had long promised that if ever Han wanted to go to the South, he only had to come to Haeju and Yun could find him a reliable guide.

"There's a large zelkova tree in his yard."

"Oh, I know where you mean. Please follow me."

The patrolman went ahead and led the way to the house gate, even going so far as to knock at the door and call for Mr. Yun.

Mr. Yun was indeed at home. There was also one other guest, who looked familiar.

"Oh, did you have trouble finding the way?" Yun asked as soon as Han had sat down.

"Trouble?"

"I mean, because you came here with a patrolman."

"He was most kind. I just asked for directions, and he goes and brings me here himself!"

"Is that so? Then, if it hadn't been for that patrolman, you would have had trouble finding the house."

Yun seemed glad. The guest, who sat glued to the warmest part of the floor as if it were his very own spot, glanced over and asked, "Was the train on time today?"

And immediately thereafter, "Who knows whether he is a kind guide or on your tail? Ha, ha . . ."

He laughed. His voice, too, seemed familiar. Just as Han was thinking "I know that man and yet I can't think who he is," the man took a drag on his cigarette and laughed again, "Are you sleeping well these days?"

They had met only a couple of times before, when the man had sat in a swivel chair, wearing a white doctor's coat with a stethoscope in hand. Han barely recognized him outside of the examination room in his ordinary clothes. He was a doctor of internal medicine in Pyongyang, whom Han had visited several times on account of his insomnia, before stopping on account of the high cost of the medicine he prescribed.

"It's Dr. Sim! What a surprise to meet you here."

"I guess so. Ha, ha."

Dr. Sim laughed several times, as if he had suddenly become jovial. It was not long before Han realized that the doctor was in Haeju for the same reason as himself.

"So, Dr. Sim, you're planning to leave Pyongyang for good?"

"I'll come back in the open after reunification. Ha, ha."

"Well, how are things? With your hospital you can surely make a living unlike many of us, why not wait for reunification since you've made it this far?"

"What else can I do when I can barely get by?"

He rubbed two plump and oily hands together while he pleaded poverty. It was Yun Myŏnu who responded with a joke, as if the two of them were unconnected.

"You doctors are all hoodlums anyway, aren't you? It's because you can no longer get away with it that you're running away."

"Well, to tell the truth, who becomes a doctor just to get by?"

"Dr. Sim, you're not making as much money as before Liberation?"

"How can I make any money? As you have surely noticed, a People's Hospital has sprung up in every borough, then there's the Central Hospital, the Soviet Hospital, and the Red Cross Hospital; there's just so many hospitals now, aren't there? On top of that, we should be receiving two thousand won for a dose of penicillin, but those guys give them out for six or seven hundred won, and at the Soviet Hospital, if you have no money, they just give you a dose anyway, don't they? What kind of idiot would go to a private hospital these days? And we're doctors. Those shamans who used to do so well, they have absolutely nothing to do in North Korea!"

"But isn't it the case that most people who used to go to shamans in the past went because they were too scared of how much a hospital would charge . . ."

"I've been too lazy to move my arse up 'til now, so I've been stuck here watching it all, but it seems to me that anyone looking after their own interests fled immediately after Liberation, didn't they?"

"And don't some of them regret it now?"

It was the owner of the house who asked the question.

"Regret it?"

Dr. Sim jumped up, his round eyes wider than ever. Apparently, those people had amassed amounts of money far greater than the value of the land that had been confiscated from them in the North, and they had taken possession of hospitals formerly owned by Japanese, which were far larger than the ones they had left behind.

"Well, there must be competition in Seoul, what with all those doctors leaving from the North, how've they made so much money?"

"Are you crazy or what? No fool of a doctor wears a stethoscope in Seoul these days!"

"What do they do then?"

Han was really curious.

"Those of us from Severance know how to speak the 'yes-no' language, don't we? There are Americans all over the place, so why would we sit around cutting out boils and the like? If you can become an interpreter for someone in power you can earn enough overnight to loosen the belt, and if that doesn't work out, well you can trade in millions of won as a pharmacist!"

"Really, do pharmacists do that well? Better than doctors?"

"Oh really, you're such a scholar! Do you think that I'm talking about someone selling ointment in the street, like in the old days? Diazine, penicillin, and whatnot are coming in and spreading all over the country, aren't they? If you can get a foothold in that trade, they say it's a goldmine."

It appeared that Han had found the most reliable travel companion in this Dr. Sim, who was so passionate about everything in the South. The doctor said there was nothing to fear once they had crossed the border. His cousin counted General Hodge's secretary amongst his friends and was a real power player with important figures in the military administration under his thumb.

They set off for the border two days later led by an experienced guide, but because of the third anniversary of Liberation and the upcoming Supreme People's Assembly elections, security was tight, and they had to abandon the route through Ch'ŏngdan, and go instead around Sibyŏn Village toward Sangnyŏng and Yŏnch'ŏn, before crossing at Hant'an River, which flowed exactly along the thirty-eighth parallel. Thus they managed to reach the South before the anniversary.

3

This evening, once again, a party for American soldiers was being held in Sim Kiho's house at the foot of Namsan Mountain, judging from the fact that electric cars belonging to the American army had been blocking the lane behind the house since early evening, stretched out in a line from inside the property and making so much noise that the surrounding houses shook with the roar of engines.

In a Seoul that recalled the old capital of Hanyang from the era of the Great Han Empire—the same Han that featured in the country's name announced by Syngman Rhee—in that the city was lit by oil lamps and candles with the exception of those buildings occupied by the American army, such as the Bando Hotel and Minakai; in this Seoul, Sim Kiho's house glittered and dazzled once again on this night, from the dining room through to the ballroom and on into the rooms and veranda on the second floor, and even out into the garden, as if to deliberately attract attention.

Although they were cousins, Sim Kiho looked more like Dr. Sim's brother, with his big, round eyes, double chin, and bald head. Yet, perhaps on account of his rather thin lips and pointed nose, Sim Kiho paid far more attention to detail. He went down to the kitchen himself in order to taste the coffee that was being brewed and the ice cream that was being made, and he even watched on as his daughter and To Mihwa did their makeup and dressed up in ceremonial robes and bridal headgear, comparing the two of them as he did so.

To Mihwa looked by far the most bewitching of the two, while his daughter looked the least experienced. Thinking this would not do, he went back upstairs and called them in separately. He had hired To Mihwa, a dancer recently returned from Shanghai, for tonight's guest Mr. Wood, who apparently preferred inexperienced young girls now that he had tired of *kisaeng*. But there was little that seemed inexperienced about To on account of her travails here and there. Worried that Mr. Wood would lay hands on his own innocent daughter, Sim instructed her to alter her usual manner.

"Now these Americans, they think that innocence means ignorance, and they will only respect you as the daughter of a cultured family if you impress them with your refined charm. What I'm saying is that I want you to pay special attention to tonight's guests."

Next, he took hold of To Mihwa's slender hand and spoke as follows,

"Mr. Wood likes his women inexperienced and innocent. You understand? If all goes as planned, then when my friends are released, they're not likely to forget your efforts. . . . I guarantee I'll get you at least a hundred thousand from each of them . . ."

Two of his colleagues had been caught up in a profiteering incident and sentenced to three years each, despite paying a two-million-won fine. This Mr. Wood was an American belonging to Syngman Rhee's clique, director of judicial affairs in the military administration, and slated to stay on as Rhee's personal advisor once the transfer of political power to Syngman Rhee's government was complete in South Korea, Rhee having been elected president in the May 10 elections. If the likes of Wood could be properly won over, then even someone awaiting the death penalty would be free by the evening, let alone someone whose sentence was only three years, as long as the crime was not of the leftist variety, of course. And if through an event like this party they could seal what is called in English "friendship," then not only could prisoners be freed but all kinds of possibilities would open up for further profiteering and swindling.

In addition to To Mihwa, seven *kisaeng* had also arrived, armed with full instructions. At least two high officials from the military administration would accompany Wood to act as interpreters between him and the host. The *kisaeng* had been booked four days earlier in response to a request by those high officials to call specific girls from a certain *kisaeng* guild, and then partners for those *kisaeng* had been ordered too.

In general, Americans liked Korean eggs and beef. Sim Kiho had acquired eggs from a purely native species and hired a chef from a certain Western restaurant to make steaks from beef. Mr. Wood, too, seemed to very much enjoy Korean beef, for he did not refuse a second serving of the steak, which was the size of the palm of one hand. He said it was best cooked only on the outside and left rare on the inside, and when too much blood had gathered around his teeth, he washed them off with a glass of whisky before grabbing a handful of pine nuts in his rough hands and stuffing them into his enormous mouth.

With the seven *kisaeng*, To Mihwa, and the host's daughter, there were twice as many women as there were guests. To Mihwa was a sure thing and would tumble into his car soon enough, so Mr. Wood took his cut from the other women first. His wet lips reeked of alcohol and burped up meat juice, while he forced them Hollywood style onto first one woman's lips and then the nape of another's neck. Once the first round of dancing was over, everybody moved into the garden. Sim Kiho's daughter brought out the ice cream and held it under Wood's chin, all the while shooting him an amorous glance with her lips lightly parted, according to her father's orders. That was when Mr. Wood took hold of one ear and bent back her decorated head in order to plant a long smacking kiss on her lips, instead of the ice cream. Sim Kiho could do no more than quietly turn the other way and pretend not to have noticed.

"Father?"

It was not his daughter screaming but his son, who came running out of the house in search of him.

"What is it?"

"Uncle's here from Pyongyang."

"Pyongyang? Where is he?"

The atmosphere turned tense; no one knew what to say.

"There's a phone call from Tongdaemun Police Station. Here, can you take it?"

"From Tongdaemun Police Station?"

Following the separate election in the south on May 10, Mayor Chang T'aeksang had implemented a harsh decree in Seoul, according to which anyone walking around in groups of three or more, or who stood still for too long in the street, or who went into the street after six o'clock, would be shot regardless of their motivation, and so when Dr. Sim and Mr. Han Moe had arrived in Tongdaemun after six o'clock in the evening they had unexpectedly heard gunfire from behind and fallen over with fright. The shots were clearly aimed in their direction. There was no time for questions. Nothing suspicious could be found on either of them, nor in the leather bag belonging to one and the paper twine bag belonging to the other, therefore they were spared being trussed up in rope, but they were still dragged off to the Tongdaemun Police Station, and on the way had noticed how deserted the streets were, apart from armed police gathered here and there and the occasional elite car or two rushing past at high speed. This was the scene after six o'clock in this special district of Tongdaemun, where "His Excellency" Syngman Rhee might not have become president had the opposition candidate Ch'oe Nŭngjin not been illegally detained, and where Yi Hwajang was now forming the so-called cabinet.

Han and Dr. Sim felt relieved not to have been hit by a bullet, but they were dumbfounded when they were dragged off to a prison cell.

"Hey? What have we done to be treated like this?"

"No talking."

"Don't you know we've escaped from the North . . . there are hundreds of people here in Seoul who can verify our identity!"

"We don't know anything about that!"

"Then who does?"

"The top guys have all been called up because of the high security alert, who's got time for interrogations?"

The men were too young to be speaking down to Han and Dr. Sim in this manner; they gruffly asked the two their names before removing all their belongings, including the paper twine bag and their belts, and pushing them into a cell. Dr. Sim's round eyes almost popped out of his head, but he did not say a word for fear they might be bloodthirsty enough to beat him with their guns. It was only after the cell door had been locked with a clank and the guards' footsteps had not been heard for a while, that he began to complain,

"We've not even been in prison in the North . . ."

The only response came in the form of snorts of ridicule from the others in the cell. Dr. Sim and Han were surprised to find that they could barely find space to place their feet. There were many young men to be sure, but also a fair number of younger boys and old men. None of the scornful faces seemed to belong to thieves or gamblers.

Just who are they to laugh at others when they themselves are in jail, and why are there so many of them?

Dr. Sim and Han did not feel like sitting down calmly, even though there was no room for them to sit anyway. Sim shook the bars of the cell and shouted, "Is this what police do in the South? My first cousin is Sim Kiho. Please phone Sim Kiho."

Footsteps came stomping toward them. Their purpose was not to respond to Sim, however, but to shove yet another laborer into the cell. Blood was splattered all over this laborer's upper torso and he gasped for breath, but strangely enough, some of the others in the cell got up and went to him. They called each other "comrade," just like the young people in the North, and wiped the blood off him. They were talking about signing some petition. Even the young boys and old men in the cell seemed to be concerned about this talk of a petition, and soon they were debating with each other under their breath.

Han knew that a petition meant some kind of a signed letter in aid of what they believed to be right.

I wonder what their petition is in aid of?

He did not have to remain curious for long, because a hint came soon enough. The purpose of their petition was none other than to oppose the so-called National Assembly and government, which was the product of the May 10 separate election forced through by the dispatch of American tanks, bombers, and warships, and to select people's representatives for the August 25 Unified Supreme People's Assembly elections, which had been declared illegal in the South. The unified elections were apparently not merely propaganda from the North, but were going ahead in actuality. The flesh of the incarcerated was torn and their collars covered in blood.

Does this mean that people in the South support the North?

Han blinked his small, sharp eyes for a moment, eyes that had been almost singed by the reality of Seoul on the way into the city.

Indiscriminate shooting, indiscriminate arrests, a desperate war of resistance for men and women, old and young . . .

Han recalled the time he too had been thrown into a police cell for several days during the March First Uprising. He remembered how back then he too had despised the petty criminals who squeezed into the narrow cells, thinking them no better than insects. His fears grew that these bloodied warriors would find out he had escaped from the North alongside someone like Dr. Sim.

But . . . but . . . one side is just moving ahead by itself. Instead of encouraging and nurturing a political situation in which South and North might reconcile and be united, one side is going alone and ignoring the other. No matter how worthy the political policies, wouldn't it be better to first unite and agree to enforce those policies across the entire country? If you step on someone's toes and keep pushing ahead alone, then who will want to follow from behind? Isn't that why things keep going wrong . . .

This was why Han kept saying "but . . .," despite the fact that he agreed with all of North Korea's policies. He calmly adjusted his posture, as if to say I too am no petty criminal, and found a place to sit himself down, if only by squatting.

Each time the guard on duty changed and a new one entered, Dr. Sim would plead in an increasingly frightened voice, "Please call my cousin Sim Kiho. . . ." But so many people streamed into the cell, one after another, that the guards had no time to listen to Sim's plaintive cries. Laborers, students, office workers, women, female students, young boys, and old people—soon there was no more room to squeeze them into the cells, and they were dragged off to some room on the second floor.

Eventually Sim wore himself out and tried to sit down, but with buttocks the size of one of those wooden boards used for pounding rice cakes, he inevitably ended up squashing someone's shoulders. Sim and Han celebrated the much-anticipated third anniversary of the August 15 Liberation in a South Korean police cell without so much as being questioned. Finally, on the seventeenth, one of the guards on the night shift realized how powerful this Sim Kiho was, and for the first time a call went through to his house; the cousin's power proved effective, for no sooner had the phone call been made than an American soldier had rushed to Tongdaemun in Mr. Wood's shiny private car, carrying the name card of this giant in the military administration.

As it was already nighttime and too dangerous for Han to set off alone, he had joined Dr. Sim in the car and come to Sim Kiho's house.

D r. Sim was most impressed. In fact, he was so impressed it was as if he had already declared coming to the South a success by virtue of having met his cousin after a gap of many years, finding him unchanged in his energetic social climbing from the time of the Japanese occupation, and having shaken hands with such bigwigs from the military administration.

Han had a quick wash before being dragged out to the party in his wrinkled hemp suit. Mr. Wood wanted to meet people from the North and hear about life there.

"He says, how much you must have suffered in the North."

As soon as they had finished their initial greetings, Mr. Wood spoke through an interpreter.

"Fortunately, we got by."

Han saw through everything and could not remain quiet. Mr. Wood wiped his glistening lips with his napkin and asked question after question, as if he naturally had the right to speak first.

"I imagine people in the North are also grateful that America has mobilized the United Nations to set up an independent government in Korea?"

Han did not know what to say, and while he hesitated, Dr. Sim gladly cut in to answer in his stead.

"Absolutely. Everyone is secretly most grateful and happy about it."

"Apparently those guys are holding elections in Pyongyang too, and making noise that their elections are unifying North and South. So how is it up there? I bet they're treating people harshly, aren't they?"

"What can I say? If it weren't so bad, would I have left, having survived so far? But is North Korea being allowed to hold elections here in the South too? People seem to be very active, judging from what we saw at the police station."

"The United States is here in the South. The United Nations Temporary Commission on Korea is here. So there's no need to worry. The United States is still the most powerful country in the world, more powerful than the Soviet Union. Just look at France and Britain. And look at China, the largest country in the Orient. Chiang Kai-shek's Nationalist Party is still in power. The most important, and the largest and most civilized, countries are all on the U.S. side. So rest assured. It is true that communist elements are holding secret elections here in the South too. But they will most certainly not succeed. How many cannons and bombers does the United States have in China? They're not far away. Politics should be run by the right people and not by some laborers."

Mr. Wood waited for the interpreter to finish before stroking his fat belly as he first guffawed and then drank, or rather emptied, the contents of a glass about the size of an eyeglass lens, and then the most fantastic question fell from his lips.

"I heard that life is so hard in Pyongyang that dozens of people are drowning themselves in the Taedong River every day? You must have witnessed such tragic scenes many times!"

Even the shameless Dr. Sim's lips froze, and he glanced over at Han. Han quickly examined Mr. Wood's face; inside those sunken eyes pupils shone with vigor, as if he were not merely asking a question but exerting pressure for an answer, which would at the very least affirm that he already knew everything but which might possibly do something more than that. Those sinister eyes moved onto Han and hovered there, while the host Sim Kiho blushed when he saw that his most distinguished guest's question was not receiving a quick reply, and he urged them to answer.

"What are you hesitating for? There's no need to be shy about something we all know is true. There's a time and place to hide our country's blemishes, but isn't this gentleman from the United States, a friend of Korea?"

Han struggled to control himself. His eyes might well be small but they were sharp, and given what he had seen so far, it was impossible to compromise his principles. In Pyongyang half a bushel of rice cost about five hundred and twenty won, but when he had asked at Tongduch'ŏn in the South, he had been told the price was three thousand two hundred. If anyone were jumping into a river because life was hard, then would it really be the Tae-dong River, or the Han River? Han wanted to ask them about this. But he did not have the courage, or rather he did not want to act on Dutch courage. Excusing himself on the pretext that according to oriental morals it was not right to cause a distur-bance at someone else's party, he picked up his glass of pop and drank. But for Dr. Sim, this amounted not so much to a case of saving his cousin's face as seizing an opportunity to buy Mr. Wood's favor, which might help with the pressing real-life problems he would face from the following day. He no longer felt it necessary to check Han's reaction, and answered, "Oh, so many have drowned. Even the fishermen can't fish anymore because of the bodies getting caught in their nets. Ha, ha . . ."

Mr. Wood nodded in a satisfied manner, before assuring Dr. Sim, "I will introduce you to President Syngman Rhee tomorrow."

Dr. Sim quickly jumped up and asked the *kisaeng* to fill their glasses, so that he could propose a toast to President Rhee's health. After he had proposed a second toast to Mr. Wood's health, he asked about his niece's headpiece and ceremonial dress, which had been intriguing him all along.

"Did she get married today?"

"Oh, my dear cousin, you really have come from the sticks! Here in South Korea it's now the fashion to dress up like that when you invite gentlemen such as these. They like it. . . . Look, that girl's dressed up the same way!"

His niece was not the only girl wearing bridal headgear and ceremonial dress.

"Well, it makes the place look quite *nigiyaka*, I guess."[1]

Dr. Sim did not find this too strange, but it offended Han's sense of taste. He thought it nothing less than an insult to Korean customs and culture.

Just then, the sound of a gramophone started up in the next room. All the guests, Mr. Wood included, moved inside to dance, wrapped up in their ceremonial robes and ramie skirts. Han seized the chance to ask Dr. Sim if he might retire, and found a corner room on the second floor, where he lay down and stretched out his back, which made him feel as if he had turned into a shrimp during the four days spent in the police cell.

---

1. Dr. Sim mixes Japanese words into his conversation as an indication of both his status and the continuity between the colonial era and postcolonial order in the South. Here *nigiyaka* means "lively."

The sound of jazz, laughter, and applause drifted up from downstairs, and then—bang, bang—from a nearby alleyway, the sound of gunshot.

4

It was barely light when Han woke the following morning. Loud snores from the rooms to either side made it feel like the dead of night. He sat up to smoke a cigarette and found several newspapers placed to one side. The *Taedong Daily* contained an editorial with the heading, "To the New Government," another header reading "Madame Yŏngsin Im for Minister of Commerce and Industry," and an article on an important press conference with notable figures held at a high-class traditional restaurant; in other words, the political trends were stormy and unpredictable, and the newspapers were taking the same populist stance that they had under the previous Japanese colonial occupation. There was a piece on Madame Yŏngsin Im's thoughts on being appointed minister of Commerce and Industry, and she appeared to be full of confidence, having had some experience in business when she had lived in the United States.

Some experience in business? So does that mean there are as many candidates for minister of Commerce and Industry as there are bowls for sale in the main street of Chongno?

It all seemed somehow perilous.

As soon as Han heard Dr. Sim cough downstairs, he rushed down to express his gratitude for everything and slipped out of Sim Kiho's house, without either washing or eating breakfast. As he walked down through Namhan Village toward Namdaemun Street, he felt as if he might hear the sound of Japanese wooden *geta* sandals at any moment. This was close to the road leading to his eldest daughter's house, but he planned to find Mr. Sŏng, the antiquarian book broker, first and ask about his various friends' whereabouts, and so he headed toward Anguk-dong. From Chŏngja-ok onward, the road was lined on both sides with armed police standing so close together they could hold each other's hands. People in the street told him that this most forbidding line of guards was on account of the Seoul mayor, Chang T'aeksang, who would leave for work in about an hour.

Han made his faltering way along the side of the road, trying to avoid the police and use the back alleys as much as possible. Yet the alleyways, being alleyways, were not easy to negotiate either. It was difficult to find a place to step because of all the garbage and feces, and then there were the people pulling handcarts and ice-water carts, so many people who were clearly sleeping rough, and families cooking breakfast in pots they had set up on the back walls of other people's houses, having no kitchen themselves.

Mr. Sŏng happened to be at home. His face seemed to have shriveled, and his clothes, too, seemed more worn than they had been during the Japanese occupation.

"How come you've grown so old?"

"Do I have any choice? It's really wonderful to see you. I thought I'd have to go to Pyongyang to see you again. What brings you here?"

"You mean you're surprised to see me?"

"Only criminals and the like get lured down here, so what are you doing?"

"Well, they say that in the inner room the mother-in-law's always right, and in the kitchen it's the daughter-in-law, that's why I've come here as a fugitive in my own country to hear and see both sides and to see with my own eyes what is going on down here, just as I've seen in the North."

Han asked for water so that he could wash his face, and then he listened as Sŏng told him what had happened to their friends.

Some had become department heads, professors, or lecturers at schools such as Seoul University and Dongguk University, and some had entered the political fray after Liberation and become active in local politics; others, meanwhile, had grown disillusioned by the grand fantasy they had envisioned with the coalition of Left and Right and withdrawn to private life, disgusted by both sides and giving politics a wide berth, just as during the Japanese occupation. Han could not help but sympathize with these latter, and murmured, "Of course, that's only natural. . . ." Tears welled up in Sŏng's eyes as he described how the young scholar Mr. Kim, who along with Han had been a good customer of his during the Japanese occupation, had abandoned the scholarly life to become politically active on the Left, but had then been arrested in the fight against the May 10 separate elections and still remained in prison without trial; with no other means to survive, his family had been forced to sell books from Mr. Kim's precious library, and this had broken Sŏng's heart when he had taken on the task himself and begun scattering the books in different directions. Talk turned next to woeful stories of what had happened to books since Liberation, when the U.S. Air Force had moved into the Law School at Seoul University: some several hundred precious volumes had been torn apart and used to wipe down the American soldiers' guns and boots; even the Royal Library had been affected when the only remaining copy of the *True Records of the Yi Dynasty* was taken and later discovered being sold as scrap paper—although part of it was recovered, the rest had disappeared without a trace.

Sŏng himself could get by renting out rooms in his house. Immediately after Liberation, there had been plenty of Japanese settlers' libraries circulating, and business had been quite good, but now those who could afford to buy books were beginning to feel the pinch, and those responsible for institutions that collected books were absorbed with their own careers and fighting for positions day and night. The result was chaos. He was lucky that houses in Seoul were scarce, and he could rent out both the side room and the room by the gate, while the five members of his own family were squashed into the inner room, which was only a few yards' square. Their cooking pots and sauce pots were piled around haphazardly in a yard no bigger than a cat's forehead, and with six or seven people, including the children, twittering away within these walls, he was embarrassed to sit down on the veranda for even a moment.

"The children must fill up the house during the holidays!"

"Holidays, what are they?"

Sŏng tutted. His eldest son attended Hwimun Middle School and for the past few days had been out all the time participating in the election battles; his second son was supposed to have started middle school last year, but they could not afford the tuition. According to Sŏng, the official cost of middle school was just over sixty thousand won, what with the official fees and savings and the like, but before even getting that far, bribes of at least a hundred thousand won had to be paid.

"But, it wasn't even like that during the Japanese occupation. You're not sending your son to school?"

"How can I? Do you know how many children go to school in the whole of South Korea at the moment? Apart from the sons of profiteers, that is . . ."

"But, that's a huge problem!"

"Who says it isn't? If we don't change this place soon, it's going to be an enormous problem. In North Korea it doesn't cost a hundred and fifty or sixty thousand won to send a child to middle school, does it? There probably aren't many children in each family who can't go to school?"

"That's true . . ."

"That's why you have to try living in the South before you can appreciate how good it is in the North."

"So, why are you letting your eldest run around taking part in some battle or other?"

"Don't they say that the people's will is right? They're not being dragged around and beaten and shut up in police cells because they like it, are they?"

"Well, no . . ."

There was nothing Han could say. He offered Sŏng his remaining cigarettes from the North, which were in the paper twine bag his friend had been fingering, as if pleased to encounter his old handiwork. He staunchly refused the offer to eat his first meal of wheat dumpling soup there and left for his eldest daughter's house in Wŏnnam-dong, sighing as he wondered how a man who had been so gentle even during the final years of colonial rule could have become so harsh.

His daughter and two grandchildren were home alone. The two children had grown so much he could hardly recognize them, while his daughter was equally hard to recognize, because she had shriveled up just like Sŏng. When they held hands and she burst into tears, her tears did not seem to stem entirely from the joy of seeing her father after so long. Then, in another scene reminiscent of that at Sŏng's house, she ladled out some wheat thing from her outdoor cooking pot for breakfast. Once she had asked after her mother and sister, the next question on her lips was the price of rice.

"How much is half a bushel of rice in Pyongyang?"

This was followed by the same question that Sŏng had asked, "Why have you gone to all this trouble to come to Seoul before unification?"

Han did not answer, but instead asked where his son-in-law was.

"Their dad can't come home at the moment."

"Can't come home?"

"What with detectives and the Northwest boys about to attack at any moment."

"You mean, their dad is now a leftie?"

The daughter sensed the meaning in her father's tone of voice.

"Is there any such thing as Left or Right any more? Anyone here with any sense is against all politics right now. Just wait a month and you'll see, father."

She appeared to be preparing rice for him. Han was really hungry by now, but he also wanted to try this American "food aid" just once, and so he had a bowl of wheat dumpling soup. The color was white, but he immediately choked on the pungent, mildewy taste.

"I thought you said their dad had taken a job at the county council?"

"He worked there for six months or so. During the Liberated Republic, he worked in the department helping with the electric supply from the North, but he left because he said he didn't want to become a crook."

"Didn't want to become a crook? It doesn't matter where you are, as long as you yourself are honest, isn't that good enough? Why meddle in other people's affairs?"

"Oh father! There was some kind of sulfur that cost fifty thousand won a ton, and they told him to remove the price because it was going to be a hundred and fifty thousand won. He said he would look into it before changing the price, and this American guy, who's the head of the department, went mad, so then the Korean guy at the next desk, who'd worked at the Government General during the Japanese occupation, he takes twenty thousand won and slips it into their dad's lunchbox and pats him on the back. No matter how hard up he was, do you think their dad would accept that? He said there was no way he could steal from the North, because it was part of Korea too, and they said fine, and from the next day they quietly began probing into everything he'd worked on. No matter how much they dug, he hadn't done anything wrong, and they couldn't catch him. But how do you know they're not going to trump up some false charges sometime? He resigned immediately and left. And he'd only gone to work there in the first place because after Liberation he thought he should do something to help the country, otherwise why would you work for the American government or Syngman Rhee's government? He can't sleep at night and keeps beating himself up about it, saying that the six months working there are a shame that he'll never be able to erase from his past."

"What have you been living on since then?"

The daughter did not reply, but simply brushed away some flies that were attacking the bowls of dumpling soup. From where he sat in the hall, Han could see through the open doors into the inner and side rooms. With all the family's belongings piled up the way they were, it would be claustrophobic in winter, but there was still not a decent thing to be seen among them. First of all, the rice chest, cupboard, and slatted wooden daybed had disappeared from the hall; the pair of standing mirrors and treadle sewing machine were nowhere to be seen in the inner room; and the books that had once been piled up against two walls in the side room had almost all been taken away, with just a few volumes remaining.

"It looks like you've gone bust!"

"Well, here in the South we're fortunate just to be able to live in our own house."

"So they were right in the North. But . . ."

"Won't you attract attention by leaving just when the election is going on?"

"What do I care about that . . . no matter how worthy the politics, what's the point, if it only postpones unification?"

"How is North Korea's politics postponing unification?"

"Well, what's going to happen later on if we leave the South in this state and just keep moving ahead alone with all these reforms and nationalizing policies? If we keep moving ahead bit by bit, then hands that are meant to hold on to each other will end up millions of miles apart, won't they?"

"Oh father! You're still dreaming, like one of those moderates who made a clamor about a united front right after Liberation, but the political situation has evolved in the meantime!"

"Dreaming? Hm . . ."

His daughter was secretly worried. It seemed that her husband's fears had not been unfounded when he had said to her, "Since your father has stayed on in the North, he'd better not grow disgruntled with the policies there!"

Han had thought that if he could only make it to Seoul, his son-in-law would be able to lend him some money and he would not have to worry about a clean suit, as they were of a similar height and build, but neither of these presumptions looked likely to pan out. He had to sit wearing his son-in-law's casual summer shirt and trousers while his own suit was being washed. His two grandsons had grown beyond recognition but looked undernourished, and when he sat them down at his side and felt their thin wrists and calves, he could not suppress the deep pain that rose inside him. He thought of those men and women of all ages that were locked up in the police cells because of the election battles, and he recalled how anemic all their faces and bodies had looked, even though their spirits were strong and full of the energy necessary to continue the fight in jail, and then he thought of the excessive consumption of the two cousins he had seen at Sim Kiho's house the previous evening and Mr. Wood's bulging hippo-like chins, and immediately he tossed aside the wooden pillow on which he had rested his head and leapt up. He had his eldest grandson go fetch Sŏng, who lived nearby, and begged him to call all of his friends who might be able to raise some money, so that his daughter's family might eat rice and meat that evening, and then he led his two grandsons by the hand and went out to buy yellow melons, which cost three or four won each in Pyongyang but more than forty won here.

5

As soon as Mr. Han Moe's suit was ready, he went down to Inch'ŏn.

He needed to raise some cash in preparation for an auction of old paintings and calligraphy collected by a certain Japanese, at which some Korean books were also to appear. He could not bear to miss such an opportunity after all this time. According to Mr. Sŏng, the collector had a copy of the *Collected Works of Wandang*, for which Han had long been on the lookout, and this old edition was likely to appear at auction, in which case it would most likely go for more than ten thousand won, because it was not one of the more recent print editions even though it was not very old. Han had come to Inch'ŏn in search of friends who were likely to be able to lend him ten or even twenty thousand won without too much difficulty.

Luckily, his friend in Inch'ŏn, who had owned a small paper factory from before Liberation, happened to be at home. But Han's visit was to end in disappointment.

The businessman's complaints were endless.

"With Liberation, you would think that Korean businessmen could escape from under the sway of Japanese goods and relax a bit now, wouldn't you? But what do you think! First, the raw materials and fuel have changed, haven't they? Then, how can we deal with the unreasonable demands of the Federation of Laborers? At least the workers in the National Council of Laboring Unions worked with a proper laboring conscience and were skillful workers, even if they did strike from time to time, but these bastards at the federation are not laborers at all, they're nothing but a bunch of hooligans! Even if you manage to get hold of the raw materials, the goods they produce are useless, and then they use any excuse to storm the office and make ridiculous demands for alcohol, and for this and that expense! It's like the belly button's bigger than the belly, because even though you give away almost everything you've earned, you still don't have enough to pay the taxes! I managed to hold onto this factory through the Japanese occupation by keeping the machines running and thinking of the future, but have I brought it this far only to have it seized now? What do you think happened next? A mere rumor has to spread that American paper will arrive in Pusan or Inch'ŏn on a certain day and the price of paper drops overnight! The price fell so low that I couldn't even cover the cost of raw materials, so how can I make a living in this business? After kicking and screaming this long, I ended up shutting the gates. And it's not just paper, is it? From Seoul to Inch'ŏn, at least two-thirds of businesses run by Koreans, large and small, have shut up shop, and those few places that do remain are not likely to survive if we can't keep American goods out of the country . . ."

On his way back to Seoul with barely five thousand won in his pocket, Han paid close attention to the areas alongside the railway tracks and to the factory district of Yŏngdŭngp'o, but smoke rose from only a couple of chimneys, and, in many roofless factories, rusting red machinery stood exposed to the elements, like enormous graves filled with huge corpse-like machines.

It was when the train pulled into Yongsan Station that Han was to catch sight of a real human corpse and not some corpse-like machine. It was surrounded by several rail workers and had not yet been covered with straw matting, so he could see that the head was smashed in and the torso covered in blood. Judging from his clothes, the dead man was also a railway employee, but the faces of the colleagues who surrounded him, turning alternately pale and red with fury, suggested that he had not been hit by a train or died through some mistake of his own. Everyone who heard the story raged with fury and was busily telling others what had happened, as if it had happened to them.

Apparently the dead man had been a member of the support staff at Yongsan Station. He had rushed to the south-facing platform on account of some urgent business at Yŏngdŭngp'o Station when the train was already moving. He jumped and clung to the side of a car that happened to be reserved for American soldiers, and an American army officer, who had been standing in front of the door, shouted something at him. The support worker had said he would move to another car, but with the words "God damn," the American officer had kicked the worker in the chest with his boots, sending him flying. When the station workers reached him, they discovered his head had hit the iron bar of the next track and he was already motionless. Meanwhile, the American officer had pulled out his gun and was leisurely stepping back into the car of the disappearing train.

Han's small but normally sharp eyes blurred, and he felt dizzy as his train continued on to Kyŏngsŏng Station.

What on earth do they see when they look at a Korean? I'd heard that racial discrimination was bad here, unlike with the Soviets, but how on earth could they do something like that . . .

The following day he took his five thousand won to the Antique Art Society's auction hall, alongside Mr. Sŏng. The hall was on the second floor of a Japanese house in Chin'gogae that had formerly been a branch of Edogawa.

Books were not the only items on display. There were also some paintings and calligraphy from both the Koryŏ and Yi dynasties and some several thousand pieces of pottery. Han was pleased to see so many familiar faces, but it was clear that Americans in army uniforms had replaced the Japanese—they walked in wearing their boots and restlessly looked around.

"Do those people also buy some things?"

"Some things? They buy almost anything that's expensive, that's my worry."

Sŏng removed his hands from a book he had been examining and stepped back when he saw an American officer looking down over his shoulder.

Han finally found the old edition of *Collected Works of Wandang* for which he had been looking so long. The book was noticeably popular with people milling around, amongst them Han found several friends who shared his tastes and whom he had been wanting to meet again.

"Well, who is this?"

"Oh, when did you get here? Isn't it the first time we've met since Liberation!"

"Well, talk of the devil . . ."

"We must stay away from this *Collected Works of Wandang* then, since Mr. Han Moe is here and he's been working on that one for a long time!"

Han's hands trembled as he held the five volumes of Wandang's *Collected Works*, stored in a box case decorated with a phoenix tree, but he secretly felt rather relieved; not only were his friends pleased to see him, but they adhered to the custom amongst Korean friends of shared taste of deferring to whoever most earnestly desired a particular item. Han gazed at the beautifully stained covers, as light and soft as lambskin, and at the unconventional yet elegantly written characters, which were somewhere between the Song and the Ming style and composed on thick paper the color of the white of an eye. He could not prevent his mouth from watering as if his eyes were caressing a beautifully colored flower or fragrant meal.

At last, the auction began.

The Americans all sat astride chairs lined up on both sides, still wearing their boots, while each had their own regular broker or buyer who sat beneath them on the floor.

For the most part, it was the Koryŏ celadon that caused the greatest excitement amongst the Americans. But they also jumped in without fail on the most expensive works of calligraphy and painting, and some of them also launched bids on the *Collected Works of Wandang*, for which Han held such great expectations. Sŏng's first bid was five hundred won, in response to which a broker working for one of the Americans tried to break his spirit by jumping straight to three thousand won. Han glanced at Sŏng and dipped his lotus-bud-shaped beard, which trembled a little. Sŏng responded by calling out three thousand five hundred won. The other side immediately leapt up another thousand to four thousand five hundred. Han's forehead burned. He only had five thousand won, and it looked as if this would go much higher. Whatever it might take, this was the one book he did not want to let slip away. Once it fell into their hands, it would leave Korea, and there would be no further opportunity to buy it. He had Sŏng call out his final bid of five thousand won. The American officer glanced over at Han and smiled, and then he tapped the shoulders of the broker sat in front of him and said, "Go on, go on." Six thousand won. Han's face blanched with shock as another buyer, sitting in front of an American on the other side of the room, stepped in and bid seven thousand won.

Noticing that Han had withdrawn from the bidding, one of the Koreans with similar taste stepped in, but he could only hold his ground, and his breath, up to ten thousand won before he too fell by the wayside. Only the Americans were left, and the atmosphere turned into one of a card game or sport, unbecoming to the purchase of a valuable antiquarian book. If one raised the bid by a thousand, another would raise it by two thousand, and the first one would then raise it by another three thousand, as they whistled and clicked their fingers, until finally the *Collected Works of Wandang* went into the possession of an American officer, whose whistles had been ear-splitting, for twenty thousand won.

What does Wandang's Collected Works *mean to them?*

Han rubbed his eyes, as if they were full of sand.

The two sat there a bit longer while a piece of Koryŏ celadon was brought out. The level of tension in the room changed with the appearance of this inlaid piece decorated with a bird and willow tree by a river, and bids were shouted out from every direction. All the Korean bidders had dropped out after 50,000 won, when it became a fight between the foreigners; there were murmurs that the man who dropped out at 290,000 won, just before the piece went for a final price of 300,000, was the French representative from the United Nations Temporary Commission on Korea.

The likes of Han's five thousand won meant nothing in this place. He could not bear to stay there any longer and nudged Sŏng to leave before the auction was over.

"What can Koreans buy in a place like this?"

"You think that's only the case here? It would be okay if it were only antiques and paintings, wouldn't it? But the problem is that the entire economy has become like that!"

"But why have those bastards got so much money?"

Whether intentionally or not, Han had started calling the Americans bastards. Sŏng followed suit when he answered.

"Ah, it's because of those bastards' dollar, isn't it? One dollar is worth about two thousand won at the moment. Now those bastards back there are only lower-level officials, but they earn about two hundred dollars a month. Now how much is that in Korean money? It's four hundred thousand won, isn't it? That means they come to Korea and earn four hundred thousand won each month and then, thieves that they are, they're not idiots, so they end up with more than their salary. Ha!"

"..."

Han walked on, expressionless.

"If those bastards throw in just ten thousand dollars, then they've already raised twenty million won in funds, haven't they? We struggled against Japanese capital when one won equaled one yen, but how long do you think we can last out against

American money when the difference has increased two thousand times in just three years? Eh? Americans, they're told to come to Korea freely, to invest as much American money as they like, to take anything they want whether material or immaterial . . . that's aid in name only, are the people receiving aid saying that? Ha!"

". . ."

Han's slightly embittered lips remained closed, and he walked on.

"If you think about it in terms of that *Collected Works of Wandang* just now, we bid five thousand won, but still couldn't buy it. Those bastards bought it for twenty thousand won, but that's only four times more than five thousand, isn't it? With money worth two thousand times ours they paid four times more, so to those bastards that twenty thousand won is nothing more than words. They've really got it for free because in their money they've paid no more than ten dollars. And I bet in their country it's hard to buy a decent five-volume book for ten dollars."

"My word, you're right!"

"Until last year I couldn't understand why anyone would call America imperialist when they don't even have an emperor, but now everyone understands that, even complete idiots."

". . ."

Han had not thought about this before. He could not suppress an urgent interest in this monster called the "dollar," and this was not because he had suddenly become a leftist, but because he had not been able to do anything to stop a book that he had really wanted to buy from slipping through his hands.

Those Japanese bastards destroyed us through annexation, but these bastards have figured out how to destroy us through aid!

By this point they were entering an alley in Myŏngch'i-chŏng. All of a sudden the children selling American cigarettes and gum scattered into the alleys to hide, crouching like a flock of birds spooked by a hawk. A crowd blocks the crossroads ahead, where the former Stock Exchange had once stood. The sound of fighting can be heard within the bustle. Policemen with badges on their chests and MPs with large English letters painted in white onto bowl-shaped helmets . . . they all blow their whistles as they try to elbow their way through the crowd. They cannot get through. Then, from somewhere, comes the pop of a pistol, not the sound of a hunting gun. The crowd pulls back with a "wah," and the policemen and MPs poke their way into the gap. The crowd contracts again, as if numb to the sound of gunfire, and people rush in from this alley and that. It hadn't been the sound of a fight, but of a speech.

"Our nation is one. Why would we set up a separate government here in the South? Ladies and gentlemen! If you really want our ancestral homeland to be united and independent, if you really don't want our nation to be sundered and our brothers here in the South to become colonized slaves again, then these August 15 unified elections . . ."

A young laborer has been standing in a shop window, clutching his cap in his hands and shouting at the top of his voice, but now he finds his words interrupted by policemen and MPs dangling from his arms and legs, like a swarm of bees. The young man wriggles his legs free and kicks the policeman. The MP draws his gun.

"Go ahead, shoot me then!" shouts the young man. The policemen use their clubs to beat the young man around the face. His lips are torn and blood gushes out, but still he shouts.

"Ladies and gentlemen! We have no choice but to achieve a united independence with our own hands. The only way is for these unified elections . . ."

"That's right!"

"Yes!"

There are shouts of agreement from all over the crowd. The policemen crawl up the laborer's body, front and back, as if climbing a tree. Then a crash, as the shop windows break and

the laborer falls down onto the ground in a heap with the policemen. The crowd contracts with an "aah." They push each other
in the back, falling onto the policemen as they swoop in to attack.
There is no doubt that the crowd is attempting to prevent the
arrest of the laborer.

"Step on the bowls of shit!"

"Squash the bowls of shit down into the ground!"

The "bowls of shit" referred to the helmets and caps that the
policemen and MPs wore. Here and there in the midst of the confusion, young men, older women, and boys held lists of signa-
tures and were adding names as people in the crowd quickly
signed up. A middle-school student unrolled a sheet of paper in
front of Sŏng and Han too. Sŏng quickly said, "I've signed up
in my own district."

He spoke politely to the young man. Han was flustered. When
he realized that adding his signature in such an environment
meant taking part in a desperate and bloody battle, he withdrew
his hands.

"Mr. XXX is standing in our district."

The name of the candidate flowed stealthily from the student's
trembling lips.

"It's your decision, but please sign quickly if you want to."

A flash in the student's eyes seemed to ask, "Are you with the
patriots or the traitors?" Han felt the unpleasant pressure of a
kind of test. At the critical moment, he turned away from the
student, fanning himself and adopting an aloof expression that
seemed to say, "I'm not with the Left or the Right."

Policemen were running up the street toward them, hitting
people on the head and beating them on their backs with
clubs. Breathless, Han pushed through the street with Sŏng in
his wake, as if falling though a hole, and then quickly hurried
away.

The speechmaker seemed to have disappeared, uncaught. The
policemen dusted the dirt off their clothes and fled, wielding their

truncheons at anyone who came near them, as if afraid of being knocked over by the crowd again.

No sooner did the police and MPs appear to go their separate ways than the street kids poured out of the alleyways again, flocking like birds to cover the street.

"American cigarettes for sale!"

"Buy your gum here!"

"American toothpaste! American soap!"

Han thought of his housekeeper's son, Taesŏng, back in Pyongyang. These boys and girls were about his size, but they were all trying to sell American cigarettes, gum, toiletries, combs, and knives, and other things that they carried in paper boxes or simply in their hands.

"You brats, get out of the way, get out of the way . . ."

Sŏng chased them away in anger.

6

Han returned to his daughter's house in a bad mood. But when he arrived, he discovered his daughter's family of three in even worse shape.

His eldest grandson made no attempt to get up from the stone step but simply blinked his bright-red, bloodshot eyes, while the youngest hid his face in his mother's skirts as she in turn leant against the veranda post.

"What's wrong? Have they got into a fight?"

"No."

"It's sweltering today. The kids must be exhausted, what with the heat . . ."

"Father?"

"What is it?"

His daughter's eyes burned with hostility, but fortunately there was no trace of tears as she spoke.

"I was wondering why those sons of bitches hadn't been here recently, it turns out they locked up the kids' dad a few days ago!"

Han entered the room without even removing his hat, and stood there with a blank expression for a while.

"Oh, that useless man . . ."

He blamed his son-in-law.

"Father, you think it's his fault?"

"Cultivate the body and put the house in order, only then can you govern the country. But look what he's done to this house, and now he's ruining his own body, isn't he?"

She stared at her father for a while. He looked less like her father than a member of the Korean Democratic Party or one of Syngman Rhee's gangs.

"Whatever . . . please stay here with the kids for a while."

"Where are you going?"

"He hadn't been eating well and was feeling weak anyway, I can't just leave him."

"You mean you're taking him food?"

"Yes."

"How will you pay for it?"

" . . . "

"You'll sell something else?"

"I still have our gold rings put aside for an emergency."

"You're selling your wedding rings, the ones that your parents gave you when you married . . ."

" . . . "

His daughter did not answer but did indeed appear about to sell the gold rings. Han took out the five thousand won that he had hoped to use to buy the books and tossed it toward her.

"Here's five thousand won."

"But father, you need this money, don't you? Anyway, yesterday a friend dropped by and told me that private meals have to be paid for a month in advance and cost at least ten thousand won . . ."

"At least ten thousand . . ."

He could no longer pretend to ignore the situation as her elder.

"Stay here while I go to see someone."

He meant for his daughter to entrust the matter to him and left to raise the money.

He visited three or four friends before it grew dark. But even procuring a thousand won was not easy. They were mostly friends who had been at the auction hall and had returned with empty pockets, having managed to buy only a few small pictures and letters in which the Americans had taken no interest.

He was embarrassed to return empty-handed, because even though she was a daughter, she was still a child of his who had left home to marry. Finally, he went to see Sŏng to discuss the problem, but Sŏng said he was already indebted to everyone from whom he might be able to borrow money and there was nothing he could do to help. Gazing up at the stars in the now dark sky, Han tried expanding the range of his acquaintances in Seoul. And then, he suddenly nodded as a new name came to mind.

"I should have gone there from the beginning!"

"Where do you mean?"

"If I go to see Headmaster Pak, he would lend me ten thousand won, wouldn't he?"

Pak was headmaster of the middle school where Han had worked for twenty years. Even though he no longer worked there, they had stayed in touch, and from time to time Headmaster Pak would ask Han for an appraisal when he wanted to buy an old book or painting.

"If you go there, he'd lend you money to be sure. Why wouldn't he be delighted and sure to welcome you, when he doesn't have anyone significant on his side these days? But if I were you, I would think carefully before going there."

"How come?"

"I doubt if your daughter would accept the money if it came from him, and your son-in-law might not eat those meals either."

"I see, is that because he's what these days they call the 'bourgeoisie' or something like that?"

"Well, it would be better not to go to him. More than a few people have begun frequenting houses such as his after getting into debt and got caught up in other people's political parties, and then ended up supporting some wealthy man, however absurd it might be in their circumstances, and become what we used to call 'deputies' or 'guard dogs' in the Jap language."

"What are you talking about! You think I'm going to become a runner for Headmaster Pak just because of ten thousand won? You think I'm that spineless!"

Han stormed out of Sŏng's house in anger.

The alleyway was dark, but Headmaster Pak's front gate seemed just as prosperous as in the past. Two private cars and an American military truck were parked there.

Darn, he has visitors!

The fact that Han hesitated and waivered on the approach to the gate seemed to raise the suspicions of the foreign soldiers. One man, who looked at least nine feet tall, jumped down from his jeep, shouting something incomprehensible, and blocked the way in an aggressive manner. Han was not one to simply back down and walk away in such situations. He tried to pass through without any small talk and the nine-foot giant bent down over him like a totem pole, bringing a bolt of lightning down before the gaunt Han's eyes. Han could not tell what this kind of strike would be called in the sport of boxing that these people loved so much, but it was a knockout to be sure, and he collapsed on the spot.

The following day Han summoned his daughter to the hospital in Chae-dong, where he lay prostrate in a second-floor room. All color had drained from her lips. But her anger did not stem only from her father's mishap, the broken cheekbone, now swollen up like a bowl, and the blackened and bruised eye above it. She seemed rather to think this mishap was the natural consequence of going to see one of Syngman Rhee's gang, the gang of the enemy that people were putting their lives on the line to fight, and trying to plead for those people, as if their brave battle was nothing more than an unfortunate situation. She was so furious her teeth quivered, and she burst into tears at the pathetic nature of it all.

"Father, why do you have so little judgment? How can you be so incapable of understanding the political situation? Don't you understand how extreme the age we're living in is? I visited him in prison last night. Someone came to tell me that the policeman on guard was on our side, and so I visited for a short while, but when I told him about the private meals he exploded. He told me off, saying don't I know how many comrades in here can't afford private meals, and how could I be so clueless about the situation. And then, when I told him that you're here, he was so surprised and he begged me not to let you go out too much. Do you know why he said that? He said that you would go to see someone like Headmaster Pak and end up making some absurd criticism of North Korea. Can't you just think about it a bit? What's right and what's wrong . . ."

" . . ."

Han did not open his unbandaged eye, but his lotus-bud-shaped beard trembled slightly. The daughter continued,

"Father, didn't you say that even though North Korea was doing well it was racing ahead alone and that was why unification couldn't happen? If the reactionaries heard that they would jump for joy. Which side was it that tore up the work of the Soviet–U.S. Joint Committee? Which side was it that proposed the removal of both the Soviet and American armies at the same time, and which side opposed this? And which side has gone ahead and set up its own government first? Why are you saying all these things that don't match the truth? What are you doing if not defending the traitors? Father, you're a reactionary."

"What?"

Han's one eye shot open as wide as it could.

"Who's calling me a reactionary?"

"Just think about it. Are your arguments more helpful to the democratic forces or to the reactionaries?"

"I'm nonpartisan! I am simply Korean, and I am neutral!"

"Father, you're still living in a dream world. I mean, do you still not understand how ambiguous it is to be nonpartisan right now? There's no such thing as an uncommitted middle ground at the moment. You call yourself neutral and believe that being nonpartisan is the most just approach to take, but you end up playing into the interests of the reactionaries all the time, without even realizing it. To go to that man Pak's house . . . Korean people should never go to that man's house, except to throw a bomb at it."

"I have my own sense and ideas about things, so you can take your opinions and keep them to yourself."

"Father, who's asking you to become a leftist thinker or fighter? But you have your own sense of justice, don't you? Why can't you at least support the side that recognizes the correctness of your own principles, according to your own ideas? What I'm saying is, just stick to the side that you recognize to be right. Don't you understand how drastically the times are changing at the moment? If you wander around hesitating like this, you'll be thrown to the wind. You might not be able to be a hero of history, but you don't want to be its dust, do you?"

"Dust . . ."

He spat out his daughter's words with a bitter smile.

She had left the children at home and could not stay long.

The following day, Sŏng visited the hospital.

"What on earth happened?"

"It's all because I didn't listen to you!"

It was only to Sŏng that Han could honestly express his regret at having gone to Headmaster Pak's house.

"Those bastards are crazy about boxing . . . they even pretend to box as they walk around in the street, you know. And then, when they feel like trying out a real move, they just knock someone over, anyone! There's all these people who were just walking down the street minding their own business, and the next minute they've been felled like corpses, by . . . what do they call that now . . . an 'uppercut,' where they hit you under the chin or on the eyebrow. That's why, if you see an American, it's best to keep your distance."

"But why has Headmaster Pak got American soldiers stationed at his gate? Is that the way things are these days?"

"He probably had some important American bastard visiting him. Especially since he's been making his share from that oil swindle lately."

"What do you mean, oil swindle?"

"What, you mean you haven't heard about the oil swindle here in the South?"

Sŏng stubbed out his cigarette and explained the gist of the matter.

"When they failed to pay for the electricity from the North, and ultimately refused to use it any more, their ulterior motive was to sell more of their own oil. After Liberation, the Alliance of Scientists opposed the military government's plan to import processed oil, they argued that we have a fine refining plant here in the South and should only import crude oil. If we brought in a hundred million won's worth of crude oil and refined it here, we'd provide a living for Korean factories and workers and produce three hundred million won's worth of gasoline and diesel from that hundred million won's worth of crude oil. But those shameless crooks, they accused the members of the Alliance of Scientists of belonging to the Communist Party and had them arrested and locked up, didn't they? And then, they prevented news of the debate from leaking out and gave the oil import rights to the agents of their very own oil magnets, like Texas and Sun Rising, so they could import refined petroleum, gasoline, and diesel oil, which made them three hundred million from a hundred million won."

"What thieving bastards!"

They were no longer mere bastards but thieving bastards, and a fire blazed in Han's one remaining functional eye as he asked another question.

"But, you mean to say that President Syngman Rhee just stood by and let this happen? What kind of nation building is that?"

"Just listen to you! Stood by? He's sat there stamping his seal onto all of these hoodlums' swindles in the name of aid, or agreements between Korea and the United States, isn't that why they call him the stooge of Wall Street, who sold his country and his people? And your very own Headmaster Pak is one of the ringleaders in his traitorous party. It was Pak who obtained the rights to distribute that petroleum throughout South Korea, with the result that he's made more than thirty times the amount of money he had before Liberation. Is this going on in the North too? Has the North become a playground for these foreign merchant bastards and the Korean bastards who're scraping every last drop of blood and sweat from their own people, all while filling up their own bellies running errands for these thieving bastards?"

"..."

"You've no idea what's going on right next to you, living up there in the North!" Sŏng sighed.

"No idea? Okay, let's agree I've no idea. But what has everybody in the South been doing about all these traitors in their midst?"

"Just listen to you again! Isn't that exactly why everyone's rising up? Why do you think your son-in-law has been arrested?

Do you know how many tens of thousands have died? How many hundreds of thousands are already in prison? Damn it!"

"But, why can't hundreds of thousands stand up to a few traitors?"

"Have I ever heard anything so pathetic! Do you think those few traitors are lording it over us on their own steam?"

"You're right, it's America, isn't it!"

Han forced a sad smile.

"What good are even ten Americas? Those bastards are merchants to the core. If they see that their interests are not being served, they won't stick around. In the past we were innocents, like tigers eating tobacco, but these days we know better, don't we? Don't the workers know that there's a country like the Soviet Union? And the peasants too! If they didn't know what the bastards are like it would be different, but now those bastards, if they're confronted with awareness, solidarity, and absolute resistance, not one of them will risk their life when it comes down to a fight. Just look at what's happening in China!"

"But what do those guys like Syngman Rhee and Headmaster Pak imagine is their future, when they stay in place despite losing the people's trust?"

"They'll flee to America, of course. Isn't that why they hoard dollars and precious stones? They say that Syngman Rhee's Western concubine is sitting on all the diamonds and gems in Seoul."

"And leave Korea?"

"Do you think those bastards would miss Korea? What do you think they care about Korean culture?"

"You're right! They even send their own daughters out in bridal headgear if some American bastard comes to their party! It's outrageous, to think that someone could insult their own country's cultural customs like that! Why don't they make the American bastards dress up as grooms . . ."

"Don't even mention it. They despise everything Korean even more than during the Japanese occupation, and we're surrounded by frivolous American things instead. That's why those traitors are fine with any country as long as dollars are on offer, and unification through American decadence would be most convenient for them. Then, even if they're thrown out, there's nothing to remind them of Korea. . . . Isn't that why these days the leftists are fighting globalism? What with the United States telling every country to drop their national pride and the North Atlantic Alliance being the first step to a European federation . . ."

"It's only right to fight policies like those that aim to destroy other peoples."

"And that's not the only thing that the leftists are right about."

"Well, it's a good job I didn't meet with Headmaster Pak, even if I did come off worse for wear . . ."

"That's right."

" . . ."

Han said no more. Sŏng was not a chatterbox by nature, but he also was not one to sit in silence, and soon he raised a new topic.

"Recently I've been wondering about something . . ."

"What?"

"You would know the answer better than I, but if Pak Yŏnam or Kim Wandang were alive today, what side do you think they'd be on? That's what . . ."

"Well, that is an interesting question! And?"

"Well, Yŏnam exposed the *yangban* nobility with satire and was always interested in economic thought, so there's no way he wouldn't be a communist today."

"And Wandang?"

"What did he mean by 'seeking the truth from facts'? Wasn't he advocating the science of what is actual and casting aside the empty idealistic philosophy of Neo-Confucianism? Wandang was a leader of the Practical School, so if he were around today he would be a giant of social science. What do you think?"

"That's a difficult question . . ."

Han listened to Sŏng's opinion some more, but he did not offer his own response.

H an spent two more lonely days lying prone in the hospital and gazing at a test chart for colorblindness, which was affixed to the wall across from his bed.

Was I colorblind when I looked at North Korea? I could see the whole, but there were certain things I couldn't see properly . . .

There was no end to the noise of passing cars in the street outside the window. He did not even need to look to know that what sounded like the whistle of a hawk speeding by were actually the jeeps driven by American soldiers, and it was American army trucks that shook the building and made a snarling sound, which sounded like some giant monster straining itself.

I have seen it now. I have seen South Korea until my eyes have burst! I don't want to see any more! But the fact that I don't want to see any more is a sign that I'm no reactionary!

He had been angry with his daughter for calling him a reactionary. He had not come through the thirty-six years of Japanese colonial rule living in a servile manner. He had always liked people who knew how to protest, like Mr. Kim, whose family had been selling off his library since he had been imprisoned for taking part in the fight against the May 10 elections and whom he had considered a friend despite their age difference. Kim had also favored Yŏnam and Wandang most of all and even owned a few of Wandang's pieces of calligraphy, despite a lack of interest in that art.

As for Han, of all the books he had collected, he had read those by Yŏnam the most, beginning with his *Diary of a Journey to Jehol*, and he had also read extensively in Wandang's voluminous collected works, although in a print edition. His regret at missing out on the old edition of his *Collected Works* this time had stemmed less from his compulsion to collect everything than from the spirit of a disciple who revered Wandang himself.

If Yŏnam or Wandang were alive today, would their sense of justice and spirit of practical thought lead them to join the leftists or not? No, they would not merely join, they would be standing at the forefront leading the way!

Han could not but agree with Sŏng. His forehead burned when he realized that he deserved the scorn not only of his own daughter and the people he had seen in the Tongdaemun Police Station cells, or the middle-school student and laborer in the Myŏngdong alley, but also the scorn and a reprimand from the sages whom he still revered today, such as Yŏnam and Wandang.

Calling me a reactionary was going too far! But it is true that I have been conservative! Conservative? Am I really a conservative?

He sat up in bed with a start. He picked up a fan and tried to cool his still throbbing face in fits and starts.

Conservative? But that's not who I really am! The conservatives are noxious pests who block the progress of their country and society in any age! Am I really conservative?

Han was supposed to rest in the hospital for another couple of days, but discharged himself with his one eye still bandaged. He did not feel like returning to his daughter's house in his depressed state of mind, and instead climbed up to the Blue Cloud Pavilion, which he had frequented when he lived in Seoul before.

The pavilion appeared bare through the once-dense pine grove, but it was perfect for taking in a view of the center of the city, even with just one eye. At the foot of Namsan Mountain in the distance, he could see the site where the Residency-General had stood forty years before. In the place of the Japanese flag, an American flag flapped above what was now the American military police base.

He walked along the ridge of the hill to the Half Misty Gate. From there, he could look down as if at the back of his hand upon the Tŏksu Palace, where the UN Temporary Commission on Korea was based, and Kyŏngbok Palace, where Syngman Rhee had set up his traitorous cabinet in the American military administration's wake. American army billets were crammed into the courtyard in front of the Main Hall and American army trucks wriggled about like a swarm of ants. In the midst of it all, shiny sedan cars were entering and exiting the two palaces.

He felt indescribably sad and depressed to witness such chaos. He recalled his youth, when he had watched with his own eyes the scene of Hanyang in the final years of the kingdom. The scene today seemed little different from back then, when Itō Hirobumi had sat in his two-horse carriage wearing a top hat, and Song Pyŏngjun, Yi Wanyong, and the rest of the Ilchinhoe gang had been pulled in and out of the Tŏksu and Kyŏngbok Palaces in their rickshaws.

You bastards, are you cooking up those Ilchinhoe games again?

His sigh was resolute, but tears collected in his one unbandaged eye.

7

Mr. Han Moe picked up his paper twine bag and left his daughter's house in Seoul as soon as he could remove the bandage from his eye. He left without visiting Sŏng or any of his other friends again, and without waiting to see his son-in-law, who had little hope of either a trial or release.

He decided to take the Tongduch'ŏn route by which he had arrived. He spent four days in Tongduch'ŏn trying to find a guide, but no one volunteered amidst claims that the security was just too intense. Even staying more than a few days in such a small town might expose his true intentions, and so he set off alone, and with confidence, on the road that he had traveled no more than one month earlier.

After walking thirty ri he reached the Hant'an River: a cock crowed twice somewhere and lights flickered in the windows of both the civilian and official residences in Chŏngongni, the first village on the northern side.

He held his breath as he looked around to his left and right. All was still. He quietly took off his jacket and tied it onto his back, along with his bag. It was already autumn, and although the water was shallow it was as cold as ice and the stones were slippery. No matter how carefully he trod, the water made a noise. And then, before he made it half way across, he fell over with a loud splash. He managed to stand up again, but this time, before he could fully right his body,

Pop, pop,

Pop, pop, de de de . . .

The sound of the rifles came from a fair distance, from the hill to the west of the iron bridge, and not from only one or two guns. Bullets covered the river, splashing up water like a rain shower.

After a while, the shower of gunfire came to a halt.

Everything was still once more; not even the shadow of a person on either the north or south bank of the river, and no sound in the water.

—February 1950
Translated from *Munhak yesul*, 1950

GLOSSARY

ILBO: A pen name of the fiction writer, translator, and scholar of drama Ham Taehun (1906–1949).

ILSŏK: A pen name of the linguist Yi Hŭisŭng (1896–1989).

KUBO: A pen name of Pak T'aewŏn (1909–1986), modernist writer and member of the Group of Nine.

KUJō TAKEKO: A Japanese poet and educator (1887–1928) known as one of the three beauties of Taishō.

NOSAN: A pen name of the historian and essay writer Yi Ŭnsang (1903–1982), who was also a poet specializing in the traditional, short form of the sijo.

PINGHŏ: A pen name of the pioneering modern short-fiction writer Hyŏn Chingŏn (1900–1943).

SATURDAY SOCIETY (TOWŏLHOE): A new-style drama group formed in 1922 by students in Tokyo.

SINBOK: A pen name of Ch'oe Yŏngju (1905–1945), a writer, translator, and editor of children's fiction.

SŏGYŏNG: A pen name of the cartoonist and film scenario writer An Sŏkchu (1901–1950).

SŏHAE: A pen name of the writer Ch'oe Haksong (1901–1932).

SUJU: A pen name of the poet Pyŏn Yŏngno (1897–1961).

WŏLP'A: A pen name of the poet Kim Sangyong (1902–1951).

YI SANG: A pen name of the modernist poet, fiction writer, artist, and member of the Group of Nine, Kim Haegyŏng (1910–1937).

YŏSU: A pen name of Pak P'aryang (1905–1988), poet and member of the Group of Nine.

YUN: The children's fiction writer Yun Sŏkchung (1911–2003).

WEATHERHEAD BOOKS ON ASIA

Weatherhead East Asian Institute, Columbia University

LITERATURE

David Der-wei Wang, Editor

Ye Zhaoyan, *Nanjing 1937: A Love Story*, translated by Michael Berry
Oda Makato, *The Breaking Jewel*, translated by Donald Keene
Han Shaogong, *A Dictionary of Maqiao*, translated by Julia Lovell
Takahashi Takako, *Lonely Woman*, translated by Maryellen Toman Mori
Chen Ran, *A Private Life*, translated by John Howard-Gibbon
Eileen Chang, *Written on Water*, translated by Andrew F. Jones
Writing Women in Modern China: The Revolutionary Years, 1936–1976, edited by
   Amy D. Dooling
Han Bangqing, *The Sing-song Girls of Shanghai*, first translated by Eileen Chang,
   revised and edited by Eva Hung
Loud Sparrows: Contemporary Chinese Short-Shorts, translated and edited by Aili
   Mu, Julie Chiu, and Howard Goldblatt
Hiratsuka Raichō, *In the Beginning, Woman Was the Sun*, translated by Teruko
   Craig
Zhu Wen, *I Love Dollars and Other Stories of China*, translated by Julia Lovell
Kim Sowŏl, *Azaleas: A Book of Poems*, translated by David McCann
Wang Anyi, *The Song of Everlasting Sorrow: A Novel of Shanghai*, translated by
   Michael Berry with Susan Chan Egan
Ch'oe Yun, *There a Petal Silently Falls: Three Stories by Ch'oe Yun*, translated by
   Bruce and Ju-Chan Fulton
Inoue Yasushi, *The Blue Wolf: A Novel of the Life of Chinggis Khan*, translated by
   Joshua A. Fogel
Anonymous, *Courtesans and Opium: Romantic Illusions of the Fool of Yangzhou*,
   translated by Patrick Hanan
Cao Naiqian, *There's Nothing I Can Do When I Think of You Late at Night*, trans-
   lated by John Balcom
Park Wan-suh, *Who Ate Up All the Shinga? An Autobiographical Novel*, translated
   by Yu Young-nan and Stephen J. Epstein
Yi T'aejun, *Eastern Sentiments*, translated by Janet Poole
Hwang Sunwŏn, *Lost Souls: Stories*, translated by Bruce and Ju-Chan Fulton
Kim Sŏk-pŏm, *The Curious Tale of Mandogi's Ghost*, translated by Cindi Textor
The Columbia Anthology of Modern Chinese Drama, edited by Xiaomei Chen
Qian Zhongshu, *Humans, Beasts, and Ghosts: Stories and Essays*, edited by Chris-
   topher G. Rea, translated by Dennis T. Hu, Nathan K. Mao, Yiran Mao,
   Christopher G. Rea, and Philip F. Williams

Dung Kai-cheung, *Atlas: The Archaeology of an Imaginary City*, translated by Dung Kai-cheung, Anders Hansson, and Bonnie S. McDougall

O Chŏnghŭi, *River of Fire and Other Stories*, translated by Bruce and Ju-Chan Fulton

Endō Shūsaku, *Kiku's Prayer: A Novel*, translated by Van Gessel

Li Rui, *Trees Without Wind: A Novel*, translated by John Balcom

Abe Kōbō, *The Frontier Within: Essays by Abe Kōbō*, edited, translated, and with an introduction by Richard F. Calichman

Zhu Wen, *The Matchmaker, the Apprentice, and the Football Fan: More Stories of China*, translated by Julia Lovell

The Columbia Anthology of Modern Chinese Drama, Abridged Edition, edited by Xiaomei Chen

Natsume Sōseki, *Light and Dark*, translated by John Nathan

Seirai Yūichi, *Ground Zero, Nagasaki: Stories*, translated by Paul Warham

Hideo Furukawa, *Horses, Horses, in the End the Light Remains Pure: A Tale That Begins with Fukushima*, translated by Doug Slaymaker with Akiko Takenaka

Abe Kōbō, *Beasts Head for Home: A Novel*, translated by Richard F. Calichman

Yi Mun-yol, *Meeting with My Brother: A Novella*, translated by Heinz Insu Fenkl with Yoosup Chang

Ch'ae Manshik, *Sunset: A Ch'ae Manshik Reader*, edited and translated by Bruce and Ju-Chan Fulton

Tanizaki Jun'ichiro, *In Black and White: A Novel*, translated by Phyllis I. Lyons

HISTORY, SOCIETY, AND CULTURE
Carol Gluck, Editor

Takeuchi Yoshimi, *What Is Modernity? Writings of Takeuchi Yoshimi*, edited and translated, with an introduction, by Richard F. Calichman

Contemporary Japanese Thought, edited and translated by Richard F. Calichman

Overcoming Modernity, edited and translated by Richard F. Calichman

Natsume Sōseki, *Theory of Literature and Other Critical Writings*, edited and translated by Michael Bourdaghs, Atsuko Ueda, and Joseph A. Murphy

Kojin Karatani, *History and Repetition*, edited by Seiji M. Lippit

The Birth of Chinese Feminism: Essential Texts in Transnational Theory, edited by Lydia H. Liu, Rebecca E. Karl, and Dorothy Ko

Yoshiaki Yoshimi, *Grassroots Fascism: The War Experience of the Japanese People*, translated by Ethan Mark